Prole Nation

Prole Nation

By RC Murray

Author of *Legally* STUPiD: Why Johnny doesn't *have* to read

Prole Nation

Published by
Lighthouse Christian Publishing
SAN 257-4330
754 Roxholly Walk NE
Buford, GA 50318
United States of America

www.lighthousechristianpublishing.com

To Gloria, the joy of my life and wife of my youth.

Chapter One

"Relax," said the night man. "We are programmed to receive. You can check out any time you like, but you can never leave!"
Don Felder (*The Eagles*), "Hotel California"

Kathy took a sip from her Diet Coke then set it on the sales counter next to a bowl of assorted chocolates. Satellite radio was churning out another '70's hit through the store's intercom system as she reached for a Hersey's Kisses and looked over at the digital clock under the cigarette display. Almost noon. Three more hours to the end of her shift. Three more hours!

Bob Seger was telling her *"You're still the same,"* but Kathy disagreed. She'd fallen far and fast and landed like a sack potatoes. At least she was no longer *tiffany-twisted*, she mused as she shoved a chocolate morsel between her lips.

Two years ago, she was the head of the English Department at a 3-A high school. Now she struggled to pay rent on a duplex apartment and keep a reliable car, having to work the cash register at a right-off-the-interstate convenience store, just to make ends meet. The early retirement they forced on her left her with a monthly check that didn't go very far with today's double-digit inflation. She missed her old job, her used-to-be friends and her Mercedes, but she missed her self-respect most of all. As the Kisses melted in her mouth, its sweetness failed to improve her bitterness.

It was bad enough having to serve the endless appetites of an ignorant populous, who streamed in and out of the store for gas, tobacco and alcohol products, snack foods, lottery tickets or fishing supplies. But she also had to take orders from an uneducated, retired Marine, who daily showed his utter contempt for her, "the over-educated, white trash *infidel*." On this thought, she turned back quickly to the chocolates and grabbed a fun-size Snickers bar. She assured herself she wasn't prejudice. Jamal was prejudice. Redneck Southerners were prejudice. But nice, little Catholic girls from New Jersey were not prejudice.

"Are ya feelin' sick?" Jamal's deep voice bellowed from behind her, causing her to jump.

"Huh?" She asked, her nasally accent concealing how much he'd startled her, "Why do you ask that?"

"'Cuz yur face's red," he said, grunting as he bent over to pick up several tiny ribbons from Hersey's Kisses that lay on the floor behind the counter. *"Don't leave yur trash on d'flo'r.* I fig'ur yur blushin' 'bout somethin' yur thinkin', or yu'r sick."

She didn't reply to his reproof about the trash but tried to smile as she bit a chunk from the Snickers, surprised he was so observant. She studied him as he twisted his huge body to move several cases of soft drinks from one side of the aisle to the other. A large, nasty scar on his right cheek seemed to be illuminated by the sweat on his round, black face. She'd always wanted to ask him how he got the scar, but they rarely had casual conversations.

Jamal's resentment for her bore itself out in whiny sarcasm and hateful stares. As she now stared at him, she noticed he was shaped like a pear. A six-and-a-half-foot, black pear with a shiny black, pumpkin head – no neck. She was sure he'd been kicked out the Marines for being overweight. He did say he was forced to retire. At least they had that much in common. Still, he was in charge, not her. And he was *stupid.*

"Life ain't fair, ya know it," he mumbled as he re-adjusted the unsightly stack of Fayetteville *Observers* some customers had rifled through, as though the top ones didn't contain the same bad news about the economy, the war and the sheer hopelessness that convinced the entire country of some impending national judgment. Jamal suspected though they were looking for coupons, a sales gimmick brought back to get people to at least buy a paper, if not read it, which few people did anymore. During the last four years, newspapers, magazines and book publishers had been folding around the world, especially in the U.S.

"Is he clairvoyant?!" Kathy thought, again startled. She wondered if she should even be thinking that. Could he hear her thoughts?

"Things weren't s'pose to be like d'is," Jamal went on, still mumbling more than actually talking. "'Bama promised change for d'better, *not d'worse.* D'gov'ment done messed up ever'thang now."

Oh, that again! Kathy sighed with relief he was only talking politics again, his favorite subject. Not hers. He was right though. Americans had wanted change and they got it – *18 percent inflation and 16 percent unemployment.* And the recession- turned-depression was the least of America's problems. In her bitterness, Kathy decided America's taxing situation was what it deserved, especially for idiots like Jamal.

She laughed at herself for thinking he could read minds when he could barely read the instructions on the cappuccino machine? Even Jamal's religion was mostly about politics, which was more tolerable to her than his theology. In the last eight months of hearing him preach his political gospel, she'd learned he belonged to an all black church that fused Christianity and Islam, whose Jesus was more like the Jesus of the Koran than the Jesus of the Bible.

The "Kingdom" will come, he'd say, but first the white man would have to pay for his sins against the black man. Though she wasn't a practicing Catholic or one of those Bible-thumping Baptists she resented more than Jamal, she didn't recall reading any biblical accounts of God promising to punish one specific race of sinners.

A buzzer went off at the counter, disrupting her thoughts and his mumbling.

"Yes," she answered the customer service call from pump 2, leaning toward the gooseneck microphone and pressing a button on the switchboard. "May I help you?"

Kathy smiled to herself when she realized she'd said the word 'may' and not 'can.' Josh Athol would be pleased. He was such a stickler for proper grammar.

"Turn on the pump!" An irritated voice came over the speaker.

"Sir," she responded. "Are you using a credit or debit card?"

"Neither one. I'm gonna fill up and pay cash," the voice came back, sounding even more irritated.

"Then you'll have to leave a $150 deposit first," she explained.

"I don't know if it'll hold that much," the voice came back, clearly angry now. "Just turn on the pump!"

"I'm sorry, sir," she said, trying to sound sympathetic. "I can't do that."

The caller didn't call back, but Kathy and Jamal could hear his explicatives from inside the store. Jamal walked to the double glass door and leaned against the doorpost, watching the disgruntled customer speed away, almost hitting another customer's car as it pulled in from the side road that led back to I-95. Jamal then expressed some explicatives of his own when he realized the angry customer had left the fuel hose and nozzle stretched out on the pavement.

"Ya piece of dumb *bleap* white trash," he mumbled loud enough that Kathy could hear him. "Ya prob'bly didn't have no money in the fus' place."

When he punched open the door, a tiny brass bell tied to the door handle tingled loudly. Jamal waddled outside and across the station parking lot as a young woman hurried inside. She wanted menthol cigarettes and light beer. Kathy didn't even card her. It wasn't necessary anymore, now that the federal government had standardized the legal drinking age at 18 and smoking at 16.

State laws concerning every aspect of society – education, health care, family life, social values – were being replaced by federal laws. Congress called it the *Children's Rights Amendment*. Kathy liked some of the changes but questioned the federal government usurping the Constitutional rights of the states, and that thought bothered her because she was starting to think like those *stupid* Southerners and cowboys.

As the girl hurried back out the door, Kathy also wondered why tobacco, alcohol and greasy fast foods seemed to be the only products unaffected by the terrible inflation that swept the nation two years ago. Now she really didn't like where her thinking was going because she was starting to think like Josh.

Just because she'd lost her job and all the *things* that meant anything to her – *just as he predicted* – didn't make him a prophet. Besides, he'd also said the federal government would one day start rounding up *"enemies of the state,"* putting them in camps just like the Nazis did in Germany back in the 1930's. That hadn't happened – *yet.*

Jamal hustled back inside gasping for air with every step. His face was dripping with sweat, his dingy green polo shirt was soaked, and he smelled like a locker room. It was another hot August day. The whole earth seemed to be struggling for its next breath, but global warming had nothing to do with it.

"You need to sit down, Jamal," she told him, like a mother scolding a stubborn child. "Here, let me get you at bottle of water."

He didn't argue. He climbed upon a large stool near the back side of the counter and waited for the promised water bottle. As Kathy walked back to her end of the counter and a smaller stool, he watched her. She wasn't hard to look at for a white woman in her mid-50's. He liked her shape, especially as she walked away. He also liked the ruffled blouses she wore, always low-neck, always tempting him to look.

Kathy's dark brown hair was thinning on the top; he could tell that because he was a foot taller than her. She kept it colored to hide the gray, but the roots along the top of her scalp often showed her real hair color, which was more gray than brown. White women like to color their hair; black women like wigs and assorted hair *stuff*, as he called it. It was all *vanity*. Women were vain. That was why he'd never married.

But he did like to look at women, something that had gotten him in trouble as a Marine and as a store manager. In fact, he was transferred to this store from Jacksonville because a high-yellow girl accused him of inappropriate contact. All he did was touch her hair to see if it was a wig!

Kathy sensed his eyes groping her but pretended not to notice. Jamal had very little use for white people, but he did like to look at women – white, black, yellow, brown – it didn't matter. Every day she watched him as he watched women come and go, and in this part of Benton County, most of their female customers were poor whites, blacks and Hispanics who lived in run-down trailer parks or on farms nearby, or they were wealthy Northerners stopping by on their way to or from Florida.

Not many people traveled long distances these days, gas being over $9 a gallon. Incidents like the guy trying to get her to pump the gas before paying were common. Last winter, when gas went over $9 a gallon, there was rioting in the streets. Some gas stations in L.A., Charlotte, Chicago, Atlanta and Miami were torched by rioters venting their anger at the high gas prices and government lies that no one was gouging them.

But even the ignorant masses understood someone was deliberately controlling the supply of oil and gas in order to increase demand and inflate prices. It was too bad, she thought, that more people couldn't stay focused or angry long enough to change things back from socialism to a free, capitalist economy.

She thought about that bogus "hit list" of oil company executives that made its way around the internet. It supposedly contained names and addresses of top executives and urged a lawless public to take action against the greedy devils controlling their lives. Kathy suspected it was probably a government-sponsored hoax, one performed by the Department of Homeland Security, the ATF or FBI, who used the riots and phony hit list to declare martial law in a dozen major cities.

No arrest of the subversive hit list's author was ever made. Seems the names and addresses were as fictitious as the government's excuse for suspending civil liberties.

"I've got to stop thinking like this," she thought. "I'm getting more and more paranoid – *just like Josh.*"

Josh Athol was one of the English teachers in her school. At first they were friends, but his radical teaching practices forced her to take action against him. Kathy sighed a moment when she thought about him. Had he been *friendlier*, she might have overlooked his crazy ideas about returning to the basics of learning.

No! That wasn't true. She wasn't a woman scorned. Josh made it clear his fundamentalist beliefs forbid extra-curricular *activities*. She respected him for that and wondered how he could love his wife that much. She never loved her husband like that, which was probably why the silly twit divorced her when he found out about the assistant football coach. *Called her a cougar!* It was the first time she'd ever heard the term. At least he didn't know about the others. She wouldn't have gotten a good settlement.

She counter-sued her naïve husband on grounds of mental cruelty, getting the Mercedes and the house, which she sold back to him after their youngest chose to stay with her father. Their son was a college student at the time, but he also sided with his father. Kathy won in divorce court but lost her family.

She decided to go back to her maiden name and move south, to start over. North Carolina needed English teachers, and she was a seasoned veteran, well-rehearsed in the latest *research-based, field tested* teaching strategies supported by the NEA, to which she'd belonged since 1988 when she completed her bachelor's after 12 years of part time studies and fulltime housewife.

She started teaching with great expectations of touching the lives of kids in her classroom and maybe proving to her own kids why she'd chosen her career over family. If only she'd known the NEA and the public school system itself would betray her 22 years later! Maybe Josh was right. The whole stinking system is corrupt. *Life stinks then you die!*

Her mind drifted from how she was betrayed by the school system to how she betrayed Josh. She could still see him carrying his last box of personal reference books, files and papers down the hallway, forced to pass by her classroom. She was co-instigator with Brookie, the assistant principal for getting Josh fired for "refusing to meet the needs of *diverse* (non-reading) learners," which in layman's terms meant he refused to accept the modern education theory about *learning styles* (that some children learn best by *doing*, not reading).

Josh was subversively asking other teachers how they would teach a child to understand abstract concepts like *love, liberty* and *honesty* with *hands-on* activities. He flatly refused to teach using small group settings (group learning), refused to grade holistically (overlook grammar, spelling and sentence structure errors), and he wouldn't allow his students to *visually express* (not write) how they *felt* about a particular theme in something he'd read to them (thematic visualization).

He actually expected his students to read their *own* literature assignments – not him read *to/for* them – and write their *own* essays! As Superintendant Ferrell said, Josh Athol was too rigid for his own good. He had to go.

"I'm sorry that teaching didn't work out for you," she remembered saying as Josh walked by her that afternoon. "Maybe you can teach in a Christian school."

"Maybe," he said, pausing only for a moment. "I'm not worried about me, and you don't need to worry about me either. The Lord will take care of me and my family. You did what the system programmed you to do. But your *religious* zeal for the public school system and these *Different but Equal* teaching strategies will be your downfall some day because this system you love so well considers you as much a threat as it does me. *You know too much.*"

He didn't wait for her reply, just walked away. That was six years ago. Someone told her he'd joined the sheriff's department. If so, she hadn't seen him, nor did she wish to. His insulting comment about her being "programmed" and especially her supposed "*religious* zeal" for the public school system would mean nothing – *except that things came about exactly as he predicted.* She'd been forced from her job by those she had blindly obeyed!

While she was busy weeding out classical educators like Josh, the system was purging itself of all teachers who'd come through Outcome-Based Education, Student-Centered Learning and even No Child Left Behind. Starting two years ago, any teacher with 20 or more years in the classroom was forced into early retirement by the federal government, ostensibly, to create more jobs for "an *army* of *new* teachers," who were supposedly better trained to understand the needs of today's children.

Both assertions were boldface lies! For 20 years public schools had had trouble filling classrooms with certified teachers, and for the last three, 70 percent of the younger teachers were quitting before the start of their second year on the job.

"Did ya eat lunch?" Jamal grunted, breaking her from her thoughts.

"Not really," she admitted. "I ate some crackers and some candy. That's about all I'll eat until I get home."

"W'ah, I'm goin' in d'back of d'sto' to eat m'ah lunch," he told her as he slid off the stool, plopping his nearly 300 pounds supported by hard-sole shoes that hit the tile floor with a *clack*. "Buzz m'a if ya need help wid anythin'."

As he disappeared through the stockroom door, Kathy realized Linda Ronstadt was singing to her, telling her "*You're no good.*" She tended to agree but wondered why she felt more guilt for the deceitful way she'd treated Josh than the deceitful way she treated her husband and children. She'd tried to achieve her American dream by cheating her way to the top then found out when she got there, it wasn't real. The dream was nothing but a nightmare.

She helped herself to a pack of cheese crackers from the small snack rack and walked around to the double doors to take a look at the world outside, the world that had beaten her twice – in her marriage and her career. It seemed to be beckoning her to try just one more round. As she nibbled on a cracker, she noticed a baggy pants teenager strolling toward the store from a wooded area that concealed a trailer park just up the road.

He held his britches up with one hand, and with the other, he seemed to be text-messaging on a cell phone. Even though it was August, he wore a hooded gray, pullover sweatshirt. *Stupid*, she thought. As he drew closer, Kathy realized he was one of her former students. She rushed back behind the counter and turned to one side, trying not to show her face when he burst through the double doors, ringing the little brass bell, which announced his arrival.

Tyrone didn't even give her a glance, almost as if he didn't want her to see his face either. He went straight to the beer refrigerator and began plucking cans of beer from a six pack, seemingly placing each beer on the floor by his feet. She could see him in a distorted way through the convex mirrors in each corner of the store.

He was bending over the open refrigerator door in a way that seemed peculiar, but she didn't want to say anything in an accusing way. Then he stood up and walked casually by a large snack rack, snatching a family-size bag of potato chips before bolting for the door. She knew better than to try to stop him.

Kids like Tyrone couldn't get jobs when they were *given* (literally) their high school diploma because they were unable to read. Employers didn't want to hear about their *learning styles* or *learning disability labels*. So now, a generation of *diverse* learners like Tyrone was putting the "hands-on" learning style theory into effect by stealing everything they could get their hands on!

"*Jamal*," Kathy pressed the button for the stockroom as she spoke into the gooseneck microphone. "You may want to come out here. *We've just had another shoplifter.*"

She could hear Jamal cursing all the way to the stockroom door through which he crashed and continued on to the front doors, as if he might catch a glimpse of the culprit leaving the scene of the crime. Tyrone was long gone by then, having jumped a ditch and run into the wood line. Kathy imagined there was probably a beaten path there that led back to the trailer park, from which most of their *non-paying* customers came and went.

"I know this one's name," she told Jamal, who stood in the doorway mumbling. "His name is Tyrone, probably 18 or 19 years old now."

"Call the shur'ff's office and r'port it," he mumbled, too exasperated to ask how she knew Tyrone's name. "Wha' dis 'un take?"

Jamal's store was hit at least three times a week. Sometimes the punks were armed, for which he used to have a little something for them. He pulled his Glock on a punk at his store in Jacksonville three years ago. Scared the kid so bad, he wet himself as he ran back out the store, crying "Don't shoot! Don't shoot!"

The feds seized his Glock there at the store four months later then raided his home that evening, taking every gun he had. Their warrant was the *NCIS Improvement Act*, better known as the *Veterans Disarmament Act*.

Jamal had been medically retired from the Marine Corps in 2006 after surviving an IED attack against his convoy near Ramadi in 2005. He was the only survivor in the Humvee, with blood and body parts from the only three white people he ever cared about splattered all over him. Jamal suffered a broken leg and TBI but mostly

PTSD. And because PTSD was on his VA medical file, the government he had served for 20 years of his life stole his 2nd Amendment right to defend himself and his store, ostensibly because he *might* be a danger to himself or others.

Jamal's blood boiled whenever he thought about it. Nearly five years ago, the ungrateful government – *both* houses of Congress, including *both* political parties and a supposed-to-be *gun rights* president, *even the NRA* – were afraid of Jamal and millions like him, so they enacted a law that the new administration was now using to disarm veterans.

Why? Jamal knew why. Anyone with any common sense knew why. It was because he was a Marine, trained in the use of firearms and military tactics. If it weren't so, why hadn't they bothered to round up the illegal guns owned and used by criminals to commit crimes? *Their purpose was never to reduce crime but reduce resistance!*

If he still had his pistol, he'd use it to defend himself, even Kathy and his other employees. But he wasn't going to use it to murder anybody, not even the white and black trash or the Hispanic punks who came in the store to rob him. He wasn't crazy. The war was hard on a lot of veterans, what with repeated deployments to Iraq and Afghanistan for nine years now. Every day it looked like Iran, Syria and Pakistan were going to be added to the Middle East bus tour.

What kind of way was this to reward veterans, declaring war on them, pronouncing them guilty of a crime they *might* commit?! It was like racial profiling, only it was committed against those Americans sworn to protect and defend the Constitution. **That was it!** *Once a Marine, always a Marine.* Yeah, that was the reason. He was disarmed because somebody was planning on taking over the country. *Or maybe they already had.*

It wasn't fair. And it wasn't right. He suffered enough in service of this oppressive nation! Taking his pistols, rifles and shotguns was too much. For over six years now, he'd lived with nightmares about the explosion. Chaplain Leland was a good man, and it didn't matter if he was white, and *Southern* white at that. The driver, Pfc. Dayton was a little sweetheart, everybody's little sister. And Gunny Murphy was the only white man he'd ever called his friend.

The Army doctors in Landstuhl who removed the bone fragments imbedded in his right cheek determined that the bone splinters came from Murphy's left thigh. It grieved him to think about it. It was Murphy who had stood by Jamal when Jamal's ex-girlfriend charged him with sexual harassment. He'd warned her she was going to ruin her career if she didn't quit messing with that married white guy – an *officer* at that. *Served them right that they brought smoke down on themselves by trying to file charges against him!*

Pastor Chavis here at *Falcon Manna Praise Tabernacle Church of Christ of Prophecy* and Pastor Odum at *Trinity Holiness Full Gospel Church of God in Christ* near Maysville had counseled him about his feelings of guilt for having lived when his fellow Marines died. They reminded him that he had been caught up in a *white man's war against their Moslem brothers*, that the Father had chosen to spare him when he released his wrath upon the others, not that they were personally *bad* people but because they were guilty of *white sins*. Jamal wanted to agree with them and go on with his life.

Even his mama had told him to let it go, saying, "D'ose white dudes an' d'at white chick wo'd lon' since be done furgot you b'now."

She was right, of course. Mama was always right. But Jamal was torn between his lifelong racial hatred and his genuine love for three dead white people.

"Oh, he took some beer and chips. Anyway, the sheriff's office is sending a deputy out to get prints and a copy of the surveillance DVD," Kathy interrupted his thoughts. "I told them the kid's name and where he was heading. He'll be in the county jail by sundown."

"Yeah, and in Kuwait w'in 30 days," Jamal added sarcastically. "D'ay don't play games wid d'ese punks no mo'r."

"That just doesn't make sense to me," Kathy said, popping a top on another Diet Coke. "I mean, why take a sociopathic punk like that, send him to a war zone and put a gun in his hand?"

"Weapon," he corrected her.

"Huh?" She asked.

"*Weapon*," he repeated. "D'ay call 'em *weapons or rifles*, not *guns*."

"Whatever," she responded, taking a sip from her Coke then biting a chunk from a cheese cracker. "It just seems to me you can't force somebody to fight a war for you without risking him going off on his leaders."

"It happ'ns," Jamal admitted. "But lot of us 'ave f'ot in wars we didn't want to. For d'most part d'ough, ya ain't fight'n for d'gov'ment. Yur fight'n for d'guy to yo left and right. D'ay d'ones d'at keep ya 'live, so ya wanna keep d'em 'live."

What he said made sense, even though she had no military experience. It had become government policy now to ship out repeat, non-violent offenders to the war zone. Congress paved the way for it, somehow with that all-inclusive Children's Rights Amendment. This was one of the measures she disagreed with because it – *more than many other areas in which the amendment was now applied* – essentially said the state now owned the children – *and apparently adults too.*

Repeat offenders 17-21 years old, especially males, were carted off to a special 12-week basic training camp in Kuwait that was ran by joint U.S. forces. Upon graduation, they were required to serve 12 to 18 months combat service, usually with the Army or the Marines. If they served their time honorably, they could reenlist with a promotion or go back home and report to a federal parole board. Those who were killed in action, however, did not get the same life insurance and few of the veterans benefits afforded to volunteers and draftees.

Their families got a small indemnity from the government, but they couldn't even be buried in a veterans' cemetery. Kathy had to admit that as harsh as this new arrangement seemed to be, it was helping to get juvenal and some gang-related crime under control, and it kept the government from having to draft as many law-abiding Americans since re-establishing the draft last year.

"*Aaaah…….*" Jamal growled then added some colorful language to go with it as he watched what appeared to be another baggy-pants, gangster-wannabe approaching the convenience store. "We got 'nother one."

"I don't know that one," Kathy said, as she peered around Jamal's massive form to see the approaching storm.

She quickly retreated back to her counter, setting down her Diet Coke and putting away the rest of her cheese crackers. As the stage set itself for the show to begin, satellite radio began playing John Lennon's imaginary world of peace, a world without possessions, hunger, greed or God. Jamal ambled toward the rear of the store and began straightening items on each shelf, pretending not to be watching Iago as he made a beeline for the door. The tiny brass bell announced his arrival.

"Yo, m'on," Iago said, nodding at Jamal and pointing at him with his right index finger, thumb cocked back.

He headed straight for the soda refrigerator, walking with a defiant bounce, his long dreadlocks swaying from side to side. He grabbed a 20 oz. Pepsi, twisted open the cap then began drinking it down, all of it. Some spilled out over his grungy beard, but he continued until he'd emptied the bottle. Then he belched, smiled and turned toward the counter.

He had a vicious look that made Kathy shiver. Jamal took one look at him then at the metal baseball bat he kept under the counter, near where Kathy was standing. He began moving toward the counter, figuring to nudge her aside.

Iago placed the empty bottle on the counter, belched again then grinned, showing off a sparkling gold tooth that he apparently wanted her to see. A spider-web tattoo ran down one side of his neck into a dingy, oversize t-shirt. Standing so close, Kathy could smell his intense body odor. He wasn't one of their local punks.

"M'on, d'at wuz good!" He laughed to himself, realizing how uncomfortable he was making them both. "It's hot out d'are."

Kathy tried to smile and nod her head in agreement. Jamal continued to edge his way behind the counter. Iago liked the odds, a skinny white woman and a whale of a brother.

"I need som' gas," he told them, trying to belch again but to no avail.

Kathy and Jamal looked at him then at each other then outside then back at him. They'd both seen him walk into the station parking lot.

"No, m'on," Iago laughed, realizing why they were so puzzled. "M'a van ran out of gas on m'e 'bout half mile up d'road. Ya got a gas can I can use?"

"I can sell ya one," Jamal spoke up, now at the edge of the counter, facing Iago. "Got some 3 gallon c'tainers right ova d'are."

Iago looked up at Jamal, sizing him up. It was a face off – a huge black American and a medium-size, black Jamaican. Jamal's cold expression was intimidating. *Even though he was overweight and out of shape, he was still a Marine gunnery sergeant and not the least bit impressed with this punk!* After several seconds, Iago grinned again then shuffled toward the aisle to which Jamal was pointing. On the bottom shelf, he found a dusty row of bright red, plastic gas canisters. He picked one up, blew off the dust and looked at the price sticker on the side: $17.95.

"M'on, yur crazy!" He said then swore. "I ain't payin' d'at kind of money for no gas can! I jest need a half gal'n or so to get d'van started d'en I'll drive it up hea' to fill it up. Ya can sell m'a a whole tank full d'en."

Jamal and Kathy said nothing, just stood there behind their counter fortress. This guy seemed like he was getting ready to go off. Jamal knew he could take him in a straight fight. He just hoped he wasn't packing a pistol or knife.

Iago put the canister back on the shelf then looked around with growing frustration. Finally fixing his eyes on the refrigerator, he marched down the aisle, made a right face then jerked open the refrigerator door, grabbing a half gallon carton of milk off the shelf. The price on the shelf said it was $4.51 plus tax. Iago sneered at the price then marched back up the aisle with the carton, plopping it on the counter. He pealed a $10 bill from a roll of bills in his left front pants pocket then snatched the carton of milk up as he headed for the door.

"D'ats fur d'soda an' d'milk," he told Kathy as he was almost at the door. "I'll pump whateva' change's left in d'is carton."

The tiny brass bell tingled while Kathy looked at Jamal, as if asking what to do. He lifted his left hand in a waving motion, as if to say, "Stay where you are."

As Iago marched across the station parking lot heading for pump #1, he torn off the plastic ring on the cap then opened the carton, dropping the ring to the pavement and stuffing the cap in his right front pants pocket. He started pouring out the milk on the pavement as he walked, then stopped and drank down as much as he could stand until brain freeze made him stop. He shook his head wildly and coughed then poured out the rest, trying to shake out the last few drops of milk.

He lifted the handle on the pump and stuffed the nozzle into the now empty milk carton then looked back at the store window, waiting for Kathy to turn on the pump. She didn't and he was about to lose his cool. Inside, Jamal was losing his cool too. He told Kathy to call the sheriff's office again then leaned the ball bat upright, so he could grab it more easily. Outside, Iago finally exploded.

"***Don't mess wid m'a, m'on!***" Iago said, cursing as he dropped the fuel nozzle and milk carton and began stomping his way toward the door. He was having a bad day.

Two days ago, he and Leo were taking their time, sighting-seeing their way back north after making a pickup in Miami. They were leaving Savannah, heading north on U.S. 17 but decided to grab a biscuit and coffee at Hardees. Seeing a street preacher standing on the corner giving out Bible tracts, Iago had to play with him.

He lowered his passenger side window as they stopped for the light. Grinning, he asked the preacher what he was selling. *It was the preacher's fault.* He tried to hand Iago a tract that had the words "Heaven or Hell" on the cover then he asked him if he died that day if he was sure he'd go to Heaven. Still grinning, Iago pulled his .25 caliber semi-automatic and put it in the preacher's face, asking him the same question.

He'd have left him alone after that had the preacher not been so arrogant. Iago hated people who were so sure about what they believe, about right and wrong, good and evil, God and Satan. That preacher looked directly into the barrel of the pistol and said defiantly that he was sure he was going to Heaven then he added he wasn't afraid to die because of his "relationship" with Jesus. *So Iago popped a few caps in his face.* Leo had thought his playing with the preacher was funny up till then. He was superstitious or something, said you didn't kill preachers.

Leo floored it, running a red light and having to dodge on-coming traffic. Then he got off the back roads where they were safer, considering their cargo, and headed straight up I-95. When they stopped for gas near Florence that afternoon, Leo drove off while Iago was in the bathroom. He later called Iago on his cell phone and told him to find his own ride back to New York. He told Iago he was "bad luck."

After being stranded in a state full of redneck white dudes and in-bred brothers, Iago was beginning to believe he was bad luck. Then this morning he saw the soccer mom jump out of her minivan and run in a convenience store just like this one. She not only left the keys in the van, she left the engine running. Iago walked right up to the van, opened the door and sat down in the driver's seat, closed the door and drove away.

As he headed up the street, he used the rear view mirror to inspect the back seat and make sure he didn't have any kiddie passengers he'd have to drop off at the curb. There was a child's car seat behind him but no occupant. Whether she intended to grab a cup of coffee, cigarettes or just leave the air conditioner running, the dear lady had done wonders for his self-esteem. He wasn't bad luck after all.

That's what he thought. He spent the next hour on his cell phone, calling Leo to report his good luck and to check on the delivery of their goods, particularly his share in the sale of those goods. He had to be careful what he said, as the new and improved Patriot Act had given the FCC, FBI, ATF and Homeland Security the authority to listen to all calls. He thought himself clever when he asked Leo if their sister had gotten home safely and if the folks were happy to see her.

To each of these questions, Leo was short with his answer, confirming everything was "cool," that he and the "family" were looking forward to seeing him. It bothered him a little that Leo wasn't concerned he might want some sort of concession for having abandoned him in South Carolina.

After talking with Leo, he tried to call home and talk to his mother in Kingston. But within minutes after he got her on the phone, his cell phone battery went dead. *And his charger was in his bag in Leo's Camry!* He threw the phone in the passenger side floor and cursed just to hear himself curse. His mother didn't approve of his gang life and refused to accept any money from him. She was always begging him to come home. At least this time he didn't have to hear her say she was praying for him.

Maybe he wasn't that lucky after all. He was sure of it less than half an hour later when his fuel light came on. He had failed to notice how much gas was in the van when he stole it, and now he was 15 minutes north of the last exit for Fayetteville and at least five from a town called Doone. He was hoping he could make it to the next station when the van's engine died, a little less than a mile from this station and convenience store. *And now he was having to deal with these wanna-be heroes!*

The tiny brass bell announced Iago's re-entry, not that Jamal and Kathy weren't expecting him. She was on the phone, trying to get help. The Eagles were on satellite radio, taking them all down a dark desert highway. It was Kathy's favorite song, but she wasn't able to enjoy listening to it right now.

"Drop d'phone!" He ordered after whipping out his pistol and pointing it at her as he approached the counter. "I said drop d'phone."

She dropped it, causing it to bounce off the counter then fall to the floor. The dispatcher could be heard asking the caller to repeat what she'd said. Iago knew they could trace the call in seconds. He also knew he was on a surveillance camera at that very moment. But he didn't care. His mind was running wild. He wanted to shoot them both and make a run for it. But he didn't have a car!

"Let her be. She ain't done nothin' to you," Jamal said, sliding between Kathy and Iago's gun. "I to'de her to make d'call. Figured d'at wuz why you wuz testing us."

"*What?!*" Iago demanded. "What ya talkin' 'bout, m'on?"

Jamal told him he figured he was with the North Carolina Department of Agriculture, that he was there testing them to make sure they obeyed a state law about not allowing customers to dispense gas into unauthorized containers. He was lying through his teeth, of course, trying to buy some time for both of them. If that deputy didn't get there soon, he'd have to distract this punk somehow and take his ball bat to him. He was pretty sure he could hit a homerun with that frizzy head! Still, he wished he had his Glock.

Jamal wasn't trying to be a hero, just a Marine. It wasn't as if he was trying to protect Kathy or that he particularly liked her either. He didn't. But intelligent, dependable and *honest* employees were hard to find and Kathy was all three, something he couldn't say about his other three girls or even his assistant manager. Kathy was worth more to him than what he could afford to pay her, so he told her to help herself to all the sodas, snacks and chocolate she wanted.

He didn't make the same offer to the others. Didn't have to for they tended to steal small items from the store on a regular basis. Kathy came to work, did her job and went home. Except that she never went to church, she lived the same lonely existence he lived. That, and both of them having been forced into an early retirement was all they had in common.

"You 'tink I work for d'gov'ment?" Iago asked, almost grinning again. "M'on, yur crazy. If I worked for d'gov'ment, why do I gotta gun in yo face?"

"Maybe ya jest wanna scare us," Jamal told him, coolly.

"I don't need no gun to do d'at, m'on," he said, shoving the pistol in his right rear pocket then whipping out a long, lock-back knife from his left rear pocket.

He had the blade open and locked in place before they realized what he was brandishing now. The blade alone was at least six inches long, with part of it serrated so it would rip the flesh. Iago had calmed down some now and realized using his pistol here would trace him back to the preacher he was sure he'd killed back in Georgia. He could take care of these two with his knife then unload his pistol on somebody when he got back to New York.

"You ain't playin' me, are ya?" Jamal asked, just to see his reaction, his eyes looking down at the bat that almost touched his left leg.

"Nah, fool! I ain't playin' you!!!" Iago shouted then tried to stick the knife in the Formica counter top.

It wouldn't stick, so he tried it again with more force. Seeing this distraction as his chance, Jamal reached down and grabbed the bat, quickly passing it to his right hand. But as he raised it in the air, Iago swiped his right forearm with the knife, cutting a long, deep gash. The bat dropped to the floor with a loud *clang!* Jamal grabbed his forearm with his left hand and cursed Iago's mother.

Iago lunged forward and made an upward swipe with the knife, this time slashing Jamal's throat from left to right. The serrated edge ripped open the main artery in his short fat neck while the razor end sliced through part of his windpipe. Jamal's hands went for his throat, having immediately sensed he couldn't get his breath.

With Jamal's center of mass now fully exposed, Iago lunged forward again, this time plunging the knife in the middle of Jamal's huge chest, just under the ribcage. Blood was gushing all over the counter and onto the floor. It all happened in a matter of seconds, too quickly for Kathy to react, not that she could. She couldn't catch her own breath and was unable to move her feet. She was controlled by fear.

Jamal understood he was about to die, and this was just not the way he ever imagined it. His murderer wasn't a white man but one of his own race. What would Pastors Chavis and Odum say now? How would Mama explain this outrage? His whole life's energy had been wasted hating one particular race of people when now he realized all men were equally evil! When Iago dared to step forward to stab him again, Jamal grabbed him by his skinny neck and began to squeeze. He was sure he could rip his ugly head off if he tried.

Iago wasn't expecting the counterattack. He tried slashing at Jamal's arms and stabbing at his chest again, but Jamal had a much longer reach. He was suffocating under his deadly grip and felt like his neck was about to break. He tried to jump onto the counter or pull himself away, but Jamal was too powerful for him. Iago started to feel faint. He regretted not using his pistol.

Jamal suddenly relented. He was barely able to see the face of his murderer whom he was now murdering, and he didn't want to leave this world with that image in his mind or answer for it when he faced the God he now figured had been trying to talk to him the last seven years. He released Iago and the hatred that had consumed him for 44 years then he fell forward across the bloody counter top, mouthing a prayer only Jesus could hear. *"I'm sorry, Lo'd. He's yo's to deal wid."*

Iago staggered backward for a moment, coughing and cursing then he lunged forward one more time, this time plunging the knife in the middle of Jamal's back, its sharp point piercing vertebra and slicing into the spinal cord. Jamal's body flinched only slightly then went limp. His eyes were still open, but the world around him was growing dim. The last thing Jamal saw was a blurred figure approaching the doorway.

The brass bell's tingle seemed louder than ever. Still frozen in her corner behind the counter, Kathy snapped her head toward the door as did Iago who was wiping his bloody hands on his t-shirt. A small Hispanic boy stood fixed in the open doorway, his mouth ajar. He saw a pool of blood covering the tile floor in front of him and an enormous black man stretched across the counter, drenched in blood with a large knife sticking out of his back. As if snatched from behind, the boy leaped backward out the door then raced across the parking lot toward his mom standing beside pump #3, apparently waiting for the pump to be turned on.

Kathy suddenly found life in her lungs and her feet, both at the same time. She screamed for all she was worth and tried to make a run for it toward the door, but she slipped on Jamal's blood that was oozing out in all directions. Iago quickly plucked his knife from Jamal's back then went after Kathy, jerking her to her feet, while himself slipping on the blood he'd shed.

"Ya gotta car?" He growled, holding the bloody knife against her throat. "Answer m'a! 'Ave you gotta car hea'?"

"Yes," she whispered, afraid to open her mouth too much, feeling the edge of the blade cutting into her flesh. She pointed outside, toward the far end of the store. As she pointed, she was aware that his sweaty body odor now included the stench of blood.

"Where's d'keys?" He asked, dragging her behind the counter where he suspected she kept her keys.

He was right. A large key chain holding her apartment and car keys, personal trinkets and a small leather pouch containing a bottle of pepper spray lay atop her hand bag on a shelf under the counter. Kathy looked at the pepper spray longingly, hoping he wouldn't know what it was.

"*Don't even tink 'bout it, lady*," he told her. "You touch d'at stuff and I'll cut yo head off. Now let's see where d'at little brat done went."

He began dragging her back around the counter toward the door, this time avoiding the still growing pool of blood. He could see the little boy talking to his mom, pointing toward the door. No real threat, he told himself and shoved Kathy forward and out the door, the little brass bell clinging one last time.

Iago wasn't sure just how he'd make his escape, how he could get her to believe he wasn't going to kill her, so she'd drive them out of there. He would, of course, but later. Not now. He was taking it one step at a time.

Not only was he having trouble adjusting his eyes to the bright sun, it was just his luck that as soon as he exposed himself and his hostage, Deputy Sherman would finally show up to investigate the earlier shoplifting. He whirled into the station then wheeled his patrol car around, so he could park directly in front of the store. Only then did the rookie realize he'd come up on a hostage situation.

"Hold it," Sherman said, pulling his service pistol as he leaped into action, his patrol car still running. "Just hold it right there."

"Well, well," Iago laughed, seeing skinny, little Sherman take an exaggerated military stance with his pistol, as if he was good enough with it to pick him off from behind his hostage. "Don't try to be no hero d'are, Barney. You better wait fur Andy to get hea'. So you jest hold it right d'are yo'self. We got some place t'go."

Kathy was in another world. Though it had all happened in a matter of minutes, it seemed a lifetime ago that she watched Jamal step between her and a pistol. The guy she thought hated her was willing to die in her place. That didn't make sense. Why would anyone die for someone else? Maybe, like her, he was fighting demons of his own. They could have been friends!

Now Jamal was dead and she would be as soon as this devil forced her to drive them away from there. He would kill her. She knew it. Not that she loved this life; she simply wasn't ready to die. She was afraid. She was baptized as an infant and confirmed by the Church when she was 10, but she had no confidence in religious ceremonies and wished she had a personal faith like Josh.

Iago forced Kathy to move sideways in front of him, down the length of the store to where she'd said her car was parked near the dumpster. Across the station lot, he could see the Hispanic kid and his mom hiding on the opposite side of their car. He could see Sherman crouched down, still holding his gun on them with his face full of confusion.

What he failed to see was the faded blue Dodge Ram that was parked in the far corner of the parking lot. He didn't see the silver-haired man standing by the open door of the pickup, removing a rifle from a leather case he'd retrieved from behind the seat. In all the excitement, he failed to hear the sound of a round being chambered. But he did hear the deep, loud voice calling to him.

"**Hey, *prole!***" The silver-haired man called to Iago.

Iago turned his attention away from the others toward the voice. He saw the faded blue Dodge Ram and the silver-haired man and the reflection of light off the scope of the rifle aimed at him. The last thing Iago saw was a 180 grain Bronze Point™ slug that pierced the inside corner of his left eye, spiraled through his brain then exploded from the back of his head at 2500 ft/sec. Though only slightly deflected, the round continued on a path some ten feet behind him, ricocheting off the brick wall of the store into the dumpster behind and to the left of it. There, it ricocheted again into a group of pine trees behind the store.

The force of the bullet's impact caused Iago and Kathy to fall backward onto the burning asphalt. Iago's world was already fading to black as his soul cried out in terror of the hellish darkness into which he fell.

Kathy found herself screaming again, clutching her throat where the knife had sliced into her flesh. It was cut but not seriously. She felt weak and put her hand down to steady herself as she tried to stand, but she felt something warm and wet where her fingers touched. She looked down to see a pool of blood and brain tissue flowing out from Iago's dreadlocks, which lay sprawled out on the pavement like Medusa's hair. What used to be his left eye was now purple pulp. His mouth was wide open, his blood-smeared face was frozen in a look of surprise, and his gold tooth didn't sparkle anymore.

Kathy fainted.

The silver-haired man started to eject the shell in his rifle then stopped. No. There would be a pretense of an investigation. Just a pretense.

"Sherman, call for an ambulance and CSI," he shouted as he carefully put his rifle back in its case and behind his seat then he reached for his badge clipped on the sun visor. "I s'pect we'll find another body inside."

"Yes, sir," Sherman saluted after he put away his pistol.

The silver-haired man clipped his badge on his belt then slowly walked across the station lot toward his victim and Kathy. He had a serious limp that favored his right leg. As the silver-haired man neared the dead and the fainted, the deputy eased up to the store window, close enough where he could see inside. The silver-haired man refused to even look at Iago, but he painfully bent down on one knee beside Kathy and shook his head.

"I thought that was you," he said, almost whispering. "You've aged some, Kathy."

He slid one hand under her legs and another under her head, gently picking her up and moving her into the shadow of the building. He then plucked a white handkerchief from his back pocket and wiped the blood under her chin. She had a nasty cut, enough for two or three stitches, but he had saved the hostage.

"Inspector Athol, you were right," Sherman said, excitedly. "There is a body in there, a huge black dude laid out on the sales counter. Looks like another black on black crime, huh. *Two down, 38 million to go.* Hey, what was it you called that guy?"

He didn't respond, just looked up at Sherman through his dark photogray glasses, sneering at his racist comments and insensitivity in general. Sherman was a bigoted idiot, just like his namesake ancestor. He then looked back at Kathy, though his eyes kept trying to look over at Iago ten feet away. He refused to let them. He held the handkerchief to Kathy's bleeding chin, hoping she wouldn't awake before the rescue squad got there. Didn't feel like talking about *old times* with her. But the sound of the sirens approaching ended all hope of that.

"Josh?" Kathy asked, waking up in a panic, "*Is that you?!*"

So much for going fishing today, he thought.

Chapter Two

"Don't know much about history,
Don't much biology,
Don't know much about a science book,
Don't know much about the French I took..."
Sam Cooke, "Wonderful World"

"Well, if it isn't Inspector Callahan," Sheriff Westin said jokingly to his unwanted guests from the Department of Homeland Security. "Mr. Dodds, Mr. Peyton, I'd like y'all to meet our very own Dirty Harry, *Inspector Joshua Daniel Athol.*"

The three men were standing in the hallway outside the Sheriff's office when Josh entered the courthouse, his cased rifle tucked under his left arm. A hush fell over the entire building as he limped past office doors and rows of desks, each covered in desktop computers, phones and paperwork.

Several deputies chuckled, a couple patting him on the back as he went by. He ignored the VIPs and reported directly to the Sheriff, whom he'd heard referring to him as a Hollywood anti-hero. Josh couldn't see all that well, but he could hear a squirrel chewing on a pine nut at the top of a 200-foot Carolina pine tree.

"Not me – I'm not tall enough," he told Sheriff Westin, still ignoring his guests, whom he recognized from previous unannounced visits. "I brought my rifle in like a good little boy. Please ask McNeilly not to scratch it up."

"Good man," Westin said, pushing his glasses higher on the bridge of his nose, watching Josh as he turned and limped toward an empty desk in the far corner of the room. "Get your report done then take the next three days off while we placate the media with our…our… *investigation*. Oh, by the way. In case I'm asked, why were you at the crime scene? I thought you were gonna go fishing this afternoon."

"I thought so too," Josh said, turning to look at his mentor. "I drove out to Rhodes Pond but found out their bait store had closed up. A fellah who was putting in his jon boat told me I could buy some bait at the Flash Mart right off I-95.

"I got there just before Sherman came wheeling in the parking lot like a teenager on a joy ride. Already figured something was wrong when I saw a Mexican young'un come running out of there hollering his lungs out. He was telling his mama something, and I understood the Spanish words *sangre* and *hombre muerto*. Then I heard the scream inside the store. I reckon I was in the wrong place at the right time."

"Reckon so," Westin agreed, nodding his head approvingly, then as he led his guests into his office, he added instructions he didn't want to see Josh's reactions to. "Oh, speaking of Sherman. I'm gonna need you to work with him, Nichols and Hooper Friday night. We gotta show a large presence at the Board of Education meeting. They're expecting trouble. *Ha ha!* Can't imagine why anybody would be disappointed in our *wonderful* school board or our *great* public schools."

He went into his office with the feds following on his heels. Josh placed his rifle case across his borrowed desk and smirked. If he was a cussing man, he'd say something meaningful about his next assignment. As he made himself comfortable, Hooper slipped over to him and whispered that he needed a favor from him.

"Hey, Friday night, would ya mind lettin' that idiot ride with you?" He was earnestly pleading, his huge hand resting on Josh's shoulder. "We don't get along."

"Come on, Hoop," Josh smiled, returning the whisper. "That idiot's an equal opportunity bigot. He not only doesn't like black folks; he doesn't like Hispanics, Asians, Native Americans, Arabs, Jews, Baptists, Southerners or anybody that isn't a card-carrying Democrat."

"Yeah, I know," Hooper grinned. "But will ya keep 'em off my back and away from me. I can't 'ford to lose my job over d'at *federal snitch*."

Everyone knew Sherman was a federal hire – someone placed in every local and state law enforcement office by the federal government through the auspices of the Department of Homeland Security. The constant unannounced visits by the feds were probably due to information supplied by Sherman. He was a rat. Everybody knew it.

Interference by Homeland Security personnel was more than an aggravation. Violent crime had increased 270 percent over the last three years, but the feds saw local law enforcement reaction to it as a greater threat to security than the rising crime rates. Most states had long ago set up a Violent Crime Task Force, but Southern and most Western states had been resistant to federal interference.

Despite the enforcement of the NCIS Improvement Act and several other gun confiscation measures, there were more murders, rapes and armed assaults than ever in history. Most veteran law enforcement officials and all criminals knew by confiscating guns, the federal government had declared open season on law abiding citizens.

Sure, younger, less violent criminals were being carted off to serve as surrogate soldiers to fight in a war that had no end. The professional politician that promised to end the war began expanding it within a year after taking office. War was good business anyway. And besides, it helped keep the American people distracted from the increasing federal intrusions into their daily lives. The rate at which the federal government had grown in the past three years was scary, even to some liberals.

State governments were mere puppets – except in those Southern and Western states where storm clouds of succession were growing stronger, generally those states formerly designated by the media as "red" states but now called "white" states with symbolic malice.

Federal troops were too far stretched to confront dissident state legislatures head-on, so the president and his rubber-stamp Congress incited class and racial unrest through their allies in the news media, public education and especially entertainment. For most Americans, however, the race card was wearing thin.

North Carolina's liberal governor and other Democratic governors found themselves in a fix, wanting to support their Democratic president while needing the support of their state's military leaders. As a matter of policy, they were now refusing to send National Guard troops to support the war over there because they feared civil war could break out at any time right here. Most local governments and law enforcement agencies were holding out against both state and federal demands, trying to maintain some sense of community control.

Sheriff Dave Westin and the sheriffs in surrounding counties were under a lot of pressure to carry out ridiculous policies from Raleigh and Washington while maintaining law and order within their jurisdiction. They did not oppose *peaceful* secession but were sworn to work with National Guard commanders to put down all pockets of *violent* rebellion, should any appear. That hadn't been necessary – *yet*.

The one light of hope was the rise of a third political party, the *American Party*. Its pro life, pro family platform was reflected in its slogan: "*We'll keep the **Bible**, our **Guns** and the **Constitution**. You can keep the **Change**.*" The new party found an immediate attraction among evangelical and fundamentalist Christians who'd been used by Republican *socialists* for decades. It also attracted blue collar, pro life, *God & guns* Democrats who were sick of being called *racists* and *rednecks* by their *communist* leaders. The new party was a coalition of *former* Republicans, Democrats and Libertarians – *tea partiers* – the news media liked to call them.

This triple source of new members enabled the new party to pick up hundreds of local and state offices throughout Southern and Western states as well as several House and Senate seats during the mid-term elections. And even though the Republicans also re-gained some seats in Congress, it was the American Party that was re-setting the balance of power in government. In fact, several conservative Republican leaders had switched to the American Party during the last two years.

A proud member of the American Party, Josh was especially pleased that their candidate was a contender in the presidential race this year, much to the chagrin of the *Democratic* news media and Hollywood, who tried to paint the new party as underclass illiterates, racists and right-wing Christians. This was why the media now referred to the former "red" states as "white" states. The inference was clear.

The contrary was reality. It was that **50** percent of the country, those non-tax-paying, functionally illiterates – *proles,* Orwell called them, *fools,* the Bible called them – that had given inner party *scorners* control over the country, not those *simple*, tax-paying Americans now ready to take back the country or start a new one. Josh put his trust in God, not government, but he believed the American Party was the country's last best chance to avoid civil war.

"Okay," Josh smiled, musing about the political climate that he predicted six years ago. "It's my turn to watch Comrade Sherman anyway."

He suspected Westin gave him the assignment for that reason. Why else would they need an Incident Response Team inspector with the Violent Crime Task Force to work with a few deputies just to keep order at a school board meeting? There were little more than a dozen like him but scores of deputies.

Then again, since the federal government had delegated local school boards accreditation and teacher certification authority over home schooling parents and Christian schools, local school board meetings were sometimes entertaining. Josh knew the greatest hurdle home schooling parents or Christian school administrators had to get over was not simply the blessings of a biased public school board but the federal requirement that they use a federally-approved curriculum.

Josh also knew that federal curriculum was based on modern education theories and teaching strategies that were proven failures – *whole language reading, holistic grading, group learning, learning disability labels, learning style labels, thematic visualization* and *block scheduling.*

Even harder to swallow, the federal curriculum mandated Christian parents expose their own children to *Darwinism, moral relativism* and *socialism,* which Josh called the *Fundamentals of Humanism.* He could understand why so many parents around the nation were up in arms. *A federal public school curriculum violated the 1ˢᵗ and 10ᵗʰ Amendment!*

He logged onto the computer and began completing the pages of forms and reports required to justify his use of deadly force. Detective McNeilly came by to pick up his rifle, which he receipted to him with an admonishment that he could save him a lot of paperwork if he'd only use department weapons. He also said he was running a ballistics check on the "pea shooter" found in Iago's back pocket, and that he expected results in the next hour.

Half hour later, when his cell phone began vibrating, Josh noted the time. It was 5 p.m. Joy was checking on him.

"Did you catch any fish?" his wife asked, her voice sweet and cheerful, a great improvement in her disposition since being forced into retirement two years ago. Teaching was a job she loved to hate and hated to love. Teaching at *Northside Baptist Academy* this year was helping to fill a void.

"Nah," he told her, still punching keys on his keyboard. "Something came up, and I had to come by the courthouse. I should be home in an hour or so. I'll call ya when I leave here."

She didn't want him to hang up, knowing something was wrong at his end. But there were some things he didn't feel like talking about on the phone. And this was something he didn't want to have to tell his wife at all. Still, he hated cutting her off, knowing how sensitive she was and how she'd know something was wrong then worry herself sick about it until he came home.

"*You are the man*," McNeilly was back, this time with Detective Bennett. "You took out a naughty one this time. We just watched the surveillance video. That dude was bad news. He killed the manager, Jamal Wheatley then…."

"Yeah," Bennett interrupted. "Turns out that little pistol of his was used to kill a Baptist minister in Garden City, Ga. two days ago. They caught it all on traffic cameras. But even before that, the ATF was already following our little friend and his companion after they picked up 250 kilograms of cocaine in Miami. The feds figure there must have been some disagreement about killing the preacher. Your buddy was dumped off in Florence that afternoon."

"Phone traffic between the two punks didn't pick up again till this morning," McNeilly added. "Seems your buddy was bragging about some new means of transportation and trying to find out about their *sister's* arrival. He probably thought he was being clever on the phone. According to the feds though, he was headed for a landfill in Newark had he made it home. They're a small time gang, all of them from the Caribbean – Jamaica, Haiti, Puerto Rico, Cuba. But they have certain rules you don't break. Killing preachers is bad luck."

Josh wanted to comment that it was too bad the feds themselves weren't as superstitious. Since passing the *Hate Crimes Protection Act* nearly three years ago, all three branches of the federal government were violating the 1st Amendment rights of Baptist and fundamentalist churches around the country.

At first it was intimidation though public ridicule. The few African-American churches that had stood on the wrong side of the last presidential election were the first to suffer direct persecution. Late last year, Baptist ministers in San Francisco and Key West were arrested for supposedly *"inciting hate among their congregation by preaching against homosexuality."* Every arrest after that made national news, proving to Josh there was a media-backed, federal campaign to paint Bible-believing Christians as *enemies of the state.*

Multiple class action lawsuits were filed against KJV Bible publishers for not censoring key passages in the King James Bible, which calls homosexual behavior *sodomy* and further calls such behavior *"an abomination unto the Lord."* Though their lawsuits remained stalled in state courts, nearly all of the larger Bible publishers had stopped publishing the KJV Bible.

The apparent objective was to remove all negative references about sexual perversion from the Bible then fundamentalists wouldn't be able to call it a *sin* anymore. Josh figured their next step would be the confiscation and burning of KJV Bibles.

Hollywood and the news media added fuel to the fire, recently promoting a fictionalized account of David Koresh as a fundamentalist preacher rather than leader of an extremist, non-Christian cult. Bible-believing Christians were high on the government's list of hate groups with new sanctions and laws passed each month to force compliance into what the president called the *norm* of 21st Century Christian beliefs and practices.

Josh compared this government-sponsored persecution of Baptists and fundamentalist Christians to the persecution of Jews in Germany just 80 years ago. He figured concentration camps couldn't be too far in the very near future. In fact, he knew the good folks at Homeland Security had already built several dozen "containment camps" in remote areas around the country, a large one right here at Fort Bragg. He had little doubt who these camps were for. The prediction he gave Kathy six years ago was close to reality.

****

"I thought you were gonna call when you left work," Joy said, scolding him as she met him at the door. "Why didn't you call? What's wrong?"

He looked her in the eyes as he made his way through the doorway, which she seemingly blocked while waiting for an answer. His shaded glasses were no help. When his beady, gray eyes met her big, blue eyes, she knew he'd done something he regretted.

"*I killed another man today*," he told her, sighing as he walked into the kitchen where he searched the refrigerator for he didn't know what. "That makes four now."

"*Oh, Josh*," she said, closing the door. "I'm sure you had no choice. Did you at least save somebody's life?"

"Yeah, *Kathy*," he told her bluntly.

"*Kathy!*" She repeated, "Kathy? Not *Volkschulen High School's* Kathy?!"

"One and the same," he said. "Seems she now, or rather, she *used* to work for the Flash Mart off I-95 near Doone. Her store had a visitor today who wanted something more than gas. He killed the store manager and would have killed Kathy after using her as a hostage to get away."

"So *Miss Backstabber* was working for a convenience store," Joy mused, after concluding it was okay for Josh to have taken a life to save one, *even if it was Kathy*. After a long silence, she asked, "I don't s'pose you're wantin' supper?"

Joy was always trying to mother him now that their three kids were grown. She needed someone to take care of, but he needed to be alone right now. He shook his head, smiled at her then walked into his study, which had been their son's bedroom, now converted to an office.

Easing the door shut behind him, Josh looked at the pictures of his wife and kids hanging on the wall. There was also a colorful calendar of the North Carolina mountains as well as black and white prints of Robert E. Lee and Stonewall Jackson strategically positioned over his computer desk, next to son's old bunk bed. Then he looked at the bronze-plated plaque of the Ten Commandments, hanging by the closet door. His eyes immediately fixed upon the sixth commandment.

"*My God, what have I done?!*" He cried and fell on his face in the floor, "What have I become? Lord Jesus, *please* help me!"

From the other side of the door, Joy could hear him crying. She wanted to go to him but knew this was his *God & I* time. Josh was no killer. He'd completed two secret, special operations in Nicaragua in the early 1980's, had jumped into Grenada with the 1st Ranger Battalion and served with the 82nd Airborne Division during Just Cause and Desert Storm then with 3rd Ranger Battalion in Somalia.

In 21 years as an Airborne Ranger, he'd never killed a single enemy soldier. But in only four years with the sheriff's department, he'd killed four men, two in the last three months. Joy didn't understand it either.

****

"Hey, did ya hear the one about the black dude, the Mexican and the Jew?" Sherman asked, breaking a long silence as they drove the country back roads to the county courthouse for the school board meeting.

His three days off passed by quickly. It was Friday evening, not quite dark but getting there. Josh wondered why they had to schedule these meetings so late in the day, except perhaps to make formal appeals as inconvenient as possible. He had picked Sherman up in his Dodge Ram at the department's Overhills annex.

"*Uh uh,*" Josh said then turned toward the rookie deputy, shaking his head. "Don't really care to either."

A set of headlights nearly blinded them as Sherman felt his attempts to strike up a conversation rebuffed. Another long silence ended when a whitetail leaped across the road in front of them, forcing Josh to hit the brakes slightly.

"That was close!" Sherman overstated the situation.

"Not really," Josh said. I saw movement in the wood line and was already slowing down for him. It's a full moon tonight, so the deer are moving."

"Do you hunt?" Sherman asked.

"Used to," Josh answered, not elaborating.

"I know ya like to fish," the deputy came back. When Josh didn't respond, he asked, "You don't talk much, do ya?"

"Sometimes," he answered.

Sherman cursed under his breath then complained, "I can't figure out you guys."

"*How's that?*" Josh looked at him across the seat through the shadows.

"You *Southern* guys," he went on. "I can't figure you out. I always thought you guys were all Rebel flag-waving rednecks and loyal members of the KKK."

"*You thought wrong!*" Josh responded, his voice terse, "Sounds like you've gotten your information from the wrong sources."

"Public schools in Indiana and Ohio where I grew up use the same history textbooks you guys use down here," Sherman countered.

"If the public school system is your only source of information about the South, Southerners or even *Mr. Lincoln's War Against the Southern People*, you have a very skewed understanding," Josh shot back, this time with venom in his voice. "Public schools really didn't get started until after that war, where it was force-fed on the South with the objective of *re-educating* Southern children, mostly not to believe in *states' rights* but also to dumb them down."

"States' rights?" Sherman repeated, his words subdued by the *thunking* sound of the truck's tires passing over the concrete segments of the Cape Fear River bridge. "I've heard that argument before. But the whole world knows the Civil War was fought to free the slaves and save the Union."

"*What does the world really know?!*" Josh retorted, "The world knows the little bits and pieces of information fed to it by *unelected elitists* during the last 150 years. If Southerners were fighting to preserve slavery, why were the **85 percent** of Southerners who owned small farms and businesses – **no slaves** – willing to fight and die for someone else's slaves? And I *betcha* didn't know there were laws that allowed *planters* owning 20 or more slaves to stay home and run their plantation during the war.

"As for saving the Union, the only time these so-called *United* States have been *united* during the last 150 years is when an *outside* force attacked. *Maybe that's why our government has to invent outside enemies like Nazis, Communists or terrorists to keep from losing its control over its precious Union!*"

Josh allowed the bitterness in his voice to subside. Sherman kept silent.

"If you tell a big enough lie – *long enough*, the whole *stupid* world will believe it, especially the *proles* that put these devils in power," he said, sighing. "Just so you know though – *most Southerners are not a bunch of racists*. But we still hate Yankees though, especially Yankees baring notorious family names."

That said, he grinned, which Sherman could see through the street lights as they neared the courthouse. He wasn't sure if the grin made jest of his last statement or if it was the punctuation mark that concluded this Southern history lesson.

Inside the meeting room inside the county courthouse, parents and Christian school faculty members were already gathering. Josh located Nichols and Hooper then gave all three deputies an assigned area of the room to watch. Sgt. Rushton with the Millingham Police

Department caught Josh by the arm and let him know he had three officers inside the room and three outside the building.

The county Fire Marshall then pulled them both aside and warned them if more than 300 people came to the meeting, he might need their assistance in getting the new arrivals to go to the overflow room and watch the meeting on a large, flat screen television. Josh nodded his support and informed Nichols, Hooper and Sherman separately. Rushton did the same, only he used his radio. As they separated, Josh was taken by the symbolic differences in their uniforms.

The policemen wore their dark blue uniforms while the deputies wore their kaki, almost gray uniforms. Though his own uniform wasn't as flashy as his deputies, it was gray. He chuckled to think about it. Both policemen and deputies wore their standard side arm and radio, and all but Hooper and Josh wore the new stun gun-taser.

The new stun gun-taser had the capacity to send a stream of 775,000 volts up to three feet away without having to touch the victim with probes or shoot darts. Josh didn't like stun guns or tasers. They reminded him of cattle prods and the violent excesses of the 1960's civil rights protests that played to a stereotype of Southerners as redneck racists. Racism was not exclusive to Southerners or white people.

Josh found a seat in the back of the room from which he could watch the show. Sitting and standing for long periods were not easy for him. He adjusted his seat several times, crossing his legs one way then another, slumping then sitting up straight. No position was comfortable. He sometimes imagined he could feel the metal pins in his right hip and thigh pressing against a raw nerve.

Josh watched with the sort of innocent curiosity of a child as the county's education *experts* gathered at the long, semi-circular table at the front of the room. Benton County had five elected members on its Board of Education, with the superintendent now officially serving as a sixth member and secretary. A seventh chair at the table was reserved for another unelected education expert, the North Carolina representative for the National Education Association.

Until the current administration's executive order giving accreditation and certification authority to county boards, Ms. NEA's *de facto* membership was only symbolic. Josh's innocent curiosity vanished as he stared at the demagogues busily talking to each other about their self-importance.

A sudden jolt of pain shot down his leg, forcing him to shake. At that moment a face from the past appeared in his mind. It was Sgt. 1st Class Ballard, the racist admin NCO from 8th PSYOPS who'd accused him of slandering *his* president. That was over 19 years ago, only months before the Battle of Mogadishu, action Josh never saw.

During a unit barbecue in the field, Josh inadvertently referred to President Clinton as a *"draft-dodging womanizer."* No one in the 3rd Ranger Battalion had a problem with the truth. But Ballard wasn't a Ranger, and he had a reputation for filing EO complaints. He wouldn't let it go, even lied about what Josh had said.

Though he refused to reprimand one of his best noncommissioned officers, the battalion commander reluctantly agreed to transfer 1st Sgt. Athol immediately to Fort Bragg where he would be allowed to retire within six month. A month later, however, when Josh was to make his 300th and last airborne jump, he had a double parachute malfunction and landed hard on Normandy Drop Zone. He broke three bones in his right ankle, plus his right tibia and femur, his pelvis and two vertebrae, L4-5, crushing the disc between them.

A year and three surgeries later, Josh was medically retired as a master sergeant with 60 percent disability. The VA later picked up the 60 percent rating on his spine and orthopedic injuries and added a disability rating for his high blood pressure. He spent the first nine months continuing to recover, mostly hunting and fishing.

In 1995 he moved his family to Wilmington where he completed a bachelor's in secondary education to teach English then a master's in the same field. He taught high school English in Pettigrew County for two years then he and Joy both got teaching jobs in Benton County. His teaching career ended less than four years later. Joy's teaching career ended four years after that.

Joy had started teaching in 1978 but quit two years later when Rachel, their oldest was born. She returned to teaching in 1989 when Abigail, their youngest started kindergarten. In between those years, she had home schooled Rachel and Nathan, who were only 14 months apart. When Joy returned to teaching, all three of their children were enrolled in Christian schools.

There was no double standard on their part. Josh and Joy were Christians. The public school system was a *humanist* system at best, *anti-Christian* at worst. They were willing to try to help public school kids gain the academic knowledge they needed but would not lend their own children to *The System* and allow it to destroy their developing Christian faith.

"Ladies and gentlemen, we need to get started," the vice-chair said, leaning into his microphone. "Would everyone please take a seat?"

Josh watched with some concern as a platoon-size group of potential trouble-makers began grabbing seats among the home schooling parents and Christian school administrators. He'd had run-ins with some of them back when he was a deputy, recognizing them by their foul language, which they shared with everyone. Proles!

Josh knew they were public school parents because he'd had to break up fights at ballgames, started by these parents who'd try to provoke visiting spectators, especially when their school's team was losing. Like Orwell's proles, *sports* were everything to them. Why were they here except to disrupt the appeal process for home schoolers and Christian schools?

If their presence wasn't enough, he watched a well-dressed, middle-aged lady in a dark blue business suit find a seat near the front. Her shoulder length dark hair couldn't conceal a large white bandage under her chin. It was Kathy. *Now what was she doing here?!* Why wouldn't these people let Christians alone and allow them to educate their own children? This night was not going to end well.

Several elementary, middle and high school administrators stood behind the board members, centered on their superintendant, as if they were his personal body guards. Josh recognized one of them, a hefty one with dyed black hair and scornful frown. It was Brookie. He wished the night was over. Too many bad memories here.

"Mr. McNair," a very large man in a gray suit stood, addressing the board chairman, giving his name and title.

"I'm here to appeal for a curriculum waiver on behalf of *Back Swamp Christian Academy*."

"The board recognizes *Back Swamp Christian Academy*," McNair responded. "Go ahead, Mr. Cunningham. Make you appeal."

Josh knew that three of the five elected board members were sympathetic to home schoolers and Christian schools. The other two were not. They, with the superintendant, usually voted against any appeal for waivers, citing their supposed *concern* for the education of children whose parents they called *radical Christians* and *secessionists*.

With no consensus, appeals were neither approved nor disapproved, thus allowing home schoolers and Christian schools to continue to operate from quarter to quarter when they had to re-appear before the board. It was a typical bureaucratic circus. Tonight was the third meeting since the charade began.

"Mr. Chair," a heavy set, black lady stood and interrupted the proceedings. "I gots ev'dence why d'at school don't d'serve d'fava of d'is board. D'ay prej'dus at d'at school. I know cuz d'ay wouldn't let my chil' enroll d'ar."

A stir of mumbling filled the room. Board members placed their hands over their mics and discussed with each other the merits of this charge. Grinning like a fat-faced Cheshire cat, Ms. NEA passed a note down the table to Superintendant Ferrell. Upon reading it, he chuckled, his double chin flapping like an ugly iguana.

"That's a pretty serious charge," he said, pulling his microphone to him. "If it's true, there's no way this board can consider an appeal from such a school."

"Well, it's not true. So I wouldn't get all excited about it," Cunningham retorted, looking at the fat lady with amused contempt. "I do know Ms. Harrington though. I conducted the achievement tests for her son myself. We did not refuse to admit her child as a student but told her he'd have to go back four grade levels.

"You see, we test every child at the beginning of the school year to determine where they are *academically*. If I remember correctly, Ms. Harrington's son tested at a 4th grade reading level and I think 5th grade math. Because we emphasize reading skills most of all, we told her he'd have to start as a 4th grader, not an 8th grader."

"That's sounds reasonable to me," McNair said, grinning at the superintendant and Ms. NEA, who sipped a large coffee mug, wearing a hateful scowl.

There was more mumbling throughout the room. The board members said nothing though the administrators standing behind them whispered among themselves, a few pointing at the large group of parents supporting *Back Swamp Christian Academy.*

"It don't t'me!" The fat lady said then cursed Cunningham and the school board as she and five others pushed their way down the row of seats to the main aisle then out the door. A disturbance apparently caused by them in the hallway was met quickly and effectively by Rushton's officers.

"May I continue now?" Cunningham asked, still standing and feeling much bolder.

McNair, his vice-chair and board member Susan Powers nodded their approval. The other two board members, Superintendant Ferrell and Ms. NEA just sat there, bitterly sullen. Josh knew Powers. She was a former public school teacher herself but quit because she wasn't allowed to actually teach. She ran for the board on a platform that public schools were *"illegal, immoral and a complete waste of taxpayers' dollars."* Josh thought it was curious that she sat right next to Ms. NEA, separating her from Ferrell. Probably strategic on her part, he thought.

"Our academy is an accredited member of the American Association of Christian Schools, and we're also accredited by the National Council of Private Schools," Cunningham continued. "We use the best phonics-based reading curriculum, both Christian and secular, including A Beka and Alpha Phonics. We use A Beka, Bob Jones and Prairie Fire Press for science, history and geography. We cannot abide with any science curriculum that would teach our children they evolved from lower animals then have to teach them so-called *safe sex* and *sociology* when they act like animals."

Several people laughed at his comments. Even a few members of the board chuckled out loud.

"We will *not* teach our children a politically-corrected view of history or some *socialist-humanist* concept of world events," Cunningham continued. "In addition to in-depth American history and world geography, we also teach church history, which no *government* curriculum includes.

"We do include art, music and foreign language as part of our studies with textbooks and study material generally based on our teachers' preferences. We use Saxon math from kindergarten through 12th grade…. and by the way, our graduates score 200 points higher on the math section of their SAT than the national average, 300 over the state average.

"Most of all, what we emphasize most is *reading skills*. That's why our kids are reading before they leave kindergarten or they don't leave kindergarten. We even promote phonics and phonemic awareness in our K-4 day care center. By the time our students finish the 4th grade, they've developed a 25,000 word *reading* vocabulary. *We'll never sacrifice that kind of reading skill for a whole language-based, **federal** curriculum that has been proven a failure for 60 years!*"

An eerie hush fell over the room when Barry "Bear" Cunningham raised his voice to emphasize the failure of whole language reading programs, public school's doll baby. Ms. NEA scribbled another note and pushed it by Powers to the superintendant. As he read the note, Josh noticed Kathy standing to speak.

"*Oh, no,*" Josh whispered out loud.

"He's only partly right," she said, her Jersey accent piercing the silence. "Mr. McNair, I'd like to comment on what Mr. Cunningham has said."

"And *you* are?" McNair asked.

"Her name is Kathy Alighieri," Ferrell interrupted, nodding to Ms. NEA who responded with a nod as she sipped her coffee. "She's a retired English teacher. Yes, I think we can let her speak. Ms. Alighieri, I heard you were involved in a nasty hostage situation recently. It's good to see you're okay. You *are* okay?"

"Other than being jobless *again*, I'm fine," she answered sharply and stepped to the front of the table, turning to address the crowd.

Ms. NEA and the superintendant gave each other a glance that suggested both were about to regret letting her speak. Kathy might not be the zealous public school ally she was before they forced her to retire.

"What Mr. Cunningham has said about his school and Christian school curriculums verses a mandated *federal* curriculum is true," she began, her voice loud and clear, thanks to many years practice in classrooms filled with unruly *diverse* learners. "He misses a point though. If you happen to know the Constitution, you know this meeting is *unconstitutional*. The government has *no* right to establish a federal public school curriculum because *education is a state right only*, reserved by the 10th amendment!   Besides, *they're your kids, not the government's kids!*"

Ferrell started to say something about her shouting, but Powers put her hand over his microphone and gave him a look that sent shivers down his wormy spine.

"And what Mr. Cunningham has said about reading being the most important thing in his school is what used to be the most important thing for *all* children," Kathy continued. "For the first 200 years in this country, mothers taught their kids to read at home. *All schools were **home** schools*. Even when church-run community schools began in the late 18th Century, the emphasis was on learning to read.

"You see, when a child has been thoroughly taught *how to read*, that child can then pick up *any* book, anywhere and *read how to learn*. The reason the government went into the education business in the first place was to put restraints on reading skills.

"When whole language came along and real reading skills were replaced with *memorized* reading lists, *children's vocabularies became **16** times smaller!* Kids who could have developed that *25,000* word vocabulary by the end of the 4th grade now only develop a *memorized* vocabulary of about *1,500* words, *words they can't even* *spell because they also don't teach spelling or grammar rules.* ***They deliberately limit reading skills so they can control knowledge, so they can control us!***"

"Hold on, lady," the superintendant found his backbone and snatched the microphone away from Powers. "You're not going to use this meeting to put public schools on trial. Sir, I expect you to escort this woman to her seat or better yet, out of this room, *right now.*"

Josh realized Ferrell was looking at and therefore speaking directly to him, despite his desire to go unnoticed from his back row-Baptist seat. He stood up.

"For what reason, *sir?*" he asked, his deep voice thundering from the back of the room. "What has she done?"

The entire room turned to look at Josh, murmuring. Seeing Josh more clearly in the light, Ferrell called Brookie from the lineup of body guards.

"*Who is that guy?*" he asked. "He looks familiar."

"That's Joshua Athol," she whispered. "He was an English teacher, used to have a mustache and longer hair. I think it was darker then too. He worked with Ms. Alighieri. In fact, she helped us get him out of the classroom."

"My, how the winds do change," Ferrell mumbled then spoke up. "If she causes any further disturbance, I'll hold you responsible, sir."

"Again, *sir,*" Josh said, deliberately patronizing. "What disturbance has she made? *You invited her to speak.* So long as she doesn't use offensive language or make accusation against individuals, she has the Constitutional right to say whatever she wants to about *your* schools."

Several people chuckled. Some laughed out loud and made rude comments about the superintendent and even worse remarks about the school system. The local newspaper reporter and a television news reporter with his camera crew who'd been sitting near and standing behind Josh left the room, clearly aggravated. They didn't cover this kind of news, news that painted the public school system in a bad light.

"That's okay," Kathy said, smiling at Josh from the front of the room. "I'm finished. If this board refuses to recognize Mr. Cunningham's school, the other schools here and all the home schooling parents, it doesn't matter. This board really doesn't have any *right* to decide anything. Again, I say, *this meeting is unconstitutional!*"

She returned to her seat. The room was silent, as if everyone was waiting for something to be decided. Cunningham stood and looked around the room.

"*Thank you, ma'am,*" he said, nodding at Kathy then turning to his supporters surrounding him. "She's right, folks. This board has no authority over us. We answer to God and our children's parents, *not government.* Let's go home."

He turned and left with at least 40 others, causing quite a disturbance. Around the room, other church-run schools and scores of home schooling parents made the same decision and began leaving the room like they were leaving a theater after the movie was over.

Some of the remaining trouble makers that Josh had noted earlier started leaving too, only they were not so quiet or peaceful. They cursed out loud and shouted obscenities at other parents. Hooper and one of Rushton's police officers had to escort them out of the room, where they became even more belligerent. Nichols and another police officer went outside to help.

Despite the disturbances, it was obvious that McNair, Powers and the vice-chair were elated. Ms. NEA, the superintendent, the other two board members and a host of school administrators were not. Ms. NEA quickly jotted off another note and tried to shove it by Powers, who snatched it from her and tore it up.

"Enough with the note passing, witch!" She growled, *"You're not a voting member of this board!"*

Ms. NEA had taken all the insults she could stand for one evening. Her eyes exploded with hate as she snatched her coffee cup from in front of her and viciously tossed the still very hot brew in Powers' face. Powers jumped to her feet, at first screaming in pain then anger. Ms. NEA sat there calmly, pretending to apologize for *"spilling"* her coffee.

Her face glowing red from the scalding and rage, Powers would later make no apology for her response. She turned and hit Ms. NEA with a downward right hook that smashed her stubby little nose, knocking her backward out of her chair. Powers then pounced on her, punching her with a left then a right then repeating the process – for as every good teacher knows, *repetition is the key to learning.*

Brookie and Ferrell raced to Ms. NEA's defense while the other administrators scattered. When Superintendent Ferrell tried to pull Powers off Ms. NEA by grabbing the back of her hair, he was tackled by McNair. Both men rolled in the floor, trying to score a hit on the other's nose. When Brookie slapped Powers across the side of her head, she was knocked to the floor by one of the other female board members, one who had previously supported The System.

"I think I see now what kind of folks y'all be!" she shouted.

Almost in shock at how rapidly the situation had gotten out of hand, Josh grabbed his radio and called for backup as his one remaining deputy, Sherman, finally stepped into the fray. In the far corner of the room, Josh could see Rushton on his radio, apparently doing the same thing. That was when he noticed Kathy hopping onto the table that separated the dispersing crowd from the brawling board members. She slid across to the other side and jumped in the middle of the fight, kicking Brookie in the behind as she tried to get up.

Sherman had Powers in a headlock but was being pounded on by the board member now siding with Powers and McNair. Kathy could see that he was occupied and that his pistol and stun gun-taser were an open invitation. She chose the stun gun-taser, ripping it from its holster. Sherman didn't even realize it was taken. His right ear was bleeding, and his face was scratched. The angry board member was now pulling out his hair.

Kathy studied the device a moment, trying to figure out how to turn it on. It wasn't that complicated. As Brookie once again tried to stand up, Kathy pointed the stun gun-taser at her behind and pressed the release button on the handle. The sound of the 775,000 volts of electricity filled the room.

Brookie collapsed on the floor, her body convulsing as its blood sugar turned to lactic acid and her neuromuscular system went haywire. Kathy grinned with satisfaction then turned her new weapon on Ms. NEA, who was finally getting on her feet, her nose bloody, blouse torn. She too fell to the floor, shaking violently. Seeing his colleagues get zapped by Kathy did not inspire Ferrell to any acts of bravery. He tried to crawl by her on the floor. She pointed and fired her fun gun one last time, temporarily paralyzing the county's number one education expert, who plopped onto his side in a prenatal ball, trembling.

At this point, it was Josh who leaped onto the table and slid to the other side. He didn't even bother to disarm Kathy. Just threw his arms around her, lifted her up and body slammed her onto the table, face down. He then easily took the stun gun-taster out of her hand, and while holding both hands behind her back, he cuffed her. By now Rushton and Sherman were cuffing the new rebel board member and Powers.

"*Why are ya arresting me?*" Kathy asked, shouting. "Why don't ya arrest them? ***They're the traitors!***"

"I know," he said, leaning over to whisper in her ear. "*Seems like I told you that some time ago.* But this is not the way to fight 'em."

"What is?!" she demanded, trying to whisper, her eyes now filled with tears.

"*Pray*," he whispered, lifting her onto her feet. "Learn how to pray."

Chapter Three

"Hope you have got your things together.
Hope you are quite prepared to die.
Looks like we're in for nasty weather.
One eye is taken for an eye."
John Fogerty (*Creedence Clearwater Revival*), "Bad Moon Rising"

"The 13th tropical storm of the season was named today. Tropical Storm Michael has formed in the Atlantic from a tropical depression that started off the southwest coast of Africa six days ago. Michael is now about 180 miles east of the Lesser Antilles and currently packing winds of 60 miles an hour, heading west-northwest at about 12 miles an hour."

Joy was watching her favorite channel, the Weather Channel, and reading the newspaper while Josh drank his coffee and read another chapter from a book she had given him for Father's Day, ***Controlling the*** [Ignorant] ***Masses***. The word "*Ignorant*" was inserted into the title with an editor's insert, like an afterthought.

It was pretty interesting though a little wordy, written by a former public school teacher. Its title gave away the whole book. Governments control the ignorant masses by *making* and *keeping* them ignorant. And public schools are governments' primary means of controlling knowledge, with a little help from news media and the entertainment industry.

"You don't s'pose they named that storm for the angel Michael?" Joy asked, only half expecting Josh to answer. His usual response was a grunt or an "*uh huh*."

"If they did, let's pray he doesn't come this way," Josh smiled and sat his book aside. He'd just finished that chapter anyway. "I reckon I better report to the Sheriff's office, see if I can't get the media off Dave's back."

"The paper seems to be trying to put all the blame on three members of the board itself, including the chairman of the board. They also claim there were not enough law enforcement officers there," she told him, pointing to the front page article then frowned, seeing him prepare to leave. "I wish you could stay home just one Saturday."

"Me too," he said, standing by the kitchen sink, rinsing his coffee mug. "The media will say whatever they can to make Dave look bad. I'm sure they don't mention their reporter and WREL's TV reporter got up and left the meeting before the ruckus ever started. They didn't like the way the meeting was going. Didn't wanna report the truth. Now they're making up the news based on what they hear from their sources – *probably Ferrell, Brookie and that NEA hussy.* I'm sure they haven't talked to McNair or Powers or any of the home school or Christian school parents who attended the meeting."

Joy joined him at the sink and took his coffee cup from him, saying she was going to wash dishes anyway. She didn't like him or anyone else messing around in her kitchen. Josh smiled at her, noticing how the morning light showed the gray streaks in her light brown hair. Though she was only a year younger than him, Joy was just now starting to show her age. He kissed her forehead then gave her a love pat on the behind as he headed for the master bath to brush his teeth.

****

"Why does this Inspector Athol's name come up every time Benton County has some major incident in the news?" Special Agent Dodds asked as he sat in Westin's office, seated across from his desk.

"Josh Athol is one of my best officers," Westin answered, the furrows of wrinkles in his bald scalp coming together in a v-shape – *body language that warned he was clearly irritated.* He then pushed his glasses higher on the bridge of his nose, another sign he was losing his patience with Dodds. "He's highly educated, got an associate's in criminal justice, plus a bachelor's and a master's in English. He also has an excellent military record – Airborne Ranger, master blaster, sniper – *you name it.*"

"Really?" Dodds questioned, "So why didn't he escort this Alighieri woman from the school board meeting when he was directed to do so by the superintendant? Is she not the same lady for whom he used *unnecessary* deadly force on a murder suspect a few days earlier? Sounds like he's got something special going with her."

"Back off, Bozo!" Westin barked, sitting forward in his seat, his entire scalp glowing red. *"Don't you dare besmear one of my men!* Inspector Athol arrested Ms. Alighieri *after* she actually *did* something. As far as him having any affection for her, let me tell ya this – *That woman helped get him fired from his teaching job six years ago because he wouldn't pass proles!* And before you try to blame him for her actions last night, it was your *rat* Sherman whose taser she snatched. *If you wanna make an issue with how this department handled that incident, start with your inside man!"*

Dodds looked across the room then out the window. He mumbled that he didn't think that would be necessary, that he wasn't going to send a derogatory report about the school board incident to his regional director. He defended Sherman though, saying he understood that at the time Ms. Alighieri grabbed the taser, he was fighting two very angry women. Although he agreed, Westin didn't say so.

"I also have some problems with some of Athol's affiliations," Dodds said, opening a manila file folder holding several documents, the top one containing a picture of Josh. "We think Mr. Athol's sympathies lie with those Southern and Western states' secessionists, rather than this government. We know he belongs to a number of organizations, a couple of which are questionable: *NCOA, DAV, UNC-W Alumni, JBS, SCV, LS, the American Party.* Oh, and he's a *former* member of the *NRA.* Wonder why *former* member?"

"I s'pect it has something to do with the NRA endorsing the *Veterans Disarmament Act,*" Westin said sarcastically. "Ya know he's also an *independent, fundamental, KJV-only, Bible-believing Baptist.*"

"We know," Dodds said smugly, not commenting further on the NRA or VDA. "You're a Baptist too. *Pentecostal Freewill Baptist,* I believe. You're the former *Reverend* Westin, aren't ya ."

"*Pastor,*" Westin said, shaking his head. "Not *reverend.* You Gestapo scumbags don't know all ya think you know. I s'pose now it's a federal offense to be a *Baptist.*"

"Not *yet,*" Dodds grinned. "When it is, we'll let you know. As for Athol, his right wing affiliations seem to set a pattern. I want you to know we're *watching* him and a couple other members of your department – *especially you.*"

"So is that like a *storm watch*?" Westin asked, deliberately sarcastic again. "Let's see, that should be followed by a *storm warning* then *storm adversary*. What comes after that?"

"You'll find out, *sir*," Dodds said, standing. "Oh, don't bother to get up. I can find my way out."

"I'm sure you can," Westin responded as Dodds closed the door behind him. "Have a wonderful day, *punk.*"

Dodds slipped down a side hallway and avoided the media circus waiting in the big hall to see the Sheriff. On his way out the door, he bumped into Josh on his way in. The two gave each other glancing stares that lasted only seconds but enough time for each man to realize he knew the other and there was no lost affection between them.

As he limped up the same hallway, Josh saw Westin leave his office and head toward the big hall. He followed him.

"Well, if it's not *Pravda Americana*," Westin told the group of TV and newspaper reporters. "And what information may I supply for you to twist today?"

In typical rudeness, a host of reporters all spoke at once, each shoving microphones or handheld recorders in his face. They demanded to know how the situation got out of hand, why there were not enough officers at the school board meeting and especially why Inspector Athol had refused to arrest Ms. Alighieri when he was ordered to do so by Superintendant Ferrell.

"For one thing, I take my orders from Sheriff Westin, *not* your public schools' superintendant," Josh spoke up, his deep voice scaring some of the reporters but sweet as music to Westin. "For another, he didn't order or ask me to arrest her but *escort* her from the building. And finally, for me to do that at that time, what was she doing that would require that action?"

There was a short silence then one of the reporters who'd walked out last night in frustration now spoke up boldly.

"She was causing a disturbance," he said, looking to his fellows for support.

"*Really?*" Josh asked, "And what kind of disturbance was she causing? Was she using foul language?"

"No," the reporter admitted.

"Was she making slanderous accusations or threats against members of the school board?" Josh asked, patronizing the reporter.

"No," he admitted. "But she was making slanderous accusations against the public school system."

"*And that's against the law?!*" Sheriff Westin interrupted with a question.

There was a long silence. Mics and recorders dropped to their sides. They seemed disarmed.

"Well, it is true, is it not, that Ms. Powers started the fight by striking Ms. Waters," one of the reporters finally blurted out.

"No, *it's not true*," Josh responded, mockingly. "If you hadn't left early last night, you'd have witnessed Ms. Waters deliberately tossing hot coffee in Ms. Powers' face. If she threw hot coffee in my face, I'd punch her lights out too. The superintendant and one of his school principals then attacked Ms. Powers. I'm not condoning what she did, but I suspect Ms. Alighieri was just trying to even things up."

"Well, Sheriff," the same reporter still pressed for dirt. "Don't you think your deputy was negligent in letting Ms. Alighieri take his taser?"

"No, I don't," Westin admitted. "At the time, all our other officers as well as city police officers were responding to a larger incident outside. Deputy Sherman was trying to subdue one board member while being assaulting by another board member at the time Ms. Alighieri grabbed his stun gun-taser off his pistol belt."

"Well, *what if she'd grabbed his pistol instead?*" The reporter asked, sarcastically.

"Then you'd have had even less of a story," he returned the sarcasm. "Our officers' side arms have a new safety device that locks out use by anyone except the officer to which it is issued. I won't go into details, but you can rest assured it works."

Josh smiled confidently as Westin disarmed the reporters' every question. He knew they'd find some way to twist what he and Dave told them, but no matter how they twisted it, they didn't have the story they wanted. As the red journalists slowly disbanded, he was grateful Dave had refused his request to carry his personally owned side arm, a .327 magnum. It wouldn't have had the new safety feature. At least he was allowed to use his Model 700; that is, whenever McNeilly decided to give it back.

"Glad ya came by this morning," Westin told Josh as the two walked back to his office. "I 'preciate the help with those maggots. Do ya think my a'sessment of Sherman's actions was fair?"

"Yeah," Josh admitted, sighing. "He did the right thing last night. I just don't like that bigoted punk. He rubs everybody the wrong way."

"He's not a bigot," Westin told him, offering Josh a cup of coffee as he re-filled his cup from a pot near his desk. "He's just baiting y'all, looking for something to pin on ya. He's already got you tagged as a Southern secessionist. Dodds was in here earlier. He says they're '*watching*' several of us, especially us *Baptists* types."

"Maybe the Lord will come get us before Dodds does," Josh mumbled.

"Amen," Westin smiled, raising his coffee cup in the air. "But if he doesn't, then we have to be like the three Hebrews facing the fiery pit. Whether he chooses to save us or not, we're gonna keep serving him."

The two men were much alike though they disagreed on some issues, including Biblical ones like eternal salvation and gifts of the spirit. But they served the same master, and they agreed on most things political. Josh considered him one of his best friends though he was 10 years his senior.

Westin was a local boy and a retired sergeant major who'd served nearly 30 years with Special Forces in Alaska, Hawaii and Korea. Unlike Josh, he was haunted with confirmed combat kills in Vietnam, Grenada, Panama and Iraq, as well as covert operations in Central and South America, Lebanon and Jordan.

When he retired 20 years ago, Dave went to a local Bible college for his denomination then preached in a local church until he resigned in order to run for Sheriff almost five years ago. He had no prior experience in law enforcement, but he won the election anyway and had since transformed the Benton County Sheriff's Department into one of the finest in North Carolina.

****

As Josh was about to get in his truck, he heard a lady's voice calling him.

"Thanks for posting my bail," she said. It was Kathy.

"What's that?" he asked, turning to face her as she approached.

She looked worse for the wear. Still wearing the same, now wrinkled pants suit, her hair ruffled and makeup smeared, she'd apparently just been released from the county jail.

"Thank you for posting my bail," she repeated, smiling with all the feminine charm she could muster in her ragged state.

"Kathy, I'm not allowed to do things like that," he told her. "Let me see your release form. It'll tell ya who posted your bail."

He looked at the yellow copy of the county form and saw the name *Back Swamp Christian Academy* as the person responsible for bail. Josh smiled.

"Looks like you've made some new friends," he chuckled, showing her where to look on the form. "A bunch of *fundamentalists* have posted your bail."

She didn't know what to say, just smiled and dipped her head, for once in her life too embarrassed to look a man in the eyes. Josh sensed the awkwardness too but didn't know what he could say to defuse it. Finally, she looked up at him.

"Josh, what's going to happen to me now?" she asked, almost pleaded. "What kind of sentence am I facing?"

"Oh, you'll appear before the magistrate next week and get hit with a fine for public disturbance and interfering with an officer in the performance of his duties," he told her matter-of-factly. "You'll get probation time too. No jail time since you have no criminal record. Jails are too crowded with violent offenders anyway. What you may have to worry about though is being sued by Brookie, Ferrell and Waters."

"Nah, I don't think I have to worry about them," she told him with sincere confidence. "I know too much about each of them *personally* for them to take any personal action against me. I won't even need a lawyer."

Her confidence was almost like her old arrogance, which Josh resented. Though she was changing, she was in many ways still the same old Kathy. He told her he wished her well and suggested that she visit her new benefactors, that they might be able to help her in more ways than she realized. She said she'd consider it and finally let him go home to his wife, whom she envied now more than ever. In fact, she was jealous.

****

"Hurricane Michael is pounding the eastern coast of Puerto Rico with sustained winds of over 100 miles per hour," the radio weather report stated.

Josh turned the volume down and shook his head when the report added the hurricane was on a path that could take it straight to the Carolinas. His partner, Rick Koznowski, slowed the Task Force SUV to make a turn. He didn't like the news either. Bad news seemed to be the only kind they ever heard anymore.

They were cruising the outskirts of the county, looking for anything suspicious and listening to both their police radio and the local FM station. The report on the coming storm was preceded by a report of a body found near Orangeburg, S.C. It was the body of a well known white supremacist.

His hands were tie-wrapped behind his back, and he'd been shot in the back of the head, execution style. A white supremacist found dead in a mostly black neighborhood? It looked to Josh and Koznowski like somebody was trying to stir up trouble in their sister state.

Prior to that report, the local news was still repeating a media spin that Friday night's school board brawl was the result of one of the board members over-reacting when an NEA representative *"accidentally"* spilled her coffee on her. It also said *"Detective"* Joshua Athol, the arresting officer, had claimed he'd have hit the NEA representative too, that his comments explained why he was so prone to use deadly force rather than non-lethal means to capture or detain violent suspects.

An additional comment with the report really got Josh's goat. Westin's opponent in the upcoming election promised to fire *"loose cannons"* like Josh, should he be elected in November.

"Ya know, Koz," Josh mused as he stared into the endless rows of pine trees that lined both sides of the country road they were cruising. "I think I'll put in for retirement next month. Save that liberal slime ball the trouble."

"Retire?" Koz shook his head, "You can't retire, man. You've got, what, *four* years with the department?"

"Yeah," Josh admitted. "But I taught high school for six years. It all goes in the same state treasury. 'Course, I can't draw anything till I'm 60 – if there's anything left in the state treasury by then."

"I know what you mean," his partner said. "Man, I wish I could retire. I'd pack up my family and head for…. *Hey, what've we got here?*"

Two deputy patrol cars with their blue lights twirling were pulled into the dugout area next to a community baseball field. It was Nichols and Harriman. Josh and Koz pulled off to offer assistance but mostly to beat Monday morning boredom.

"What y'all got here?" Koz asked as he tugged on his shirt sleeves that fit tightly around his massive arms. Josh came around the other side, noticing the drink machine laying face down. Something or someone appeared to be under it.

"As you can see, somebody was trying to turn this Pepsi machine over to get the money out of it," Harriman said, pointing to the hole in the concrete wall. "He must have thought he could push it on its side, but it was bolted to the wall here, so he had to break it free first. We figure it must have turned over on 'em at that time."

Nichols said CSI was on its way as was an ambulance but that he didn't think the ambulance was necessary. It was obvious whoever was under this drink machine died a slow, agonizing death. Josh groaned as he got down in the prone and looked under the huge refrigeration unit then reached under it to try to find a pulse on the victim, who was wearing a hooded, gray sweatshirt with the hood pulled up over his head. *A stupid thing to wear in August*, Josh thought. He found the victim's cold neck. No pulse.

When the CSI team arrived a few minutes later, Shultz asked Koz and Josh if they would help lift the drink machine off the victim. They, Shultz, Nichols and Harriman all grabbed where they could and lifted, while

Harriman teased Koz that he ought to lift the whole thing by himself.

"I don't like to show off," he grinned. "*Ooh*, look at the way his eyes are bulging."

The victim was Tyrone though none of the officers knew him. He'd gotten a reprieve from going to Kuwait because the surveillance DVD became evidence in a murder investigation. The shoplifting case lost priority. It didn't matter now. Tyrone's days as a petty thief were over.

****

The next morning started another day with the Weather Channel and an update on the approaching storm, now a Category 2 hurricane stalled in the Atlantic, thanks to a high pressure system developing in the Tennessee Valley.

Josh flipped the channel to Fox News by habit, though he knew it didn't matter anymore what station he put it on. Thanks to the new and improved *Fairness Doctrine*, Fox News was just as liberal as the other networks. Conservative talk radio was gone as were most small town and all conservative newspapers and magazines. There was one view in the news, and the fascist liberals who controlled it thought that was *fair*.

The internet was the only source for truly independent thought and news reports, but the FCC was coming down hard on bloggers and organizations like *News and Blues, Newsmax, Lew Rockwell, World Net Daily* and *News With Views*, mostly by attacking their writers with the help from the all-powerful IRS and the now almost-as-powerful Department of Homeland Security.

While authorities were still investigating Sunday's murder of a white supremacist near Orangeburg, S.C., last night the body of an Atlanta black activist and voter registration organizer was found hanging in a dead oak tree in Forsyth County, Ga. The authorities immediately admitted the victim was not lynched, that he was already dead before his body was hanged.

Though the actual cause of death was not yet known, he appeared to have been shot in the back of the head, his hands tie-wrapped behind his back. Black activists from the local NAACP all the way to the White House were quick to condemn this murder as a hate crime though they had been reluctant to call the Orangeburg murder a hate crime.

Calling both crimes heinous, law enforcement authorities in South Carolina and Georgia were not shy about saying they were too suspicious to declare either murder a hate crime but suspected each murder was set up to look like one. When pressed to say who'd want to make it look like a hate crime, local law officials refused to comment.

A Neo-Nazi group connected with the white supremacist claimed he had been arrested by federal agents earlier in the week. The FBI and ATF immediately denied any of their agents had made such an arrest. A Homeland Security spokesman simply dismissed the group's charge as "fiction."

Josh questioned why any group would risk stirring up trouble in an already racially charged atmosphere. The president had not united the country at all but deliberately divided it down racial and socio-economic lines. Even those few, semi-neutral journalists dared not say anything, lest they lose all credibility and their jobs.

Only American Party incumbents and candidates could get away with criticizing the administration. ***That was it!*** Someone was trying to frame these murders on those *"divisive, right-winged radicals"* everyone hated – the last Americans.

"Who are you talking to?" Joy asked as she came in the room, hurrying to get ready for school, "And why did you change my channel?"

Josh flipped the station back to the Weather Channel and tossed the remote on the leather couch. He didn't realize he was talking out loud. He had to be more careful, remembering the last time he did that, he lost his promotion to E-9 and had to retire early. Still, he wished there was some way he could get a message to American Party officials. All phone calls and emails were monitored by the feds. It was both frustrating and disgusting to watch his country becoming a communist state. The proles and a few million outer party Americans had been duped into voting for change, and they got it. He hoped they were happy!

"What ya doing now?" Joy asked as Josh stepped into his study and turned on his computer, "Don't you have to go to work today?"

"Oh, yeah," he answered, sitting down at his desk. "Got to send somebody a message first."

Dave had told him the feds were watching him. Josh figured he may as well give them something to look at.

****

By Wednesday evening, Michael was a Category 4 and on the move again, this time headed northeast. The storm was headed straight for New York's Long Island. It would be the first such major hurricane to hit New England in over 80 years, and more evidence of the extreme weather patterns that followed last year's solar flares and this past May's solar eclipse. Sometimes the earth itself seemed like a sick, old woman lying on her death bed.

During mid-week prayer services at *Northside Baptist Church*, the opening prayers were about the storm, gratitude that it had bypassed the Carolinas, Georgia and Gulf Coast states. Since the oil spill, repeated hurricanes had hit Florida hard, destroying billions of dollars in personal property and the Sunshine State's all-important tourist industry. But these mean summers were each preceded by harsh winters with hard frosts that devastated the state's citrus, strawberry and produce industry.

Foremost among all the prayers requested though was the state of the nation, its bitterly divided people, its crippled economy, federally supported policies of moral depravity and especially the loss of the Constitutional right to worship unmolested.

These prayers had been made each week for over four years, even though during the last two, a federal official had sat in every service, monitoring Pastor Timothy Holmes' sermons and any political conversations of the individual members of the congregation. With visitors attending every service, no one knew who the federal watchdog might be, man or woman, young or old.

Northside was a racially mixed, independent, Bible-believing Baptist church with over 200 members, located on the Braxton and Benton County line. Most members were retired military. Nearly a third of its members were new, some driven from Fayetteville's larger, denominational, liberal churches that met emotional but not spiritual needs.

Still, Josh was sure one of their new members or visitors was a spy for the feds – a virtual devil among them. A *"soldier"* belonging to the president's *"army of civilians"* sat in every church service every time a church met, if only to ensure the preacher or priest didn't violate the *Hate Crimes Protection Act.*

This was how the feds shut down politically incorrect churches. When a church stepped over some arbitrary line of what the feds said was *"speech not protected by the 1ˢᵗ Amendment,"* it would be shut down, its pastor imprisoned and its congregation fined for *"inciting hatred."*

The first churches to be shut down by the feds were those fundamentalist, African-American churches on the wrong side of the last presidential election then those churches gay activists held responsible for California's *Proposition 8*, which was ultimately overturned by a liberal federal judge anyway.

All pastors openly criticizing *That One* and opposing gay marriage were political enemies of the state. By early 2010, many of these churches had lost their IRS designation as nonprofit, religious organizations. Within two years, their pastors were charged with violating the Hate Crimes Protection Act, even though they were careful not to publically preach against homosexuality. Their crime was being on the wrong side of the American culture war.

Josh wasn't sure where the arbitrary line was, but he was sure Pastor Holmes had crossed it more than once, and yet their church had not been raided or closed – *yet*. Maybe the American Party's rising popularity suggested the tide of American opinion was turning against the tyranny of political correctness. Maybe the administration and his democratically controlled Congress had decided to back off on their religious cleansing campaign, at least until after the November election.

It had been nearly six months since the last reports of pastors being arrested or churches raided. All three were independent Baptist churches, one in Arnold, Mo., one in Holly Ridge, N.C., the other in Ludowici, Ga. He'd heard these pastors were already released on bond or on probation. According to bloggers though, every church the fed shut down re-opened in another location, sometimes under tents on private property. Their congregations may have thinned out a little, but as one blogger called it, what the feds were actually doing was helping *"separate the chaff from the wheat."*

With the Republican Convention coming in just two weeks and the American Party candidate only four points behind the president in opinion polls, it was probably a wise political decision not to remind the ignorant but volatile masses they no longer had Freedom of Religion *or* Speech *or* Press *or* the Right to Bear Arms *or* any of the rights the founding fathers had secured for their ancestors in a document the administration treated like an anachronism. Josh appreciated at least this lull in religious persecution, but he knew it was just the calm before the storm.

At the conclusion of prayers each Wednesday evening, Pastor Holmes always delivered a short expository message from the Bible. This month he began what he said was one of the longest and hardest books of the Bible to use for teaching expository scripture, the Book of Isaiah.

This week he said he would park on Isaiah 5:20-21. Though he didn't have the wealth of scripture memorized that he had when he was younger, Josh immediately knew the verses, causing him to look around the sanctuary for the devil among them. The look in his pastor's eyes said that he knew he was about to cross the line.

"Woe unto them that call evil good, and good evil," he began, reading from his Bible as his people read along. *"That put darkness for light, and light for darkness; that put bitter for sweet, and sweet for bitter! Woe to them that are wise in their own eyes, and prudent in their own sight!"*

After reading the scripture, the pastor prayed, asking for spiritual wisdom to teach his people what God would have them to know and for boldness to say what they needed to hear, *"despite the presence of one of Satan's servants in our midst."* He concluded his prayer, as always, *"in Jesus' name"* then paused as he looked out on the faces of his people. It was plain to both Josh and Joy that Pastor Holmes was about to challenge the powers of darkness.

"May I say, we all have a concept of what is good and what is evil," he began, his voice strong but not yet thundering. "But those of us in this church have a different concept of good and evil than those who attend no church at all or whose churches don't preach the Bible but promote the vain philosophies of men. Hollywood, the news media, business leaders, public school educators and university professors, and our government leaders have a *very different* definition of good and evil than biblical Christians – *real* Christians.

"*Real* Christians know, for example, that a child is the gift of God, that God is the one who forms the child in the womb, and from the womb, God calls us. *Real* Christians know from Exodus 21:20-23 that the life of an unborn child is *equal* in the eyes of God to your life and mine. Therefore, *real* Christians know to deliberately destroy the life of an unborn child is *murder*. ***Abortion is murder!*** *All those who commit abortion and all those who support abortion are murderers, whether they be individuals or governments!"*

He paused. Several church members said "***Amen***" out loud. Heads nodded in agreement though many searched the faces of their fellow members. Holmes paced in front of his pulpit then he turned and quoted more scripture.

"*He that justifieth the wicked, and he that condemneth the just, even they both are abomination to the LORD*," Holmes said. He was pretty well worked up now. "*Abomination.* Do you know what an abomination is? It's a detestable, *vile* thing. In the Bible, there are sins that are abominations to our own bodies and sins that are abominations to the Lord. Here, we see the Lord considers not only the sin of calling evil good and good evil an *abomination* but those that commit it are *an abomination to the Lord.* May I tell you another sin the Bible calls *an abomination to the Lord?* ***Sodomy!***"

There. It was out there. It was said. Holmes felt 100 pounds lifted off his back. This was a subject he'd danced around for the last three years, trying to respect the law of the land and yet serve his Lord as he knew he should. He went on to explain that all sex sins were an abomination to our bodies – with two dozen *pandemic* venereal diseases to prove it. But he added that homosexuality was an *unnatural* sex sin because it made God's whole creative purpose null and void, for in the beginning, he made them man and woman, *not* man and man or woman and woman.

Holmes said homosexuality was an abomination to God, comparable to shedding *innocent* blood – *murder*. Holmes then offered God's way out for the practicing homosexual – *Jesus*.

"Heads bowed, eyes closed, *come to Jesus*," he said, his voice softer now as he gave the invitation. "If you've never done so, do so now. If you've been living that sinful, *perverted* lifestyle, turn from it now and come to Jesus. Let his blood wash away your *abomination*. Trust him to save you then start a new life in him."

No one came forward for the alter call that evening. Josh didn't think any of their members were homosexuals and if the fed's inside man or woman happened to be one, he or she was doubly disturbed by tonight's sermon. He was sure that if the next election didn't change the political landscape, November was going to be another long month, just like the last two.

Two years ago, a 7.6 earthquake hit the city of Los Angeles on Veterans Day, destroying much of the city's infrastructure. Then the day before Thanksgiving, America's favorite national park exploded. A gigantic volcano destroyed Yellowstone and over 500 miles of surrounding forest land, towns and communities. The death toll caused by the earthquake and volcano was over 10,000. Volcanic ash was found as far east as the Mississippi Valley. The federal government just used both natural disasters to justify its use of active duty soldiers for domestic emergencies.

Starting Halloween night a year later during the gas riots, L.A. was one of the cities spared from excessive destruction, maybe because so much of the city's streets, freeways and overpasses were still shut down from the previous year's earthquake. San Francisco wasn't so lucky. Rioters burned much of the city, including affluent areas like Haight-Ashbury.

The Speaker of the House claimed the active duty CBRNE brigade commander responsible for restoring order in the city deliberately stalled deployment of his troops, saying he needed more precise instructions about when and how to engage looters and arsonists. She charged that his delay was a calculated reprisal for the city's long-standing refusal to allow military recruiters to come onto university campuses or visit public high schools.

The administration sought to make a hate crime issue of the slow CBRNE and National Guard response, claiming it had to do with the military's bias against homosexuals and that San Francisco was known for its homosexual agenda. The president hoped to use the event to finally repeal the federal law that supported the military's **Don't ask, don't tell** policy.

He called the chiefs of staff of all the armed forces together and demanded a *"consensus"* that would do away with what he called a *"morally offensive policy"* by Thanksgiving Day. When no such consensus could be reached, he demanded the resignation of the Chairman of the Joint Chiefs of Staff. He got it *and* the unexpected resignation of all the other chiefs of staff.

During the next several days, thousands of general and field grade officers and senior noncommissioned officers throughout all five branches of the military began rendering their resignations or submitting requests for retirement. Congress was forced to intervene, placing a stop-loss block on all resignations and retirements.

Behind the scenes, democratic strategists produced lists of officers and NCOs with democratic sympathies they recommended for immediate, advance promotions to fill the vacancies of what the administration was calling *"mutinous career military personnel."*

Thanks to a near blackout by the media, the public was unaware the U.S. essentially had no top military leadership for a period of several weeks, and when it did, U.S. Armed Forces were now run by political appointees. Josh was sure America's enemies knew her military was a hollow one.

There were critical shortages of medical, legal and logistical officers, and both fixed and rotator-wing aviators. More political maneuvering persuaded tens of thousands of the officers and NCOs fleeing the active military to go into the Reserves and National Guard. Federal funds were then allocated to the states to double the size of each state's Army and Air National Guard, almost overnight. Then weapons, equipment and aircraft were transferred from the active services directly to the Guards.

It was all done in a hush and a rush, so quickly it made seasoned bureaucrats blush that the government could do anything efficiently while under a cloak of secrecy. But now that the Guardsmen out-numbered the active Armed Forces, the states were expected to take over more of the active services' roles, domestically and abroad.

This fixed some of the shortage problems for a while, but early this summer half the country's governors began refusing to release their Guard units for active service. Enlistment goals were not being met, going back even before the 2008 election, which eventually led to a reinstatement of the draft last year then criminals being conscripted into military service.

As much as he was bothered by unqualified, politically promoted officers and NCOs running the military, Josh was even more troubled by the junior enlisted ranks. Military service had been a family tradition for millions of middle and lower middle class families, but now this source of outer party Americans had all but dried up.

The number of high school dropouts accepted for enlistment had grown from 25 percent in 2009 to over 50 percent by 2011. And over half of them had police records. A third were not even American citizens. Discipline problems plagued all branches, especially the Army and Marines.

The American military was starting to look like the Roman army during the last years the Roman Empire. It was filled with conscripts and foreign mercenaries, who had no love for the nation they served. They just needed a job. Josh was sure in a pinch, they would not defend the Constitution. But then, he thought, if they did defend the Constitution, they'd be compelled to attack Washington.

Josh was most troubled by the shortages in combat arms units in the Army, Navy and Marines. Infantrymen, tankers, artillerymen and combat engineers were hard to find, their units barely at 60 percent strength, especially in the Airborne, Rangers, Special Forces, Delta Force and Task Force 160.

He understood Navy SEAL and Marine Recon units had the same problem. Despite the draft and a terrible economy, no one wanted to serve an anti-military administration that cut military spending by 25 percent and undermined the good order and discipline of the forces by accepting homosexual behavior among the ranks.

It made Josh sick to see how much the nation had fallen in four short years – *from the greatest superpower in history to the biggest joke on the battlefield.* Along with the U.S.'s steady decline as an economic and military world power, the president and her highness, his wonderful secretary of state, continued to defer all international issues to the UN, EU or NATO; that is, except the *Global Poverty Act*, which added even greater stress on the American tax payer.

The administration compromised on every issue but taxes, abortion and the homosexual agenda. Whenever Russia, Iran or any belligerent force rattled sabers, the administration responded with harsh rhetoric then sought UN resolutions. The U.S. was no longer the 'shock and awe' nation but more of an 'awe shucks' nation.

Still a darker issue about all the soldiers leaving the service bothered Josh, one he rarely mentioned to anyone except the Lord. It was something he prayed about twice a day. Sure, many of the soldiers leaving active service came home and joined Guard units. Others found more lucrative jobs with Homeland Security, which now had more agents than the FBI and ATF combined. Josh felt that many of these former soldiers were selling out by joining America's KGB.

It bothered him just as much that a very large percentage of combat experienced, combat arms soldiers were disappearing into civilian society. He suspected they were joining the hundreds of secret militias that had formed in the last three years; many of which were offshoots of the Ku Klux Klan.

And yet, the Klan itself had been mysteriously silent for three years. Sure, Neo-Nazi gangs in Boston, New York and Boca Raton could be counted on for an occasional race-related beating or murder. These crimes were always followed by protests and marches that blamed all white people in general then some retaliatory act of violence by the Black Panthers or Five Percenters. It was eye for an eye. The whole country was now blind to the forces that were fanning the flames of racial hatred.

Unlike most law enforcement professionals, Josh didn't include the KKK with skinheads or Neo-Nazi groups, though he knew there was a sharing of ideology. It was their methodology that was different now. They had changed their historic tactics and overall goals set by their founding father, Albert Pike.

Where were the big Klan marches and backwoods, late-night cross-burnings? Even their web sites lacked the fiery rhetoric for which white supremacists had been known for nearly 150 years. He was sure there was no change in the Klan's fundamental doctrine, but there appeared to be a change in its battle plan. But what was it?

Josh prayed over the thought of thousands of Special Ops soldiers that might be training for some racially motivated attack that would set off the powder keg his country had become. At least one of them was an old Army buddy, a man he almost called a friend. He wondered what led Jake to join the Klan. Jake wasn't a racist.

Sometimes Josh wished he could convince Joy and the kids to take their spouses and the grandchildren and just leave the country before they were arrested for being Baptists or before the whole country went up in flames.

But where could they go? Where could anyone go anymore that Big Brother couldn't find him?

****

When they got home from church, Josh decided to check his email while Joy checked the weather. He was glad he did for he'd gotten a response from the American Party about his warning that the party might be targeted by the feds as the source of racial tension. It wasn't just a cursory response from some administrative staffer but the American Party's presidential candidate himself, Chuck Hampton.

Hampton wrote a brief, personal letter of thanks to Josh for his concern and his continued prayers. As he read the message, Josh's suspicious nature made him think his $1,000 donation six months ago was probably appreciated too. The letter eased his suspicions though. Hampton told him his headquarters office in Dallas had been visited by two Homeland Security agents nearly three months ago. They were asking questions about campaign supporters.

He admitted the party made no requirements of American citizens who joined the party, just asked they were sincere about their love of God and country. The annual $50 membership dues covered some of the administrative costs to run a web site and send out newsletters, but it was mostly used to investigate campaign contributions. Every contribution, no matter how small was investigated to ensure the sender was a *real* person or legitimate organization and one the American Party would want as a supporter.

Unlike the other two major parties, Hampton said the American Party was not for sale. His staff even showed the feds a copy of a bank draft to a white supremacist organization that had made a campaign contribution with a credit card. When the contributor was determined to be a racist organization, the $1,000 donation was returned by bank draft several days later. Good thing they kept good records.

Hampton concluded the letter, again thanking Josh for his support and concern. The fact that he was willing to send a personal note re-enforced Josh's opinion of Hampton. He was a genuinely descent fellah.

Hampton was a retired Air Force chaplain, a conservative Southern Baptist by doctrine, originally from South Carolina. He had moved his wife and family to Texas nearly 10 years ago when he was asked by several concerned conservatives with a little financial backing to give up his semi-retired life as a part time preacher and assistant Christian school administrator to help start up a new political party, one that supported Biblical principles and followed a strict adherence to the Constitution.

Though they fielded a candidate for president in 2004 and 2008, they couldn't get on most states' ballot. But now the American Party was recognized by every state in the country, even in those states where a socialist majority hated everything the party stood for and loved everything it stood against. And it wasn't the all-white, uneducated, low income party the media had painted it to be since the 2009 tea parties.

The Republican Party received only 1% of the black vote in 2008 and were now supported by 3 percent, but the American Party's 12 percent support from African Americans in recent polling spoke well of its progress. It also had the support of 60 percent of Asian Americans, 40 percent of Native Americans and 35 percent of Hispanic Americans.

Apparently, the new *Immigration Reform Act* didn't win many votes for the Democrats or Republicans that backed it. Of the 12-20 million illegal aliens who were supposedly living in America four years ago, less than six million had taken their offer for amnesty and citizenship. Most appeared to have gone home, probably because the economy had forced Americans to start accepting the low wage construction, agriculture and service industry jobs previously relegated to illegal aliens.

Then too, because of the economy, many "white" states had passed legislation that denied government assistance to illegal aliens, forcing them to go to "blue" states where they were equally unwelcomed by other minorities, which was why so many had just gone home.

Josh especially liked the demographics of his party. Nearly half of American Party members were college graduates and professionals, while an equal number were skilled laborers and technical workers – including *non-union* carpenters, craftsmen, electricians, machinists, plumbers, nurses, paramedics, firemen, police and military and especially farmers and ranchers. About 3 percent represented the super rich *and* the super poor. The American Party represented a true cross-section of working class, *real* Americans!

"Hey, Josh," Joy called. "Come look at this!"

She had changed the TV from the Weather Channel to CNN and found a news report on a murder in Pensacola, Fla. and what police were calling arson in Beaumont, Texas.

The body of a homosexual activist was found early this afternoon in a wooded area just outside Pensacola. He appeared to have been beaten to death, his hands tie-wrapped behind his back. Then just an hour ago, a Planned Parenthood office in Beaumont was apparently fire bombed. As Josh watched the news reports, he could see right through it all.

The president was already on TV condemning both incidents as hate crimes committed by those who would divide this country just because they disagreed with certain people's lifestyle or a woman's right to choose. A democratic senator added her own comments, placing the blame directly on the American Party, which she asserted was inciting violent people to put action to the *"vicious* rhetoric *spewing* from the American Party and their *intolerant* presidential candidate."

"You'd make a great artificial reef," Josh said to the obnoxious senator.

"Oh, Josh," Joy admonished him. "You don't mean that."

"*I don't?*" he asked. He wasn't so sure anymore.

Sometimes he saw his fellow Americans not as Americans at all but as *domestic enemies*. Four years ago, over half of his beloved countrymen had voted to set aside the Constitution. For the last three years, the idiots they elected had been trying to organize a Constitutional Convention, so they could officially change the Constitution to reflect their anti-Christian, socialist ideology. Now *44* percent of those same non-tax-paying voters, functionally-illiterate proles were still doing everything possible to prevent the last Americans from saving the country! If they couldn't rule over it, they wanted the country to collapse.

****

Friday morning brought rain, but the misty drizzle they had was nothing compared to what the northeast was getting from Michael, now an historic Category 5 whose 160 miles per hour winds were pulverizing New York and drowning New England with torrential rains. The high winds had already spawned F-4 and F-5 tornados from Manhattan to downtown Boston. Eyewitnesses claimed seeing dozens of people sucked out the windows of skyscrapers as the killer funnel clouds marched through cities like dark shadows of death.

Josh hurriedly limped around the puddles as he made his way to the door, his hand shielding the rain from his glasses until he reached the covered doorway of the Overhills annex. Inside, Hooper, Nichols, Harriman, Koz and the new man, Cpl. Watie, were watching Joy's favorite channel.

"Have ya ever seen anything like this before?" Koz asked Josh as he poured himself a cup of coffee and joined them at the long table in front of the TV. "This is like an act of God or something."

"Koz," Harriman shook his head. "It's a storm. *Every storm is an act of God.* Do you think it's a *government* project?"

"I know what ya mean, Koz," Hooper said, finishing the last sip of his coffee. "I been thinkin' the same thang m'self. If it ain't d'end of dis world, it sh'o look like d'end of dis country."

"What's that?" Sherman asked as he hurried in from the rain to join the others.

No one answered. Hooper tossed his Styrofoam cup in the trash can and grabbed his patrol hat off the table. He and Nichols left at the same time though in different patrol cars. Harriman soon followed.

"What were they talking about?" Sherman demanded to know.

"The weather," Koz answered, pointing at the TV as he excused himself to go to the bathroom.

"Oh that," Sherman said to Josh. "Yeah, that's bad. Glad I don't live up there. I thought you guys might be talking about the church burnings."

"What church burnings?" Josh perked right up. It was rare that Sherman ever said anything he wanted to hear.

"You didn't hear about the church burnings?" Sherman chirped, smiling as if it was some sort good news, "Yeah, some six or seven churches were torched in three states, I believe. Yeah, three. Mississippi, Alabama and Tennessee."

"What *kind* of churches?" Josh demanded. It mattered to him. "Were they black churches hit by the Klan or just churches in general hit by Muslim extremists or some other anti-Christian group?"

"Oh, they were all Baptist churches," Sherman answered, almost like he was proud to say it. "Let's see, one of the churches in Mississippi was a Southern Baptist church, the other Reformed Baptist; another Southern Baptist and two independent Baptist churches were burned in Alabama; and a Freewill Baptist and Primitive Baptist church were burned in Tennessee."

Josh asked no more questions though he wondered where Sherman got such precise details. It was almost like he was reading from a script. As Koz returned from the bathroom, Josh changed the channel to Fox News, again more by habit than choice.

A reporter was at the scene of a smoldering independent Baptist church in northern Alabama. The small, wooden frame building was little more than ashes. What was left of the pews could be seen inside the scorched sanctuary. A large brass cross leaned on a clump of charred rubble that used to be the pulpit.

The reporter noted what the public was seeing there was repeated at six other churches, which he emphasized were all Baptist churches, which he also emphasized were known for what he called "divisive, *outdated* views" about morality.

The scene then went back to the Fox newsroom where pundits were already spinning their explanation of events. They read a report from the Vatican that condemned the burnings and asked those who committed these crimes to restrain themselves from further acts of violence. The pope himself then asked all Baptists and fundamentalists throughout the U.S. and the world to stop preaching hateful doctrines that incited violence against others and themselves.

Finally, Fox News pundits spun the news events and message from Rome to suggest that the American Party should appeal to its *"core supporters"* to tone down their *"venomous rhetoric"* and *"allow the country to heal."*

Koz turned off the TV. He'd heard enough. He was a member of the American Party, but he wasn't a Baptist or even a committed Christian. He was just sick of hearing so many people blaming these simple, Bible-believing folks for things he knew they weren't guilty. The news reports were striking a raw nerve in him. No wonder this country was suffering from so many natural and man-made disasters! It harassed and arrested good people then praised and rewarded bad people.

"Maybe I should've moved South instead of East," Watie said, the deep lines in his dark, ruddy face barely moving when he spoke. "*Way* South, like Brazil."

Watie was a Cherokee. He'd come highly recommended to Sheriff Westin from the sheriff in Granite County. With tourism nearly non-existent in the mountains now, tribal leaders on and off the reservation had crime under control there with little need of a large sheriff's department. Though he was reluctant to move his family away from the home of his people, Watie had agreed to accept a transfer, if only to keep a job. It was the first time he'd been away from his mountains since he came home from the Marines 12 years ago.

Josh and Koz agreed with his comments about Brazil. Watie didn't talk much, but when he did, it was usually something thought-provoking. Josh wondered if Watie was hinting at the 40,000 Confederates who left the South in the late 1860's and settled in Brazil, rather than live under Yankee oppression. He'd have to ask him about it one day. They left Watie with Sherman to man the annex while they went on patrol. They were sure Watie could handle a smart-mouth punk like Sherman. Besides, Hooper had already told him to watch out for Sherman, that he was a federal rat.

"So, what's happening, Chief?" Sherman was heard trying to strike up a conversation with the new man as they closed the door.

****

"*Man*, I'm getting tired of hearing that kind of crap," Koz said as Josh pulled their Task Force SUV onto Overhills Road then NC 210, heading north in a light rain.

"What *crap* is that?" Josh asked, glad he'd been able to get Koz to at least *try* to stop cussing. "Are you talking about Sherman's mouth or the biased news media?"

"*Both*," Koz smiled.

He liked Koz, who was 15 years his younger. Koz was a body builder and Navy man, former SEAL with eight years active service, but he left the Navy about six years ago because his career was adversely affecting his marriage. He returned home to Baltimore where he got a job with Wells Fargo as a security guard. When he later heard through a friend of a friend that the newly elected Sheriff Westin was looking for "*former military with some law enforcement experience*," he thought it was a long shot but applied for an opening as a deputy and got hired. His wife was from Little River, S.C. anyway, so the move south was welcomed.

Sharon was a sweet lady and faithful member of the *Anderson Creek Holiness Church*. She homeschooled their three boys, who ranged in ages from seven to eleven, and they were real boys, always fighting or into mischief yet devoted to and protective of their mama. On special occasions, Koz went to church with the family but not on a regular basis.

He preferred to sit at home and watch the History Channel, Discovery Channel, Animal Planet or Military Channel and drink beer. He drank too much too often. Josh believed something was eating at Koz on the inside, and he'd often try to bend the conversation to get him to open up. Usually though, Koz would set himself up for questioning by the questions he was always asking Josh.

"Josh, have you ever heard of some Aztec prophesy about this year being the end of the world or something like that?" Koz spoke up after offering Josh a mint from a tin container he pulled from his shirt pocket.

"I've heard about a *Mayan* prophesy that said something about the end of this *age* taking place December 21, 2012," Josh answered, accepting one of the mints. "Is that what you're talking about?"

"*Mayan, Aztec.* What's the difference?" Koz chuckled. "I figured you'd heard of it. You read more than anybody I know. I think they made a movie about it a couple years ago. *What do ya think?*"

"I wouldn't know about any movie. Haven't been to one in four years. Nothing Hollywood produces anymore is worth $20 a person. As far as the Mayan's prophesy, I don't know, Koz," he sighed, looking out across the dark morning sky. "There's really a whole bunch of prophesies that point to this year being a year of great change, and we've seen quite a bit of change the last three years.

"The Chinese supposedly have a prophesy that called for this year to be the end of time. And I've read where even Nostradamus was supposed to have predicted this year to be the end of the world as we know it. As far as prophesies themselves go, I know God speaks to some folks directly whereas the rest of us have to rely on what he's told us in the Bible."

"And what does the Bible say about 2012?" Koz asked, apparently believing he was going to hear some startling news.

"It doesn't," Josh shook his head. "We can only read the *signs of the times*. No man can know *the day or the hour*."

"But it does say Jesus is going to come get his people, *I mean*, his *church*, right?" Koz persisted.

"Of course," Josh said, turning left off NC 210 onto a county road that led out toward a dairy farm he liked to pass by. It reminded him of his granddaddy's farm back in South Georgia, even though his Papa was long gone now. "As sure as Jesus came the first time, he will come again for those of us who believe in him. But what you're asking me about is what's called the *rapture*. You won't find it mentioned in the Bible by name."

"Why then do so many preachers talk about it like it's real?" Koz turned his head and looked away, apparently disappointed.

"I didn't say it wasn't real," Josh said, causing Koz to turn back. "I said it's not called that in the Bible. Rapture means "caught up" or "taken away," which describes what Paul was talking about in 1 Thessalonians 4, *ah'm*, let's see, verses 15 through 17, I think. Jesus himself alludes to the rapture in Matthew 24, verses 40 through 44, and John illustrates it for us in Revelation 4:1."

"*How do you know all those verses?*" Koz asked, wanting not to believe him.

"Like you said, I *read*," he told him, slowing to make a sharp turn where he could now see the lush green field and dairy cows grazing unperturbed by the misting rain. "I read my Bible every day. You can look the verses up for yourself, if you like. I'll give 'em to ya again."

"Nah, I believe ya," Koz admitted. "It's just that, I don't know. I mean, I know God is real, and Jesus is his son and when I was teenager, I trusted him to forgive me for being so stupid and save me from going to hell. Since then, though, *I don't know.* What I don't understand is why has he let all this crap happen to my country? As sure as he died for me, don't he understand I'd die to save my country – *if I could*, I mean?"

"Yeah, he understands. He's the one who taught us about that kind of love," Josh told him sighing, not wanting to tear his attention away from the big dairy barn they were passing. "You and I are the last of a dying breed of Americans, Koz.

"One problem we and a lot of hard core, flag waving Christian Americans have is refusing to believe this country might not be here at the time of the rapture, *at the end of the world*. We unconsciously believe America is still the apple of God's eye, and we're owed the same sort of special blessing as his people Israel. I've prayed long and hard about the same thing you seem to be going through."

There was a silence. Koz wanted to speak but was almost afraid to.

"And your prayers, did you get an answer?" he finally asked.

"*I'm not a prophet, Koz*," he told him sharply. "But the Holy Spirit is still my comforter and my teacher. I have a peace inside me about tomorrow. I don't worry about *when* the Lord is coming back for his church. I only need to be ready when he comes for *me*, which could come at any moment. *Men die and so do nations*. This country has been a divided nation since December 1860. We'd have been better off as two separate nations than one held together by force.

"Now those ties that bound us together by force have *rotted* and aren't strong enough to keep us together anymore. Even if the American Party wins in the next election, that's like a band aid on a severed limb. Without direct *divine* intervention, this country is going to die. *Judgment is coming on this country.* And if the Lord hasn't come by that time, those of us that are left will pick up the pieces and start another country."

Koz was silent. He was thinking. Josh was always making him think.

"The point of it all to me is to try not to worry anymore about the fate of this nation," Josh added. "I don't do a good job of it, I know. My blood pressure is testimony of that. But I'm trying. You gotta learn to do the same."

"Yeah," Koz said then sighed. "I know."

After a long silence, Koz turned on the FM radio, which he had turned off when they first got in the SUV. Neither of them had wanted to hear any more media bias. Remembering that, Koz quickly set the channel to a weather station then caught part of a report about earthquake aftershocks hitting Seattle. One aftershock was 6.1, the other 5.5. *But what about the quake itself?* He changed the station as he and Josh glanced at each other with looks of concern and surprise. *What now?*

They had expected to get an update on Hurricane Michael's destructive path through New England, but now they hear of an earthquake in Seattle! When he found another station, the reporter was shouting above the rotors of a helicopter about another quake, this one in San Francisco. They couldn't believe what they were hearing.

The Seattle quake, which hit an hour ago, was a deadly 8.1, but the San Francisco quake was an unmerciful 8.8! The reporter said other traffic helicopters over the city had reported half the Golden Gate Bridge was in the bay.

The huge forested mountains north of the city across the bay, especially Mt. Tamalpais State Park and Monte Rio, were now treeless, flattened by the quake. The city itself looked like a pile of rubble from the air with large areas on fire or smoking. Cars and trucks littered the streets and freeways; overpasses were down, the cars beneath them crushed. Thousands ran into the streets to avoid being crushed inside buildings only to be crushed or butchered by falling concrete and glass.

Without realizing it, Josh had slowed the SUV to about 15 miles an hour. The rain had stopped, but it was still very dark for mid-morning. Just as Koz was about to say something, the reporter who had been shouting began shouting again. He was getting a report from Los Angeles where another 7.6 earthquake had struck the city, this time destroying what wasn't brought down two years ago!

Josh stopped the SUV. He and Koz just sat there a moment, staring at the radio, almost expecting to hear about yet another disaster. There was too much static though and the station was lost. The two men looked at each other but said nothing.

They hardly spoke at all during the next hour until they came back to the annex for lunch. As they entered the doorway, Sherman slipped out between them. His lips were clearly swollen and purple, as was his left eye, and his shirt was torn. He was missing his deputy's badge too.

Hooper, Nichols and Harriman were sitting around the table barely eating their lunch, numbed by the news, national and departmental. They knew about the earthquakes. They'd been watching the news about it. It was unbelievable.

When Josh asked about Sherman and where was Watie, they said Watie had had to report to the courthouse, that Sheriff Westin was defending him before Special Agent Dobbs. Sherman was no longer with them. He'd said the wrong thing to the wrong man at the wrong time. For the time being, he was being replaced by Special Agent Peyton, only Peyton would not take on duties as a deputy. He'd stay at the courthouse and department headquarters with Sheriff Westin.

Baptist churches were being burned throughout the Old South, the northeast was being devastated by an historic hurricane and the west coast was nearly destroyed by three monster earthquakes. On the bright side – *if there was a bright side* – the Benton County Sheriff Department was now rat free.

Chapter Four

"Somewhere over the rainbow
Bluebirds fly.
Birds fly over the rainbow.
Why then, oh why can't I?"
E.Y. Harburg, "Somewhere Over the Rainbow"

U.S. 74 West was a scenic drive, up to and especially after you got around the Charlotte area traffic, though the road itself had seen better days. Josh was enjoying one of his favorite CD's, including a collection of Beethoven's greatest symphonies. Joy generally didn't care for the same music, but it was okay because she was sleeping, something she tended to do whenever they were on the road. When she was awake, Joy preferred gospel choirs and chorus groups with orchestra backup and fancy arrangements.

Josh liked gospel music too but preferred Southern and Bluegrass gospel and collections of those old gospel hymns sung by the likes of Tennessee Ernie Ford, Cristy Lane or George Beverly Shea. He also loved to hear more recent singer/songwriters like Ron Hamilton and Mac Lynch. Their kids grew up listening to all forms of gospel music except contemporary, or as some called it Christian *Rock*. For Josh, the two words just didn't go together. You might as well have Christian *beer* and Christian *crack*.

Josh's favorite music was actually western theme songs like "The Good, the Bad and the Ugly" and "Magnificent Seven." But if he changed the CD to "A Fistful of Dollars," Joy would wake up and change it to one of her "sleepy CDs," as he called them. He left well enough alone and let her sleep, smiling when the next song turned out to be "Ode to Joy." Probably not what old *Beety* had in mind, he thought.

Josh and Joy were heading for the mountains, escaping for the Labor Day weekend to a Christian family camp, called *The Outdoors*, where they met their kids and now grandkids every year. It had been a week since Michael had cut his deadly path through New England, taking over 3,000 lives with him and destroying billions of dollars in personal and commercial property.

America's financial center was down for the count, from Wall Street's greedy stock speculators to Boston's even greedier bankers. The UN had re-located its headquarters closer to Washington, D.C. Millions of homes and businesses were without power; tens of thousands of New Englanders were without homes. Still, the destruction in Washington state and California was exponentially far worse. Even the left-winged media described it as "destruction on a *Biblical* scale."

The death toll in Seattle alone was already at 4,400 and climbing. In San Francisco, it was well over three times that number and nearly twice that in L.A., where the damage extended from Burbank all the way down to Laguna Hills, almost as if the quake followed I-5 from north to south.

The aftershocks that hit San Francisco caused huge portions of the city to sink into the bay. The number of people missing from the three quakes was a tremendous burden to FEMA officials, who were trying to run search and rescue operations in and around damaged buildings that were subject to collapse from nothing more than a strong wind.

The president had declared the entire state of California a disaster area and most of northeast Washington, based entirely on information supplied by FEMA. Thus far, only state politicians had ventured into the demolished cities, and they only did so by helicopter. Property damage was estimated in the trillions of dollars.

National Guard units from surrounding states were sent to help, even from states whose governors had previously refused to release their Guard units for federal service. But they weren't going back on that commitment, for their Guard commanders reported to their own governor, not the liberal governors of Washington and California.

The president's response was to deploy two battalions of Marines from Camp Lejeune, plus three of the five CBRNE brigades and he ordered the immediate withdrawal of all but essential active duty troops from Iraq and Afghanistan and two of the three battalions still serving in Germany, plus a brigade from South Korea.

Rather than come home to their perspective units and families, these troops were to redeploy to the northeast and west coasts, ostensibly to back up Guard troops but more likely to prevent any possible takeover of "blue states" by Guardsmen from "white states."

Even at a time of the greatest natural disasters in the country's history, it was politics as usual. Josh was glad to be getting away from it all for a while. Sometimes he wished he could get away from it forever.

It was always politics. He often wondered who these people were that toyed with other peoples' lives like they were playing with puppets. How could anyone be so evil to do the things that were done for money and power?

Josh was suspicious of every catastrophe he heard about on the news.

There was the news of an Ebola outbreak in West Africa two years ago that killed hundreds of thousands. Was it a natural outbreak or was the CIA field-testing its biological weapons on the poorest of the poor again?

There was the news that incidences of lung and skin cancer had quadrupled in one Chinese province last year. Josh doubted it was cigarette smoke and exposure to ultraviolet rays. It was all just a game to governments and those who pulled the strings.

Try this and see how the people react. No. *Okay, back off. Now try this.* War? *Sure. There're too many people anyway. Got to get the world's population below 500,000. Fears of a flu pandemic? Global warming? Distractions. Keep the ignorant masses distracted.*

Josh remembered how the president's far left supporters came out like Nazi storm troopers after the 2008 election. Supposedly, nearly 100 retired admirals and generals came out of their closets, voicing their opposition for "don't ask, don't tell," *or so said the news media.* Active duty admirals and generals wouldn't take their stand until they were forced to do so a few years later.

By mid-November 2008, homosexuals and lesbians were protesting in the streets of California, savagely attacking Mormon and Christian churches for daring to support the legislation that prohibited gay marriage. Across the country in Lansing, Mich., gay activists stormed an Anglican church during Sunday services, disrupting worshipers by shouting obscenities against Christians and Christ and throwing gay propaganda leaflets around the sanctuary.

These terrorist-style tactics continued almost unabated for weeks, partly because so little of it was reported by their news media allies and what little was reported was minimized as not really being newsworthy. But the American people were finding out anyway, thanks to internet news, bloggers and YouTubers.

Gay activists were trying to force their agenda on the American people, believing they had the support of a newly elected, pro-gay president. Then one Sunday, they targeted the wrong church. The area around Greenville-Spartanburg, S.C. was well known to homosexuals for being a stronghold of Baptists and fundamentalists.

For the first three months after the election, all the churches harassed and assaulted by gay activists were mainline denominational churches. Then one Sunday when they singled out a large independent Baptist church just north of Spartanburg, they discovered something about Baptists. It still made Josh grin to think about it.

Baptist-like believers have been persecuted for over 1900 years, and through that persecution, Baptists have developed a mindset not unlike that of Jews, the only religious group more persecuted than Baptists. When assaulted, Baptists don't always turn the other cheek.

When 39 gay activists stormed the sanctuary of *Cowpens Baptist Church* one quiet Sunday morning, they quickly realized their mistake. Seven activists had to be hospitalized; several others left with broken noses, missing teeth and cauliflower ears. All left that church in a much bigger hurry than they entered.

When their press agents tried to paint these Baptists worshippers as violent hypocrites, it backfired. The local newspaper printed a headline that was carried around the world: **"Hurray for the Baptists!"** A paper in Denmark soon published a political cartoon depicting several injured and frightened lions fleeing the Roman Coliseum. When translated into English, the cartoon has one lion saying to another, *"That's not fair. They're not supposed to fight back."*

Almost immediately, the activists' tactics changed. The American media went into another blackout. Just as they had ignored the assaults on churches and would later cover-up military leaders' mass resignations, the news media would pretend nothing happened when a gay invasion went wrong.

There were no more church invasions and fewer violent public protests. In a few months, the entire incident faded from the American public's incredibly short memory. But now it was clear to gays and their radical supporters that Baptists and fundamentalists were the real enemy.

The gay culture warriors re-doubled their efforts to make Baptists and fundamentalists *Public Enemy Number One*. Now more than three years later, they were close to achieving that goal. Josh imagined this might even be the last year they'd have a Christian family camp to retreat to.

The local newspaper that published the famous headline was bought out within a year after the incident and closed. Last year, Cowpens Baptist Church was one of the first to be closed down by the feds. Gays used federal courts with backing from the administration to overturn Proposition 8 and every state that had laws banning homosexual marriage.

By the time state appeals reached the Supreme Court, new high court appointees had tipped the scales hopelessly to the left. What they couldn't do via public referendum or legislation, they had accomplished by media propaganda and judicial decree. Now they were going after their real enemies.

"How quickly Americans forget," Josh thought as his eyes drifted from the pot-hole riddled four-lane to the mountains off to his right front. "Right now, you think it's just Baptists and fundamentalists. Next year, it'll be Presbyterians, Lutherans and Methodists, until finally, Catholics. My beloved *fellow* Americans. ***Idiots!***"

"Huh?" Joy heard his last thoughts. He was thinking out loud again.

"Good afternoon, *Sleeping Beauty*," he told her, reaching across the console to pat her on the thigh as she stretched out her arms and legs and yawned. "We're about 10 miles from Forester."

Forester was a small town in the foothills, the home of Lattimore Baptist Bible College. There, they would pick up Abigail and her husband, Joel. Both were already graduates, but Joel had gone back last year to take some additional courses to prepare for the mission field in Brazil. Abigail taught kindergarten at the school's academy to help make ends meet. Joel worked part time at a local Wal-Mart.

After Josh and Joy picked them up, they would drive another hour west into the heart of the mountains to a barbecue restaurant in the town of Barton, where they'd meet their other children and grandbabies.

Rachel and her husband Phillip with granddaughter Sheila had left southeast Oklahoma yesterday afternoon. Phillip was pastor of a small, independent Baptist church there. Though they struggled with the loss of her income, Rachel had not gone back to her teaching job at an associate church's academy after Sheila was born. She preferred to be a stay-at-home mom, particularly with a 2-

year old who thought she had to climb on and get into everything, and especially with news that Rachel was now pregnant again.

Nathan and his wife Jenny with grandson William had left very early this morning from just outside Charleston, S.C. Nathan ran his own computer and electronics repair shop. Jenny had also decided to stay home with Will, especially now that their 18-month old had started walking and like his cousin, got into everything. She said she'd probably wait until they had another baby and when that baby was in kindergarten, she'd go back to her job as a dental technician.

Barton was a small town near the edge of the Pisgah National Forest. Labor Day weekend brought thousands of tourists to see the beautiful waterfalls or just breathe the clear mountain air, although the number of tourists was down quite a bit these last two years. Though the family camp was still another 30 minute drive up into the mountains, Josh and Joy always met the kids for lunch at Wilde Hog BBQ near the intersection of U.S. 64, U.S. 276 and NC 280.

Their BBQ was okay, but what Josh always looked forward to was their almond-crusted trout, something you didn't find back in his part of the state. Besides, he was particular about his BBQ. He had four favorite BBQ restaurants: one in Lexington, one near McGee Crossroads, one in Goldsboro and one in Wilmington – *all* in North Carolina. Some others had good BBQ, but these four were *the best of best*.

Rachel and Phillip were already there waiting for them, their minivan parked in the only shady spot on the back side of the restaurant parking lot. Phillip was carrying something that looked like a dirty diaper to a trash can as Josh, Joy, Abigail and Joel pulled up. They found Rachel and the baby, and with hugs and hellos, greeted each other under the shade.

Phillip approached moments later, smiling as he wiped his hands with a moist towelette. He was a tall, heavy set man, and as he approached 30, he was starting to lose his hair, not that you could tell with his cowboy hat. Of course, he had the boots to go with it. With his faded jeans and western style shirt, he didn't look much like a preacher, but he was a pretty good one when he got warmed up.

"We were just about to give y'all a call," he said. "My stomach's growling already. Have ya heard from Nathan and Jenny? I'm ready to eat."

"Me too," Josh said, shaking hands with his son-in-law, hoping whatever he was wiping off his hands was *off* his hands.

As the others said their hellos to Phillip, Rachel's cell phone began ringing. It was Jenny. They were about five minutes out. It seemed that Will had gotten car sick a few times, causing them to have to stop several times.

Because there wasn't enough shade to hold all of them, they decided to sit on the restaurant's big front porch to wait for Nathan, Jenny and Will. But as they came around to the front of the restaurant, Josh could see trouble sitting on the porch, so he directed his family into a parking slot, which he said they should hold for Nathan.

"It's hot out here," Joy complained to Josh. "They'll find a parking space. Let's go sit on the porch."

At that point, Phillip and Joel saw the trouble Josh had noted and urged their wives to wait with them. Four young men and three young women had taken up residence on the porch, all but one seated in the old wooden chairs, leaning them back against the wall, smoking and joking and harassing the customers as they tried to enter or leave the restaurant. A tall fellah wearing a dingy t-shirt, cut-off jean shorts and no shoes leaned against the porch railing near the restaurant doorway.

Josh could hear the lewd comments he was making to female customers, who tried to ignore him. The other three men were dressed similar to him, their female companions barely dressed at all. They were all covered in tattoos from the sides of their dirty faces to the tops of their bare feet. Orwell called them proles, but Josh's grandmother had a better name for folks like these: *white trash*. As he watched them, Josh expected to hear banjo music.

One of the women, a short, fat one wore a faded *Obama '08* t-shirt with its sleeves and neck cut out. The other two women were sickly skinny and wore tank tops several sizes too large, showing off their tattooed, nearly bare breasts. It seemed to be a game for these lovely ladies to flip their cigarette butts at customers.

At that moment, Nathan's jeep pulled into the parking lot. Seeing the others holding a space for him, he drove in front of the restaurant and edged them out of the way. As the girls all greeted each other and the babies, Josh and his sons-in-law pulled Nathan aside to inform him of the trouble on the porch.

"Ya know, we don't have to eat here," Joy came over to the men to advise them what to do, finally seeing the trouble on the porch. "There are other restaurants in this town, Josh."

"None that fix trout the way this one does," Josh said.

"Mama, ya can't let punks like that control where ya eat or what ya do," Nathan said, his blond hair blowing in the breeze, causing Josh to make a mental note to mention how much cooler shorter hair was on hot summer days. "I'll go get my *1911*, if you're worried about us."

"I keep a little something in my suitcase, if we need it," Joel added.

"Me too," Phillip said.

Joy studied the faces of her husband, son and sons-in-laws. By now, Rachel, Jenny and Abigail were wearing expressions of concern.

"*Daddy*," Rachel and Abigail called at the same time then called their husbands by name. Jenny did the same. They didn't get a response.

They watched an elderly black couple try to enter the restaurant, only to be pushed around by the tall, skinny fellah and called racial slurs by two of the females. The old man kept his cool and was eventually allowed to lead his wife inside. A few moments later, a young Hispanic couple with three small children came toward the door from the opposite side of the parking lot.

They too were met with shoves and heckling. When one of the seated punks got up and tried to get the man's wife to dance with him, two employees from inside the restaurant came out and made the punks leave their customers alone, threatening to call the sheriff's office. The man and his family were allowed to pass, though the tall fellah promised to be waiting for him.

"I've seen enough," Josh said and began walking toward the restaurant but not directly to the door.

Instead, he came around toward the far end of the porch where he'd have to walk the entire gauntlet of white trash. His sons followed in step behind him, wives and babies pulling up the rear.

Josh exaggerated his limp, hoping he might entice one of the punks to cross him. First one then the next then the next but none dare mess with him. Even their women kept silent. He was about to pass by the tall, skinny punk leaning against the porch railing, whose feet already stuck far out into the aisle. Suddenly, the punk dared to shove his foot into Josh's path in hopes of tripping him.

Josh let out a noise that sounded like a Rebel yell then kicked hard and high, catching the punk's foot behind its heel, lifting him so far in the air, he flipped upside down, landing on his face directly in Josh's path. Josh then placed a size 10 D hiking boot across the back of his neck, pressing down with just enough force to get the young punk's attention.

"If you so much as move, forget about your plans for the weekend," he told him, his voice so deep, it was scary.

One of his partners jumped to his feet only to be slide-tackled by Nathan, who was on his feet in a second, grabbing the punk by his left foot, twisting it hard as he spun around. The wanna-be tough guy let out a scream as he was forced to roll onto his face. That's when Nathan made a field goal kick between his legs, just for good measure.

He'd learned to slide-tackle playing soccer at *Pettigrew Baptist Christian Academy*. He'd learned how to quickly disable an enemy during Army Combatives training while serving with the Army Reserve in Iraq. The kick to the groan was something Daddy had always told him to do if he ever had to fight someone. That way his opponent would understand he'd do whatever necessary to end the fight.

At the same time Nathan was dealing with his adversary, Phillip the preacher and Joel the soon-to-be missionary were dealing with issues of their own. When the young buck nearest him started to leave his chair, Phillip gave the chair leg a swift kick, sending him to the floor. Taking a cue from Josh, he then placed a size 11 EE cowboy boot across the young man's scrawny throat with just a tad amount of pressure.

"If ya move, you won't be singing in the choir this Sunday," Phillip told him. Josh's brand of sarcasm was a family trait.

At the same time this was going on, the last fellah jumped to his feet and reached for what appeared to be a knife in his back pocket. Joel jumped forward, grabbed him around his neck with his left arm then pressed his right middle knuckle hard into the man's back.

"If you try to use that pig sticker, I'm gonna have to blow a hole clean though you," he whispered, bluffing the punk while trying his best to make his young voice sound deep and scary like Josh's.

Only one of the females tried to help their men. Joy caught her by the length of her greasy hair and jerked her back to her chair, strongly suggesting she stay where she was. She stayed. Hearing all the commotion on the porch, the same two employees rushed outside; the elderly black man and the Hispanic man were with them as were other male customers. Moments later, a Romania County deputy's cruiser pulled to a stop in front of the restaurant, soon followed by a second then a third.

When the arrests were made and the excitement was over, Wilde Hog's manager apologized to Josh and family and to each customer in the place, one at a time. As it turned out, two of the females causing the trouble were former employees, whose boyfriends depended on their tips and wages. They hoped to intimidate the manager into re-hiring them, and if they couldn't, they would try to hurt his business as much as possible. It seemed like a good strategy to the minds of the mindless.

****

"Mister Cunningham, I've been meaning for three weeks to come by and thank you and your school for supporting me by posting my bail," Kathy said, standing in the doorway of Cunningham's office. "I'm really sorry to have waited so long."

"Call me *Bear*," Cunningham smiled, standing up and reaching out to shake her hand. "Please come in and sit down. You're welcome about the bail. Don't worry about the delay. We've been kinda busy around here too, getting' ready for the long weekend. Today's just a little bit extra hectic. The kids get out at noon, plus we're losing one of our teachers today.

"Anyway, ah… what was I talking about? Oh, the bail money was a collection from church members, actually. When word got out by phone that evening what you'd said on our behalf, then what happened after we left, people were calling me to find out if you were facing any charges, and if there was anything they could do to help. We were glad to do it. I hope everything's going well with you now. Have you had to go to court or anything like that yet?"

Standing across from him now, she could see why he went by the nickname Bear. He was huge, as tall as Jamal, only he wasn't fat. They both took seats as one of his teachers or a secretary, she didn't know which, stuck her head in the office door to say they were gathering the kids into the chapel.

"I'll be there in a few minutes," he told her, then nodded to Kathy.

"I didn't have to go to court," she told him, watching the busy lady hurry back up the hallway. "I went before a magistrate about a week ago. He fined me for disturbing the peace and interfering with an officer performing his duties. I guess I'll be on probation for the next three years."

"That's not so bad," he told her. "I was told you went through a lot worse a few days before the board meeting. Did I hear right that some guy was gonna kill ya?"

"Yes," she sighed, pointing at her a band aid under her chin. "I'd be dead now if Josh Athol hadn't come along. Josh killed the guy who killed my supervisor, Jamal Wheatley, and was taking me hostage. That's how I got this cut on my chin."

"*Joshua Athol?*" Bear repeated, noting the band aid still covering the scar on Kathy's chin. "I know Brother Athol. He's a good man. We've done a couple combined services with his church. I think we got one coming up in a few weeks."

"I don't know why he was willing to save me," she admitted, looking at the floor in front of his desk. "Several years ago, I, ah… *I did Josh wrong*. You see, I used to believe in the school system, so much that when one of my English teachers refused to follow the teaching strategies of our school and every public school in the nation, I got him fired. How could he forgive me for something like that?"

Bear stared at her a moment, smiling. It unnerved her.

"Ms. Alighieri, didn't I hear at that board meeting that you used to teach English?" he asked, still smiling.

"Yes," she said, curious why he asked that. "I was the head of the English Department at Volkschulen High School. They made me retire though, afraid I might reveal trade secrets about *The System*, I guess."

"Ms. Alighieri," he called her by name again, this time almost excited. "Have you ever thought about teaching at a Christian school?"

"*Here?!*" She said, her voice squeaking with surprise. "Mr. Cunningham, ah…. *Bear*, I'm not a member of your church. I'm not even a Baptist. In fact, *I'm Catholic.*"

"When was the last time you went to Mass?" he asked. His questioning was getting personal and though it made her uncomfortable, she felt obliged to respond.

"I went, ah…., it was, ah…. *Easter Sunday*," she finally remembered.

"And before that?" he persisted.

"The Easter before that," she admitted and sighed. "Okay, I didn't say I was a *good* Catholic. But I was born and raised in the Catholic Church."

"Okay, you're a Catholic," he said, smiling again. "*Are you a Christian?*"

A wave of fear came over her, and she felt uneasy to the point of weak. Was he psychic? How did he know what she was wrestling with, spiritually? She felt he could see right through her. It bothered her but comforted her at the same time.

"I'm sorry," he said, standing then reaching for some materials in his desk. "Let me be honest with you, *Kathy*.

I know a little about you because I've already asked around, to include asking Brother Athol. You see, I'm in a bit of a situation here. One of my two English teachers is leaving here today.

"Her husband's finally been allowed to get out of that stop-loss thing that was holding him in the Army as a helicopter pilot. They're heading for their family farm in Alabama this afternoon. I envy 'em 'cause Alabama's my home too. Anyway, needless to say, I need an English teacher *real* bad. Yeah, I know that's bad English, which proves my point."

Kathy sat there speechless.

"What I'd like to do is offer you her job, at least until the end of the year," he told her. "We can't pay ya a lot, but it's gotta be better than unemployment and a whole lot safer than working in a convenience store. We don't take hostages here.

"Now if you decide come Christmas you can't keep working with a bunch of Baptists, I'll understand. If you have some issues but think you can hang in there with us till the end of the school year, that'd be *great*. I'd really appreciate it. *On the other hand*, if we can help you grow spiritually the way I think you wanna grow, I'm not just offering you a job; I'm offering you a church home. A church *family*. And you won't have to wait to attend services on Easter Sunday."

"Well, I, ah…, *I don't know*," she said, completely at a loss for words.

"I'm not asking you to decide right now," he told her. "I'd like you to think about it and pray about it over the long weekend. Come Tuesday morning, if I see you here, *say around 7:30*, I'll know your answer. In the meantime, I wanna give you some information about our academy and some information that may help you with the things that I think are troublin' your spirit. Oh, if you'd really like to check us out, Sunday morning church services start at 11."

He hurriedly said his goodbyes while handing her the promised material then rushed out the office door to the chapel at the other end of the school building. Kathy looked at the pile of material he'd handed her then around his office. She noted two diplomas hanging on the wall, both from Abeka Christian College in Pensacola, and several pictures, some apparently Bear's family and some of Bear with his students and faculty.

He was a strange man, forceful and yet kind-hearted. An angry voice deep inside her, one that had been silent for two weeks now, told her to drop the material in the floor and go home. She ignored it. She'd do what he asked. She'd think about it, and as much as she'd forgotten how, she'd pray about it.

****

The drive home from family camp always seemed to take longer than the drive there. Joy fell asleep within an hour after they dropped Abigail and Joel off at their duplex apartment near the Bible college. Actually, she cried herself to sleep, something she did every year as he drove home. Josh wasn't a happy camper either.

It was always hard saying goodbye to his kids for months at a time, but now he had to watch little Sheila and Will crying that they wanted Papa and MawMaw to come home with them, even though Sheila was headed back to Oklahoma, Will to coastal South Carolina. He wished he could have a little more time with them and their parents, *his kids*. No matter how old they got, they were still his kids. They just didn't need Daddy anymore, at least not like they did when they were little.

He adjusted his position in the driver's seat, but it didn't make him feel the least bit more comfortable. The crescent kick he used to put that punk in his place the other day put a hurting on his own back and hip. Josh was too old and busted up to be doing stuff like that anymore.

The pain had bothered him all weekend, but he tried not to ruin it for Joy. He took one of his three pain medicines Friday night but nothing last night. Couldn't risk being groggy on today's long drive. He wished he was already home where he could take his pain killers then lay on the floor with a heat pad under his back and his feet propped up on the couch.

If Joy only knew how excruciating his back and hip pain were sometimes, she'd worry herself sick about becoming a widow. But pain was just part of life as he saw it; it reminded him he was still alive, that God must expect him to be doing something. What, he wasn't sure anymore. He used to think he knew.

Josh's life verse, *Psalm 23:4*, promised he needn't ever fear anyone because his Lord was with him. From the time he was a little boy, Josh never allowed himself to show fear of any man or thing. Just God. He often wondered though when the Lord intended to lead him out of the valley of the shadow of death, where he'd been so long now.

As a boy growing up in South Georgia, Josh had wished he could fly like a bird. He loved to climb to the top of trees and look out as far as he could see. He'd swing high in the tree swing Papa had made for him and his brother, so high the rope would buckle, nearly dumping him on the ground. It didn't matter. Daddy said he wasn't smart enough to be afraid of heights. Maybe so.

He'd almost joined the Air Force so he could fly, but his eyesight disqualified him, so he settled for being an Airborne Ranger. Even now as he drove along U.S. 74 East near the town of Rockingham, his eyes picked up on every lucky bird crossing the sky in front of him.

"Somewhere over the rainbow bluebirds fly," Josh whispered the words to the theme song from *The Wizard of Oz* then changed them to fit his personal faith. "Birds fly over the rainbow. *Some day so will I.*"

His mind raced from topic to topic. He thought about *coincidentalism*, a term he used to express the idiot-ideas of humanists that argue all of creation was just a coincidental occurrence of random events. He knew nothing happened by coincidence, by chance. For every effect, there was a cause for it.

Sometimes he'd find himself thinking about a particular scene or line from an old movie then two or three days later, while he was channel surfing, he'd find not only that movie playing but that particular scene. He didn't believe he was psychic, but he didn't think it was coincidence that a movie he hadn't seen or thought of in a dozen or more years would suddenly be aired again only days after he was thinking about it.

He wasn't a prophet either, but he had several secret moments where he thought he heard a voice telling him something was going to happen then it happened a few days later. Nothing earth shattering, just personal intuitiveness. He remembered hearing a voice telling him his mama was ill and feeling a strong desire to call her, only to find out she'd just been hospitalized.

Then there was the dream he'd had three days before his near-fatal parachute jump in which he dreamt his right foot and leg were all but crushed, including his hip and lower back. Those were in fact the injuries he suffered when his main chute *streamered* and his reserve chute became entangled in it.

Josh changed his thoughts quickly. Didn't like thinking about that jump or the consequences of it. But he did like to think about the year he spent hunting and fishing while recovering from his injuries.

He and Joy and the kids had spent more time together than they'd ever had his whole Army career. He remembered it with a special fondness as he looked down at Joy, now snoozing away. She seemed to be content with life, though it had given her many hard knocks. He was one of them.

It was a blessing to be able to afford a long distance drive, a rare thing these days. Other than the Labor Day trip to family camp, he only made one other long drive a year. It just cost too much to drive, and besides, driving aggravated his back and hip. Still, he looked forward to his after-Christmas trip back to Georgia.

It wasn't the same with Papa, Gramy and his parents now gone, but he appreciated the time he got to go hunting and fishing with his brother, sister and cousins or just hang around the old family farm. Josh wished he could re-capture just a few moments of his boyhood, and he could when he thought about it hard enough.

He could remember the dusty smell of the red clay, dirt roads he walked along barefooted after school, weekends and summers. He remembered the sweet taste of the blackberries that grew in the ditches and along the rusty wire fences that skirted what seemed like millions of acres of peach and pecan trees.

Josh grinned when he thought about those lazy summer afternoons he and his brother spent catching catfish and bream in the spillway at Papa's pond, and those frosty mornings they hunted squirrels, rabbits, quail, wild turkey and deer.

Josh's memories were so vivid that he wished he was driving I-75 south, rather than the future I-74 corridor. But Joy would require him to drive his old truck when they went home to Georgia even though it got *gallons to the mile* instead of *miles to the gallon*. She didn't want *her* Stratus being used as a hunting or fishing vehicle, even though it got 32 miles per gallon.

It was strange how quickly the price of gas went up so high four years ago. Then when the international, *unelected* elitists who really control everything saw the election going the way they directed it, they relented on the prices somewhat as a reward to the ignorant masses for behaving the way they were programmed to behave.

By the end of 2008, gas prices were close to $1.50/gallon. But after the start of the New Year when their Marxist candidates were safely in office, they allowed gas prices to slowly go back up. In fact, prices continued to rise until the gas riots led to martial law in a dozen cities, which Josh supposed was also part of their master plan. He sighed because he wanted to fight the elitists *his way*, but the love of Christ constrained him.

Josh also wanted to feel recharged, like he used to after going to The Outdoors. Other than missing his kids, at least he used to leave there feeling hopeful and ready to get back into fray for the Lord. This weekend's family camp, however, focused not so much on continuing the fight but preparing for the Lord's return, which the guest speaker made a pretty convincing argument would be soon, very soon.

This too should have left him with a sense of great satisfaction, even joy, but he was troubled by the ramifications of what the rapture would mean. Josh was confident that he and his family would be spared the tribulation to come, but he grieved for the ignorant masses that prefer a false messiah. *But how could he reach the lost when the lost don't want to be found?!*

Perhaps he felt unsettled because he'd come to camp feeling so bitter toward over half of his fellow countrymen for voting the country into the state it was now in. He was still wrestling with his own spirit, trying to forgive them for being so stupid.

If going to camp this year did anything, he was reminded to love his enemies, and since he now saw half his fellow countrymen as his *domestic enemies*, he understood he'd have to learn to forgive them and accept them without compromising with anything they stood for or against.

Still, he thought, until the Lord separated his church from this crazy world, it would be easier to get along with fascist liberals and proles if they went one direction and the remaining, real Americans went another. There really is no such thing as *United* States anyway, only blue states and white states, he thought. We are in fact the *Divided* States of America!

He pushed the control knob, turning on the CD player while turning down the volume so as not to wake Joy. It was the CD she'd been playing before she fell asleep, one of Ron Hamilton's best, "Cherish the Moment." The title song was the last one on the CD and the next one to come up. He knew the words all too well and almost turned it off because he also knew how it would affect him.

It was a great song that reminded parents how soon their children grow up and move out. He'd never again play 'peek-a-boo' with Rachel, who used to hide behind the drapes in their first apartment. He'd never again be able to carry Nathan on his shoulders during family trips to aquariums, museums, parks and zoos. He'd never again sit and watch *Mister Magoo's Christmas Carol* with Abigail as they did every year for 17 years. His heart was already hurting before the song got started.

"Cherish the moment," the chorus began. *"Soon you'll be apart. Cling to the memory. Clasp it to your heart. Soon comes the day when you'll have no child to hold, so cherish, cherish the moment."*

By the time the song ended, his eyes were welled up with tears. He hoped Joy kept sleeping, but it was too late. He felt her warm hand touch the back of his hand, which rested on the gear shift. She gently squeezed his hand and smiled, tears filling her own eyes. He returned the smile, rolling his hand over to take her hand in his. Their kids were grown and gone, their country was about to implode, but they still had each other.

****

Kathy tried to slip in the door unseen, but she was greeted by an usher in the doorway. He handed her a weekly bulletin, shook her hand and thanked her for coming. Then he gave his name and asked for hers. She timidly whispered her response. As another usher escorted her into the sanctuary and showed her to a seat in the middle row of pews, she heard her name called.

"*Ms. Alighieri*," a deep, friendly voice called. "It's great to see ya. I hope your being here today is a good sign about Tuesday morning."

"It is," she smiled. "I thought I'd give it a try till Christmas at least, if that's alright with you."

"That'll do for now," Bear said, grinning.

She had read over the material he gave her, both that on the academy and on what this Baptist church believed. Though she disagreed with part of the school's dress policy for both students *and* teachers, she recognized it probably saved them a lot of discipline problems with teens. And she supposed she could learn to dress a little more modestly herself.

As for the doctrinal brochures, she wasn't as sure. Some moved her to at least think; others made her angry, if only because it was so contrary to what she'd been brought up to believe. One particular flyer though caught her attention, one titled "How to *Know* that You *Know* You're Saved." The key text was from 1 John 2:3-5, but the more she read it, the more she was troubled. That's why she was here.

Several ladies sitting near Kathy leaned over pews, stretching out their hands to shake hers and introduce themselves. A distinguished looking man sitting behind her with a young boy and girl stood and introduced himself, asking her name. His name was John. She didn't catch his last name. He was very attractive for a man who appeared to be at least 60.

She found out later when he went to join the deacons at the front of the church that John was a widower, that his wife of 42 years and their daughter-in-law had died in a car accident last year. Their only son had been killed in Afghanistan two years ago. His grandkids were his only family now.

Kathy thought it unusual the way these people were so open about themselves, while expressing a willingness to share the burdens of others. But they didn't know about her. She told herself if these people knew the life she'd led, they'd shun her the way she'd always heard about hypocrites like them.

The music was good. *Different* but good. She wasn't used to singing old hymns like these. She supposed because this was Labor Day Sunday, all the selections seemed to mention work and labor, like *"Work for the night is coming, when man's work is done,"* and *"Little is much when God is in it. Labor not for wealth or fame. There's a crown and you can win it, if you'll go in Jesus' name."*

The special music after the tithes and offering was particularly moving. She'd never experience anything like it in a Catholic service. As best she could tell, the very dramatic song was called "The Judgment," and the young man singing it seemed to bring the description of Christ's *White Throne Judgment* to life in such a way, it made her shiver to think how real the spiritual realm really is and how certain was the future of Christians, believing Jews, non-Christians and even Satan himself.

The young man, it turned out, was the choir director and assistant pastor, and he wasn't that young – nearly 40. Kathy had assumed Bear was the assistant pastor. He jokingly told her later, as the academy principal, he was the *assistant,* assistant pastor.

Dr. Robert Stearns was the pastor, a white-haired man who looked to be in his early 70's with a strong

Southern accent. His voice was soft at first but soon swelled in tone and volume to a point it sounded like thunder. Like the theme of music chosen for the day, Stearns' sermon was also on working or more specifically, *works*.

"*Do you really think you can impress God with the pompous, pathetic things you do?*" he asked, demanded. "Do you really believe God owes you eternal life because you have all the *outside* appearances of a *good* person? **He knows your heart!** He knows *all* your *lustful, selfish desires* – the ones you *acted* on and those you've only imagined. *You ain't gonna hide sin from God or cover it up with good works, church membership or baptism!*

"There is only one thing that separates the saved members of this congregation, other congregations and the unsaved world – **Jesus**. He is the *only* Way, the *only* Truth and the *only* Life, and no one can go to the Father without him!"

Kathy failed to hear the "Amens" around her. Her spirit was struggling to keep just out of reach of another Spirit that seemed to be pursuing her. When Stearns told everyone to turn to a specific passage in the Bible, she struggled to find the verse he was reading in her Catholic bible. The words were not the same; some words were not even there and others that were in her bible were not in the one Stearns was reading.

When he called for them to go to yet another verse, her frustration was apparent to those around her. The distinguished looking man sitting behind her slipped out of his pew, then outside the sanctuary. He returned moments later with a new Bible, a KJV, which he reached over the back of her pew, offering it to her with a whisper.

"Try using this one," he smiled.

Kathy smiled back helplessly and accepted his offer. She missed some of what the preacher was saying for the next several minutes while she re-read the passages he'd just gone over. Not only were the words different, they seemed to speak to her now like they'd never done before.

The Bible she was holding now seemed to have a voice in itself. It spoke to her spirit. *There is only one mediator between God and man, and thanks to years of misinformation, she didn't know him!* **She was headed for hell!**

"No one has to go to hell," Stearns was saying, recalling Kathy's attention. "No one is *predestined* for heaven or hell though God the Father knew before the beginning of time who'd accept his free gift of salvation, so he sends his Holy Spirit to move his elect toward that decision. He don't make you do nothing though.

"Every man and woman since the Adam and Eve have had the same choice. For *if we confess with our mouth the Lord Jesus and believe in our heart that God has raised him from the dead, he will save us.* It's that simple. It don't matter what kind of heifer you are or what secret sin you're holding on to; *give it to Jesus.* Confess it to God, *not me*, not anyone in this sanctuary. Trust *him* to forgive you of that sin and every other sin in your life, and you'll belong to him."

There was stillness in the room though many spirits, especially Kathy's were stirring. Stearns asked everyone to bow their heads and listen to the Holy Spirit as he moved their hearts and quickened their souls. He said if anyone there had not yet accepted Jesus as his or her *personal* savior, now was the time to do it. There were no assurances about tomorrow.

"With heads bowed, eyes closed, *come*," he said softly. "Come to Jesus."

The pianist then began playing a hymn familiar even to Kathy. It was "Just as I Am." The words caused her ears to ring and her heart to burst. She began weeping softly then openly crying.

A lady seated near her asked her if she'd like to talk with someone in another room about how to be saved. Kathy whispered she already knew what she needed to do. She excused her way down to the end of the pew and out into the aisle that seemed to be a mile long. It was a very difficult walk to the altar.

"*I need Jesus*," she whispered to Stearns, who greeted her down by the altar.

"Yes, ma'am," he returned the whisper. "We *all* do. Come let me introduce you to him. Please pray along with me as we talk to God."

****

Labor Day morning Josh slept in almost to 10. It wasn't that they got back late. They were home before dark. But after unpacking, Josh took two different pain medicines for his back and hip, grabbed his heat pad then stretched out on the living room floor with his stocking feet perched up on the couch.

Joy was slightly irritated with him for withdrawing this way, but she was used to it by now. At least he never took up drinking like a lot of injured soldiers do, which, when mixed with pain medications caused them to die young. She was content to keep her husband as long as she could but feared one day his injuries or his blood pressure would take him from her.

Josh awoke in his own bed, not remembering how he got there. He was sure Joy didn't carry him to bed. On those rare occasions he took all three pain relievers, he'd be out over 12 hours. He wasn't supposed to take but one as needed, but if the pain worsened, he could take a stronger pain reliever four hours later then yet the strongest of the three medications four hours after that.

Josh had recently developed a bad habit of taking one of each, usually the first two at the same time. When he did this, the only thing on his mind was making the pain go away for a while. And it generally did, for a while.

The house was filled with the wonderful aroma of coffee and bacon, two smells seconded only by the smell of frying chicken. Joy had planned bacon biscuits, but he asked for grits and eggs too. Though she pretended to protest how the things he liked to eat were going to kill him some day, she obliged his request.

She almost always gave into him. Josh could have his big, country breakfast. It would be enough to hold him over till the department picnic at Buzzard Rock State Park later this afternoon.

The Labor Day picnic was a difficult thing to pull off for a sheriff's department, if only because a good portion of its members were on duty during public holidays. That was part of the job of law enforcement. On the other hand, not everyone wanted to take part in a picnic. Law enforcement agencies are political too.

When he was elected four years ago, Westin had received the blessings of the retiring sheriff, a Republican. That was division enough for a county with far more registered Democrats than Republicans. But when Westin changed his party affiliation to the American Party a year later, he was attacked from all sides. It was bad enough that he was a novice in law enforcement. He had to go and be a radical *tea partier* too.

When he started, probably half of Westin's staff consisted of staunch Democrats or quasi-Republicans. He won the election by a hair, but despite his Constitutional conservatism, he had since won over a few That One-worshipping Democrats and most of the pseudo-Republicans; all the social and fiscally conservative Republicans in the department switched parties when their sheriff did.

Not Josh though. Josh was already a member of the American Party. In fact, he was one of the strongest influences on Westin that caused him to make the switch. That's why many of Westin's political enemies targeted Josh as their enemy as well. Among them was Westin's opponent for this year's election, Assistant Chief Winslow with the Millingham Police Department.

****

"Hey, Josh," Koz called to Josh as he carried a large ice chest — with additional things Joy had piled on it – toward the group of a dozen or more wooden picnic tables nearly hidden under the grove of pine trees. *"I was 'bout to call you."*

Joy was bringing up the rear, her arms loaded with a large picnic basket filled with a tray of deviled eggs, baked beans, pasta salad and other goodies. Several plastic grocery bags loaded with chips, buns and plastic forks, spoons and knives were dangling from her finger tips.

Josh carried all the heavy stuff. She carried all the bulky stuff. A small crowd had already gathered, some already cooking on the dozen or so charcoal grills provided by the park. Koz was there with Sharon and all three boys, who were chasing each other around the tables. Hooper was waving smoke from his eyes as he tried to keep his burgers and hotdogs from burning. His wife was there as were their son and daughter.

Josh put down the heavy ice chest with a grunt and a sigh then looked around at all the picnickers. Inspector Massey was there with his wife, both a rare sight at any department function. They were a very private couple. Massey himself, a tall, non-descript-looking former Marine Recon, was an aloof person, almost secretive. He did his job well as part of the Violent Crime Task Force was concerned, but after work, he kept to himself or his family.

Capt. Ike Dinkins and his wife were there with their daughters, as were Dispatcher McPhall, her four kids and her newest boyfriend. They and the Hooper family were the only black members of the department who openly supported Westin. Others did but wouldn't say so in public.

Hooper said his immediate family and his church disowned him when he told them he could no longer support *their* president, and that he was joining the American Party. The Hoopers soon joined Westin's church, which, like Northside and Back Swamp, was multi-racial. Westin rarely preached there anymore. Too busy. His son-in-law was now senior pastor at *Doone Pentecostal Freewill Baptist Church*. Westin's son was a pastor over in Greene County.

"Is Sheriff Westin here, yet?" Josh asked to no one in particular.

"That's what I was gonna call ya 'bout," Koz said, walking over to him, a hotdog in one hand, Coke in the other. "I don't s'pose you've watched the news this weekend. You never do when you go to that camp up yonder."

"I heard 'bout Obomi having to turn his troopies around before they could even get out of Kuwait," he said. "I figured as soon as that many of our troops pulled back, al Qaeda and those Taliban knot heads would make a play for it. They should have learned as much two years ago when they tried to withdraw troops."

"No, I'm talking 'bout *local* news stuff," Koz said, almost grinning. "Winslow ain't gotta chance of winning the election now. He was arrested in Bangkok on Saturday for child prostitution."

"***What?!***" Josh said, looking around among the bags of things Joy brought for their charcoal. He'd left it in the truck, his mind still foggy from the pain killers.

"Yeah, I found out 'bout it from Dan Rushton at church yesterday," Koz explained. "Turns out Winslow wouldn't have been sheriff very long even if he'd won this election. The SBI and FBI have been investigating him for child pornography for a while then they started looking into his Labor Day trips to Thailand every year.

"Seems the fellah promising to clean up this department was a member of some international pedophile group called *Men and Boys*. They travel to exotic places like Thailand to have sex with children. When he went over there this time, the FBI asked Thai officials to keep a watch on 'em. They did. Looks like they're gonna be watching him a while."

"Well, that means…." Josh started to say something but was interrupted.

"That means those of y'all who were thinking 'bout retiring *early* or having to look for new employment still have a job for at least four more years," Westin said, grinning, his bald head shining in the sunshine. He was in civilian clothes, a rare sight. "*Hey*, would ever' body come gather 'round a minute? I got some news for ya, just in case ol' Koz here hasn't told ya ever' thing."

Burgers and dogs were put on the backs of grills so they wouldn't burn. Parents rounded up their little ones as over 30 people found their way over by the table where Westin was standing with Josh and Koz.

"In case y'all didn't hear, my opponent in this election has gotten himself in some deep *kimchi*, even for a Democrat," Westin said, looking like he was about to start a sermon. "News of a sex crime of any type will kill the political career of a Republican and especially a member of the American Party.

"But Democrats tend to get a boost in the polls when they're caught in extra marital affairs or gay scandals. So far though, nobody's gotten away with being a pedophile. Winslow's gonna be in a Thai prison for a long time. He's become an international embarrassment for our dear governor and president. Personally, I hope they use him for an artificial reef. That's all perverts like him are good for. Jesus even said so in Matthew 18:6."

A couple men chuckled at his interpretation of Scripture, at least those who knew the verse Westin was quoting.

"Anyway, I've just come from Chief Harrison's office," Westin continued, adjusting his glasses on his face. "He called me because he's already fired Winslow and wants to hire one of my people to take his place. Maj. Hernandez and I have had our differences, but he's a good man and fine law enforcement officer. *Maj.* Ike Dinkins, I need you to take his place."

Formerly *Capt.* Dinkins approved of his sudden promotion to operations director without hesitation, as did his wife. She kissed him; his daughters hugged him. Those standing near him also congratulated him.

"*Capt.* Joshua D. Athol, I need you to take Dinkins' old job. Do ya think ya can get use to an office job?" Westin asked, watching Joy with a smile as her jaw dropped open. "By the way, *y'all gonna have to explain to me why the Romania County sheriff might wanna hire your entire family.* I'm curious 'bout that one."

"*Inspector* Samuel J. Watie, are ya here?" Westin asked as a surprised Watie stepped forward. "I haven't had a chance to thank you for helping us get rid of that skinny rat, Sherman. Please try not to hurt little Koz over there if he gives you any lip. Oh, and Koz, I expect you and Inspector Massey to train him up quickly, making sure he uses *department* rifles when he takes out the bad guys. And finally, *Cpl.* Benjamin Hooper, I'm gonna need you to take over the Anderson Creek Branch Annex."

"I don't know what to say," Josh smiled, thoroughly surprised. "*Thanks.*"

Dinkins, Watie and Hooper used this moment to say their thanks as well.

"Folks, I don't want to interrupt this picnic any longer," Westin said, seeing his wife, Su coming his way, her arms loaded with picnic supplies. "I'm hungry."

Joy gave her husband a kiss on the cheek when she thought no one was looking then went over to help Su set her things down and say hello. They were good friends, had known each other back when their husbands were in the Army. Su was a beautiful lady, a Korean, whom Dave had met early in his career while stationed there. They'd been married over 50 years.

"*Yoshua*," Don Luis Miguel Lopez called to Josh as he returned from his truck with a bag of charcoal. "We 'ad visit'r Bak Swomp Bautista *adverbio*. Ya know her?

Josh only half way listened to the young deputy, only because he couldn't understand half what he said. He was a good officer, but his English was even worse than Josh's Spanish. "Ya know Katerin' Allavarie?"

"I know a Kathy *Alighieri*," he told him as he spread the charcoal and lit it. "So, Miss Kathy finally paid your church a visit. That's good. I'll have to give 'ol Bear a call and ask him how he managed that one."

"She join church," Lopez said sharply. "She got saved; cry *hard*. Bear say she start work 'cademy *mañana*. You come t' Bautismo *miércoles*?"

Josh stopped what he was doing to repeat in his still cloudy mind the words he thought he understood. *Kathy got saved?!* That's what he said. A *Wednesday* baptism? *Unusual*. Okay. This was something he needed to see for himself.

"*This* Wednesday?" Josh asked, his heart smiling. "Lord willing, Joy and I will be there! *Hey, Joy!* Wanna hear some good news?"

Chapter Five

"Nights in white satin, never reaching the end,
Letters I've written, never meaning to send.
Beauty I'd always missed with these eyes before,
Just what the truth is, I can't say anymore."
Justin Hayward (*Moody Blues*), "Nights in White Satin"

"Ah, *man*! That's was *good* BBQ," Koz said, belching and rubbing his growing stomach as Josh drove his old truck back to the courthouse. Koz had apparently stopped working out. "Stephen's BBQ really is *the best of the best*."

They were the last to leave the restaurant because Koz had to order a couple BBQ sandwiches and a sweet tea to go, *just in case he got hungry later*. Westin, Dinkins, Watie, Massey, Hooper, Nichols, Harriman, Nichols, Bennett and McNeilly were already on their way back to work in four other vehicles. It was a Saturday training day for the whole department, or at least those not already on duty. Mostly quarterly admin stuff the state required of all sheriffs' departments, requirements dumped on the state by the feds.

When lunchtime rolled around and someone asked for a recommendation about where to eat, Josh began bragging about the *"best of the best BBQ"* in North Carolina. McPhall and three other lady officers called them *"meat-eating cavemen"* as the dozen hungry men left the office together, most not believing Josh's assessment about the "best" BBQ in the best state for BBQ. Stephen's made believers of them.

"Hey, I wanted to ask you to name some good books for me to read," Koz said, just as Josh was about to list off the names of his other favorite BBQ restaurants. "I didn't get to talk at ya this week, now that you're a desk jockey."

"What kind of books?" Josh asked, "And how are things working out with your new partner? Watie hasn't had to rough you up or anything. It'd be a shame for him to pick on a little fellah like you."

Josh had to admit, he missed their philosophical conversations too. Today though, as they headed back to Millingham, they almost had to yell above the wind, both men having rolled down their window. Koz' curly brown hair was blowing wildly, making Josh think weight training wasn't the only thing he'd given up.

The NCO in him was close to recommending a trip to the barber. But hair standards were something established by the sheriff, not Josh. Dave even allowed the men to wear mustaches. It wasn't that Josh didn't like slightly longer hair or some facial hair. He tended to have a little of both when he was in college and as a teacher. But law enforcement was a lot like the military; Josh felt it demanded a military appearance.

"Yeah, right," Koz grinned at Josh's assertion that Watie might have to rough him up the way he did Sherman. "Sam's great to work with. 'Course, he don't talk about deep, philosophical stuff like you. He talks a lot about his mountains and history. His great granddaddy was a Confederate general. Did ya know that? Oh, he and his family have started going to our church now. Liz, *his wife*, and Sharon have a lot in common, home schooling being one of them."

"Sounds like you've improved your church attendance," Josh noted, smiling with fatherly approval.

"Yeah," Koz admitted. "Read my Bible every day now, twice a day when I can. What I wanted to ask you for is a list of some books you'd suggest for me to start reading, particularly those that you seem to quote from all the time."

"You mean, like Shakespeare, Hawthorne, Twain, Dickens and Kipling?" Josh asked, knowing these were not the books or writers Koz was referring to.

"No, you know which ones I'm talking 'bout," Koz protested as they slowed down to make a turn off NC 50 and onto NC 210. "You're always talking 'bout *proles* and *illuminati* and stuff like that. Where'd you get that stuff?"

"Oh, *that* stuff," Josh grinned. "It's a long list. Are ya sure you're ready?"

It had been five days since the picnic. Josh was immediately placed in charge of patrols, first thing Tuesday morning. He was bored, but Joy was thrilled to pieces because he was *safe*. For her and Dave's sake, he figured he'd try to make the best of it.

He and Joy had a good visit to Back Swamp Baptist Wednesday night. Seeing Kathy get baptized was proof in the power of prayer if ever there was need of proof, which there wasn't. All those years following his end-of-the year, early dismissal – *firing* – Josh fought off his bitterness toward Kathy and the others by praying for them. It had worked for Kathy; maybe there was hope for Brookie and Ferrell too.

On the national scene, things continued to go badly for the administration and the Democrats. The federal troops sent to Washington and California tried to assert their authority over the National Guard troops from Wyoming, Idaho, Montana, Colorado and Texas. Rather than allow their troops to be "federalized," their governors ordered their Guard units to return home to their perspective states, leaving the disaster-stricken areas severely under-guarded.

Looting and vandalism were common place and authorities were unable to do anything about it. Gangs ruled the streets of many cities. Refugees from Washington poured into Oregon from the north while refugees from California poured into Oregon from the south, crippling that state's resources and already struggling economy.

But the combination of tens of thousands of homeless, jobless refugees was not just a west coast problem. The same homeless-jobless refugees fled the northeast for the Midwest and southward as far as Delaware, Maryland and northern Virginia. The already starving economies of those states were stretched to the limit to support their unwelcome guests, and the bankrupt federal government was helpless to do little more than promise federal aid.

Then, as if things were not going bad enough for the president, Thursday night during the Republican presidential nominee's acceptance speech at the Republican National Convention, the world heard the most shocking political speech in American history. Despite strong opposition by party elitists, the last two social and fiscal conservatives left in the Republican Party had been chosen to represent the Republicans in the 2012 election.

Both U.S. Congressmen, one from Texas, the other Alaska, stood side-by-side on the platform, as if they were going to accept the nomination together. Instead, to the surprise of the entire world, they stepped forward and declined their party's nomination and asked their supporters to support Chuck Hampton and the American Party, saying there was no real difference between Democrats and Republicans, that it was all an illusion perpetrated on the public by the *unelected elitists*, the same "invisible government" Teddy Roosevelt had warned about 100 years ago.

The convention floor exploded with shouts and screams by supporters who'd only lent their support because of party loyalty. Now they were officially released to support the Constitution and their dying nation. It worked. Though Republican Party leaders tried to push for a new nominee, there was almost no support for it.

Yesterday, Hampton's standing in the polls jumped from 36 percent to 58 percent. American Party candidates running for House and Senate seats as well as state and local offices also saw a huge jump in the polls. With the election less than seven weeks away, it looked like real Americans were going to take their country away from the elitists-controlled proles!

"Well, let me see," Josh said, his eyes briefly leaving the road to look at a fish pond they were passing. "Have ya ever heard of George Orwell's *1984*? Actually, ya may want to read his *Animal Farm* first then read *1984*.

"When you've read those books, read Ray Bradbury's *Fahrenheit 451*, John Stormer's *None Dare Call it Treason* and Alexis DeTocqueville's *Democracy in America*. After that, try reading Dr. Bill Grady's *What Hath God Wrought* then Thomas DiLorenzo's *Lincoln Unmasked* and *Red Republicans and Lincoln's Marxist* by

Walter Kennedy and Al Benson. When you've read these, try reading David Rivera's *Final Warning: A History of the New World Order*."

"Yeah," Koz said, sighing. *"That's a lot.* I reckon I'll start with Orwell then."

Josh slowed to stop for the traffic light that guarded a four-way intersection near the Johnson-Benton county line. Both men noted with curiosity the two vehicles that crossed the road in front of them.

The first was a rusty, old Chevy pickup. The driver was a clean-cut black man wearing a dark suit and sunglasses. His passenger was a white man, whose battered face was pressed against the passenger-side window. He was unconscious. Josh recognized his old battle buddy from two secret missions in Nicaragua back in the early 1980's.

Unfortunately, Master Sgt. Barefoot was now the grand dragon, sort of a middle-management leader of a Ku Klux Klan group based in Johnson County. He was a very dangerous man, partly because of his membership with the Klan but mostly because this retired Special Forces soldier was a trained assassin. Josh had seen his handiwork in person. But how did this unconscious Klansman come to have a black chauffer?

The old truck was being tailed by a government sedan, which also passed in front of Josh and Koz. Its driver was a clean-cut white man also wearing a dark suit and sunglasses, but its passenger was an unconscious black man, whose head was slumped downward toward his chest, clearly visible through passenger window. He was Josh's *Judas*, Sgt. 1st Class Ballard.

"Hey, ain't that the guy running for mayor of Fayetteville?" Koz asked as Josh made a right turn, deliberately following the suspicious vehicles, which were now a quarter-mile ahead of them.

"Uh huh," Josh told him. "Did ya happen to recognize the Klan dude in the truck in front of him? Looks like they're both being escorted somewhere, and they're both in a less than conscious state."

"Who'd want a Klansman and a black politician?" Koz asked, looking at Josh with concern. "Ya reckon we oughta call somebody?"

"I think ya better," he answered, watching the two vehicles pull off the paved road onto a dirt road that Josh knew led to a closed landfill. He used to hunt rabbits with the farmer who owned that land. "Call Sheriff Westin if ya can get him then ask him to get up with Johnson County's sheriff."

"If those guys are feds, they must be up to something," Koz said, his years of working with Josh having made him suspicious of Homeland Security agents.

"Well, I can guarantee ya they're not taking those fellahs back in the woods for a Bible study," Josh said, turning onto the same dirt road. As soon as his truck was concealed by the trees, he stopped and turned off the engine. "This dirt road becomes an old logging road 'bout 50 meters up yonder then dead ends 'bout 100 meters later. You call for backup while I go see what's going on."

He quietly opened the driver's door and laid back his seat, removing a leather rifle case. Koz was about to dial Sheriff Westin on his speed dial when Josh unzipped the gun case and pulled out a long barreled Winchester, lever action rifle. Koz' eyes grew wide when he saw the huge bore on the rifle barrel.

"Ya going hunting for buffalo?" he hissed.

"Hope not," Josh whispered. "McNeilly's still got my Model 700. I reckon I'll have to make do with this 45-70. Wish I'd put a scope on it now."

Josh cocked back the lever and chambered a round. He always kept his guns loaded, just kept the chamber empty. All those arguments about gun locks and junk like that were just another invention of those intending to disarm the American public.

He could hear Koz on the phone as he moved carefully and quickly up the left side of the dirt road until it narrowed to become a logging road, winding around to the right. He then moved to the right edge of the path, wading through the tall wiregrass, which helped to absorb the sound of his footsteps. Ahead about 50 meters, he could see the two vehicles stopped, the passenger doors open. Now he could hear voices.

"Let's just go ahead and shoot 'em," a whinny voice said.

"What would be the fun in that?" a shrill, almost girlish voice asked. He seemed unsure of his own question. "Let 'em wake up first."

Josh continued to move forward while his approach was concealed by the sedan. He then edged his way around the right side, up to the tailgate of the old pickup. In a small clearing about 40 feet ahead, two men in black suits, wearing sunglasses and surgical gloves were standing over Ballard and Barefoot, who were just starting to come around.

A tall black man guarded Barefoot, his standard issue 9 mm pistol drawn. A skinny white man guarded Ballard with what appeared to be a very worn Model 1911, .45 caliber pistol. Not standard federal issue anymore.

Their captives' hands were tie-wrapped behind their backs – *just like the white supremacist found dead in Orangeburg, S.C., the black activist found dead in Forsyth County, Ga. and the homosexual found beaten to death near Pensacola.* Josh looked behind him, hoping beyond hope the cavalry would soon arrive.

Barefoot was first to awaken. He coughed some but said nothing, just sat there looking at his captors with violent contempt. Ballard woke up jumping around on his buttocks, trying to free himself, cursing.

"Man, what y'all want with me?" he asked. "I ain't done nuthin' to ya."

"Oh, but you're going to help us bring down the mighty, *Invisible Army*," the white man said, laughing an effeminate laugh as he appeared to inspect his captor's pistol. "Barefoot, you do have bullets in this thing, don't ya?"

"What good's an unloaded gun?" Barefoot answered with a deep, angry voice, "Go on and get your business done. My people already have your names, *Special Agents Brown* and *Garrison*. You won't see the end of this week."

"I'm scared. I'm scared," Brown mocked Barefoot with a whinny voice then kicked him in the side. "We've got moles in all your local organizations, you stupid *redneck*. You can't make a move without us knowing it."

"Ya think so, do ya?" Barefoot coughed as he lay on his side, cursed Brown's mama then sat up slowly. "We know who your moles are and use them to feed you idiots bad info. The Klan today ain't the same Klan it was even four years ago. We finally know who our *real* enemy is."

Both of Barefoot's dark, muscular forearms had large, colorful tattoos. The right one was a familiar golden bayonet with three golden lightning bolts through it, all surrounded by a blue arrowhead. Above this was a black and gold "AIRBORNE" tab and above that a blue and gold "SPECIAL FORCES" tab.

The left forearm's tattoo was an orange-red circle with a white cross inside it, both outlined in black. Though Josh couldn't see all the details of this tattoo that far away, he knew what he was looking at. There would be a diamond-shaped symbol centered on the cross and inside it what appeared to be an orange-red apostrophe. This tattoo was the symbol for the KKK.

Barefoot obviously dyed his hair because he was the same age as Josh. It was pitch black, and he wore it long, gelled down and slicked back. Went well with his Elvis sideburns and Fu Manchu mustache. Even though he hailed from New England, Barefoot was a card-carrying redneck. *But he was a smart redneck.*

"I don't care 'bout the Klan," Ballard protested, still trying to work his hands free. He wore his own salt 'n pepper hair long and frayed back Afro-style, trying to look like his literary hero, Frederick Douglass, but he lacked Douglass' character and genius. *"What's that bigot got to do with me?"*

The two federal agents looked at each other and grinned.

"Ballard, you're a moron!" Barefoot shouted. "They're gonna blow your *stupid* head off with my pistol then use me for target practice with their gov'ment-issue pea shooters, making it look like they *almost* prevented your execution!

"They want the public to think the Klan's the same racist organization it used to be. They probably have some elaborate story about following us into the woods here. *Me* being the white Klansman and *you* being the black political activist – *it'll make a great story for the liberal media.* Maybe get these faggots a promotion."

"You're a dangerous man," Brown laughed and kicked Barefoot again. "Last thing this world needs is a *smart* redneck."

Josh kept his eye on both federal agents, having already eased back the hammer on his rifle. He wasn't sighted in on either agent, just ready to respond to whichever one tried to shoot his captive. Garrison was in a bad angle to him, hovering over Ballard almost point-blank. He also seemed to be the most nervous.

For that reason, Josh hoped if he had to shoot one of the agents, it was Brown, especially since he seemed most capable of returning fire. Unfortunately, it was Garrison who acted first.

"Well, fellahs, it's *show time*," he laughed and chambered a round in the .45. "I'll try to make this quick for ya, Mr. Ballard. No hard feelings now."

He took a standard military-style pistol stance, both hands on the pistol grip, pointing the 100-year old .45 at the back of Ballard's wooly head, the muzzle only inches away. Ballard was crying as Josh swung his rifle over to find his best shot. A head or body shot wouldn't prevent Ballard from being killed, so he laid the sights on Garrison's right hand.

The explosion from the big rifle echoed from over the pickup's tailgate and through the piney woods. Garrison's hand burst into a small cloud of blood and bone fragments, the bullet entering at the joint of his right wrist, shattering what bone it didn't pierce.

What used to be his right hand dangled from a bloody stump by pieces of flesh and sinew and the elastic from the surgical glove. The slug then continued its path into the pistol grip where it was deflected slightly to the inside of Garrison's left hand, blowing away three of his fingers, starting at the middle knuckle.

The pistol spun off to the left, discharging as it hit the ground. The round whizzed close by Ballard's head, but he failed to hear it. He thought he was dead, that the first shot he heard was the last thing he'd ever hear. In his mind, he was already gone, causing him to empty the contents of his bladder as he began shaking and whimpering.

Though critically wounded, Garrison screamed in pain as he fled into the woods in fear of the unknown shooter he supposed to be a vengeful Klansman. Though startled at first, Brown traced the muzzle blast back to Josh who leaned on the edge of the truck's tailgate, levering another round in his rifle.

Brown fired off one shot, which grazed Josh's right forearm and left shoulder. Before he could respond, shots rang out from behind Josh. Two large, red holes appeared in Brown's white shirt left and center of the pocket, just as he was about to fire a second shot. Brown staggered back but remained on his feet, his pistol down by his side. Then a third shot to the middle of his dark forehead caused Brown to slump over backward.

"I thought you could use a little help," Koz called out to Josh who'd already swung around, crouching between the two vehicles, preparing to take on whoever was firing at him from behind. "What's going on here?"

"Off hand, I'd say we've just saved the lives of a couple of racists," Josh said, groaning as he slowly rose to his feet, his back and hip responding badly to his crouching. "And if I don't find that other fellah before he bleeds to death, we've just killed a couple of federal agents during the performance of their duties."

A trickle of blood dripped from Josh's right forearm, and more blood oozed down his left arm from the shoulder. Joy was going to have a hard time believing his new job was safer now. He carried his rifle at port arms, ready to respond if Garrison somehow found a way to shoot the service pistol he was still wearing when he ran into the woods. Koz walked two steps behind him, his pistol raised and ready to fire, as the two approached the clearing where Ballard still sat there whimpering. Barefoot sat there, grinning like an opossum.

"*Hooah!* That was some nice shootin' there, son," he told Koz. "You too, *Preacher* Athol. I see he nicked your arm and shoulder some. *Praise the Lo'd*, you're alright. Where did ya learn to shoot like that, young fellah?"

"In the Navy," Koz answered, walking over to and looking down at Brown, who lay on his back with his eyes wide open. Blood trailed down both sides of his forehead, and it covered his chest, turning his white shirt red. His black dress coat was bunched up under his shoulders, his arms stretched out behind him.

"*Really?*" Barefoot shook his head. "Never knew they trained you Navy boys to shoot like that."

"They do if you're on a SEAL team," Koz said, kicking the pistol out of Brown's hand before his fingers froze to it.

"Oh, Navy *SEAL*," Barefoot grunted. "Well, no wonder. What's your name, young man? I wanna know who I'm thankin'."

"*Koznowski, sir*," Koz answered, finally looking at the man who'd been asking him so many questions.

"Richard Koznowski. My wife and mom call me Rick, but most folks just call me Koz. You know Josh? How come ya called 'em *Preacher*?"

"Koznowski," Barefoot repeated, watching Josh following the trail of blood leading from the clearing into the wood line. "Yeah, I know the ugly rascal. A walking dichotomy, that fellah. He's as hard as they come, but he loves his Jesus too much to be useful. I take it you're Polish?"

"My daddy was," he answered, not knowing what or if he should say anything about Barefoot's assessment of Josh.

"Catholic too, I s'pose," Barefoot said, a disappointed look on his face.

"No," Koz shrugged his shoulders. "Pentecostal Holiness."

"*Really?!*" Barefoot said, smiling approvingly.

"*Forget it, Jake*," Josh said, walking back into the clearing. "Ya can't have 'em. Besides, you'll find he's a Bible thumper too. Koz, what did Sheriff Westin say when you called him?"

There was little need for Koz to reply. At that moment the sound of several vehicles could be heard charging up the logging road, bouncing and scrapping bottom all the way. The lead vehicle was Westin's NC State-red Dodge Challenger, a car far too nice to be driven back in these woods. The second vehicle was Watie's gray Silverado. In the distant background, they could hear sirens, probably Johnson County's folks. Stealth was apparently not their policy.

"Let me guess; the cavalry's late again, right?" Westin asked as he hurried from his car, his old legs struggling to get through the tall stalks of dog fennel on either side of the two vehicles that blocked the narrow road. "What y'all got here, fellahs?"

Josh gave Westin a quick summary of what had taken place and what he supposed the two agents were up to, pointing out how Ballard and Barefoot both had their hands tie-wrapped behind their backs and were about to be executed. He then pointed to the trail of blood leading into the woods.

Watie, Hooper, Massey and Dinkins were soon standing among them. Seeing two other black men caused Ballard to come around. He started crying for one of them to cut his hands free.

"We can't do that," Dinkins tried to explain. "That'll have to be something for the Johnson County sheriff to approve. This is his jurisdiction. Besides, I think he'll wanna see the crime scene here as much like our folks found it before they were forced to shoot these guys to save your life."

"Com' on, *brotha*," Ballard pleaded. "Cut m'a loose."

"*Brotha?*" Hooper repeated with vehement contempt. "The closest thang you got to a brotha here is 'dis redneck Klansman. I s'pect he's jest 'bout as much a racist as you. Only he don't get to hide behind the gov'ment like you."

Seeing the blood on Josh's right arm and left shoulder, Westin asked Massey to retrieve his first aid kit and a box of surgical gloves from the trunk of his Challenger. A few minutes later, Massey was back with the medical supplies requested.

"Hey, Hoop," he called. "Didn't you tell me once the Corps sent you through the Army's Combat Lifesaver training?"

"You mean, you don't know how to dress a bullet wound?" Hooper asked, taking the box of gloves from him and selecting a pair. "Oh, I forgot. Y'all Recon guys ain't use to the sight of blood."

"*Oooh-rah!*" Massey said, grinning.

Massey glanced over at Barefoot, who was watching everyone, almost studying them. Hooper used an alcohol wipe to clean the blood off Josh's forearm first so he could get a look at the wound. Josh said nothing, just took a deep breath.

While the bleeding was stopped, Hooper could see a one-inch long gash was cut across his arm, probably needing at least three stitches. His shoulder wound was about the same. Hooper cleaned both wounds a second time with alcohol wipes, laughing at Josh who grit his teeth and hissed as the alcohol burned his wounds; but he didn't cuss.

"Look at you!" Ballard snarled at Hooper. "What you fussin' over dat white dude for? You'd think he wuz more 'portant to ya 'dan yur own people?"

"He *is* my people!" Hooper responded, pointing surgical scissors at Ballard, "*You bigoted* ... At least we serve the same Lo'd. I ain't sure who you serve, ya ungrateful.... *I ain't gon' say it*. I just can't understand the hate in so'body like you. Here dis man done saved yo' sorry life, and 'stead thankin' 'em, you're dissin' me for puttin' bandages on the wounds he took on yo' be'haf."

"*Well,*" Ballard said, sighing and looking down at his wet paints then off into the trees. "I s'pose I do owe ya thanks for savin' my life, First Sergeant."

"I'm not a first sergeant anymore, *thanks to you,*" Josh almost growled. "It's alright though. You didn't thank me when I spared your life 19 years ago. I don't expect any thanks from you now."

"What you mean, *spared* my life?!" Ballard barked. "I don't r'call you sparin' me from nothin'. You were dissin' our C'mander in Chief, and I 'ported it."

"You didn't just report it; you *lied* about it," Barefoot interrupted angrily, his dark eyes flashing. "You accused Athol of threatening that idiot in the White House just because you didn't like hearing his opinion of your Playboy president.

"When word got out to SOCOM forces in theater that you killed this man's career, a bounty was put on your nappy head. I know 'cause I was the bounty hunter 'bout to collect.

"But your soft-hearted, *Jesus-loving* friend here called off the dogs. Just before he got on the plane to Bragg, he made me promise not to break your short, fat neck. *And all these years, you never knew it.* Now he's done gone and saved ya again."

There was a long silence among everyone standing in the small clearing. Ballard was looking pale, like he was going to be sick. The silence was finally broken by a caravan of patrol cars with an ambulance in tow, making their way up the logging road. Josh quietly excused himself, saying he was going to track down Garrison. Watie asked Josh if it was okay for him to tag along.

"Sure," Josh said, trying to forget about Ballard. "Would ya think I was stereotyping ya if I ask ya whether your tracking skills were any better than mine?"

"Oh, no, *Ke-mo sah-bee*," Watie laughed. "Me no good tracker. But if ya need me to skin that rascal, just let me know. I've been skinnin' deer, bear and anything you can 'magine since I was 7."

****

"How ya been doin', Jake?" Westin said, sitting on the ground next to Barefoot. "Thanks for stickin' up for my man, Athol there. *Boy*, I sure wish you'd answered my request to come work for me instead getting' linked up with the Klan."

"A man's gotta do what he's gotta do," Barefoot laughed. "I 'preciate your boys, Koz and Athol though. They're good men. Ya know, I worked with Athol a long time ago in Nicaragua. He saved my butt back then too. Carried me out of the jungle with my leg broke and a killer fever.

"We had different targets. Mine was….well, mine was up close and personal. His was to destroy some piece of crap the Army thought was important at the time. I forget what it was. *Doesn't matter*. We both did our jobs then headed back to our rendezvous point. But I fell in a *flippin'* ditch and didn't link up with him. Despite Sandinistas looking for us everywhere, he stayed in the AO for 18 hours till he found me. Those Rangers mean what they say about not leaving a comrade behind. He'd be a perfect soldier if he'd ignore that conscience of his."

"It ain't just a conscience," Westin corrected him. "I knew some of that story. Thanks for fillin' me in on the rest. He'd never have told me."

"Yeah," Barefoot admitted. "I know. How's his family, by the way?"

"Grown and gone, just like mine," Westin grinned.

"Yeah, I was gonna ask about yours next," he said then lost all expression in his face. "My boy was killed in Iraq in 2008. Got a real purty flag and 'thank you' letter from the gov'ment. His mama grieved herself to death within a year."

"I'm sorry to hear that, Jake. *I really am*," Westin said. "*Is a*...is that why you joined up with the Klan? I know it ain't because you've sud'dly become a racist. And I know you don't hate Jews either. We both trained with Mossad for over a year. When was that, '87? As for Catholics, I always figured you didn't like or dislike them anymore than ya do any other organized religion."

"*Maybe ya don't know me as well as ya think ya do*," Barefoot mumbled.

"That's possible," Westin admitted. "I guess I don't know the Klan as well as I thought I did. Y'all ain't been acting like yourself lately. What y'all been up to?"

"Dave, you know I can't tell ya stuff like that," Barefoot complained then whispered. "But when the *Invisible Army* starts to march again, the whole world will know it."

****

Josh and Watie worked together well. While one followed the trail of blood, the other watched for Garrison, who might surprise them with an ambush, however unlikely. About 500 meters from the clearing, they found him leaning against a pine tree, unconscious.

He had been trying to put a tourniquet on his wrists using his shoelaces. The blood covering his shoes showed he'd succeeded in at least getting the shoelaces off one shoe with the thumb and index finger of his left hand. His other fingers were gone. He'd wrapped the shoe lace around the right wrist, but it wasn't tightened down enough to stop the bleeding. His right hand was still dangling by a mere thread, though now it had turned purple. He'd lost so much blood, Josh wasn't sure he'd last.

"I hope this fellah doesn't have AIDS," Josh shook his head, handing his rifle to Watie as he knelt down to finish the tourniquet Garrison had started.

"Just in case, maybe ya better put these on," Watie said, handing Josh a pair of surgical gloves. "Figured we might need these if we found this dude, so I snatched a couple from that box Massey had as he took it back to the Sheriff's Challenger."

After putting on the surgical gloves, Josh put the shoelace to use for its intended purpose, placing a good tourniquet on Garrison's right wrist then wrapping the stump and the mangled hand in his handkerchief, tying it to the tourniquet. After using Garrison other shoelace to make a tourniquet for the left hand, Josh picked him up in a fireman's carry.

"Come on old fellah," Watie joked. "Don't ya think you ought to let a young buck carry that load?"

"You can carry my rifle," Josh said, adjusting most of Garrison's weight onto his right shoulder, away from his, now burning, bullet-wounded left shoulder. "I've carried whitetails out of the woods that weighed more than this little fellah."

As Josh hurried Garrison back to the waiting ambulance, he was reminded of the time he carried Barefoot out of the jungle. Barefoot was talking out of his head, sometimes in a foreign language. Josh not only had to set the leg he'd broken just below the knee, he had to stop constantly to give him water to get his fever down.

Several times, he had to muzzle Barefoot to keep him quiet and not give them away to Ortega's rather unhappy soldiers, who were trying to catch them before they crossed the border back into Honduras. At one point, he had to use Barefoot's sniper rifle to wound two Sandinistas so they wouldn't follow them. Yeah, he could have killed them, but he chose to let them live. Besides, it took four to tote them out of the jungle.

Now he was trying to keep Garrison alive to find out if he and Brown were rogue agents, or if they were acting under direct orders from the Department of Homeland Security to stir up or just maintain racial or domestic trouble in general. Josh also wanted to keep him alive because he didn't want Garrison to be *Number Five*.

****

"Gentlemen, this is Capt. Athol and Inspector Watie," Westin said to the two men in black suits standing on either side of him. "That would be your Agent Garrison there, I s'pose, or what's left of him."

They were feds, FBI though. Josh was glad. The FBI and ATF agents were not as politically motivated as Homeland Security. Agents Messner and Murphy had been investigating Brown and Garrison for several months. Feds investigating feds was touchy business, which they didn't mind admitting made them very unpopular.

Their district supervisor was awful uncomfortable about authorizing them access to information on another federal agency's agents. According to Messner though, Brown and Garrison seemed to operate in a *permissive* environment, taking no particular steps to cover up what they were doing.

"These guys made it pretty easy to follow their activities," Messner explained, removing a notebook from his coat pocket. "They kept meticulous expense records, saved and submitted every receipt.

"We traced them to Orangeburg, S.C. on the day of a murder there, to Forsyth County, Ga. on the day of another murder – basically, the biggest, unsolved cases in the Southeast for the last two months have these guys in the vicinity and at the time of murders and arsons."

"*Arsons?*" Josh asked, still holding Garrison across his shoulder.

"Yeah, arsons," Murphy repeated, counting off on his fingers the churches that were burned in three states from west to east then north. "These guys never seemed to figure anyone would follow up on them. They filed their mileage report from state to state, the same states and cities where each of the churches was burned on the date they were burned."

Josh almost dropped Garrison in the dirt. He handed him off to Watie as if to say, "*Take this piece of trash!*" He didn't say it though. *Just thought it.* He was glad he didn't think it out loud. Watie tossed him over his shoulder like a large saddle bag and took him to the paramedics who were loading Brown into the ambulance, his face covered by a long white sheet.

"*It's pretty bad when your own gov'ment starts burning churches, ain't it?*" Barefoot asked, not really expecting an answer. He was on his feet now, rubbing his wrists where the tie-wraps had cut into his skin. "The next thing ya know, the gov'ment's gonna tell you Bible-thumpers ya can't go to church at all. What ya gonna do then?"

****

Garrison didn't make it, but it wasn't because Josh threw him on the ground when he realized the extent of his crimes. He was pronounced DOA when the ambulance got him to Johnson Memorial Hospital.

A newspaper reporter from Raleigh had showed up while they were loading Garrison into the ambulance, delaying its departure. She asked one of the paramedics who Garrison was and who was the other guy laying on a stretcher with a sheet over him. The paramedic told her they were Homeland Security agents, that he'd heard they were the ones burning all those churches last month, that two FBI agents had been investigating them. He didn't recall the agents' names but pointed to them. She could talk to them herself.

He also told her Garrison and Brown had been killed by Benton County law enforcement officers who were trying to prevent them from killing a *"couple of racists,"* only one of which was still there, Barefoot. The other left in another ambulance.

Seeing Barefoot standing there talking to the agents and hearing from the paramedic that he was a "big wig" with the local Klan, she just assumed the *other* racist was also a member of the Klan. She took the part of his story she wanted then sought out Messner and Murphy, not interested in talking to local law enforcement peons.

"Is it true that you were investigating these two agents about those radical, fundamentalist churches that were burned last month? Is it true they were killed as they were talking to two well-known racists here in these woods? Is it normal for one federal law enforcement agency to investigate another?"

She fired off one question after another, leading each with her particular slant. When the agents tried to clarify her wrong assumptions, she cut them off. She wanted news, not facts.

The first reports about the incident on the news wire had Messner and Murphy killing Brown and Garrison, who were characterized as little more than over-zealous federal lawmen trying to protect the public from racists like Barefoot and Ballard. Though Barefoot's connection with the Klan was emphasized, no mention was made that the other *racist* was a black man, and both Josh and Koz remained anonymous.

The FBI was deliberately portrayed as an outdated agency whose agents so envied the accomplishments of Homeland Security, that they were not only willing to interfere with Brown and Garrison while they *"interrogated their prisoners in a neutral setting"* but suggested they killed them in cold blood.

Hearing this first report on the radio and then from their district supervisor, Messner and Murphy agreed to a live interview with a BBC reporter, not willing to trust the American media to get it right. She did a *little* better. Josh and Koz were still missing from the story, but at least she cleared up the distortion about Brown and Garrison simply *interrogating* prisoners.

The similar deaths of their other victims was explained – tie-wraps and execution style murders, gas station receipts – all tying them to the area and time of the crime, *everything.* Ballard was still assumed to be a white bigot, since blacks are immune to racist attitudes.

One thing her report did do was list the name and location of each of the seven churches that Brown and Garrison burned in their effort to create or at least continue religious hatred of Baptists. She failed to lead this part of her report with the usual preface about Baptist churches *warranting* arson and other violent acts against them. This had an unexpected effect.

"*I'm Jewish*," Messner explained. "And Murphy here is Catholic. But regardless what your religion is, every American and every citizen of the world should feel personally *violated* at the thought of a government agency or rogue government agents trying to incite religious hatred by burning churches. *That's unconscionable!*"

Because the interview was live, it was carried around the world then re-played again and again in sound bites. Bloggers didn't have to wait to hear it to pass it on. World outrage was immediate. The incident became an immediate public affairs nightmare for the Department of Homeland Security and the president.

By Sunday morning, an even more serious side-effect was seen when tens of thousands then hundreds of thousands then millions flooded the doors of churches in the United States and throughout the world. It was as if the whole world finally realized their right to worship was in jeopardy. Political correctness had finally gone too far.

In most churches, however, these seekers heard only feel-good messages, not Bible-based sermons that preached the gospel of Jesus Christ – *his death, burial and resurrection*. But for those who did hear the real gospel, the effect was phenomenal. Revival broke out all over, first in the Southeast then in Western and Northwestern states up to Alaska, mostly in Baptist churches during the Sunday School hour then fundamentalist and evangelical churches during morning worship.

Then during Presbyterian and Methodist evening services, a spirit of revival took over. Men and women with broken hearts and tears in their eyes were answering to alter calls that hadn't been given. They came forward and prayed, asking God for forgiveness, and those who'd never called on him before were asking Jesus to save them. It was like a fever that spread from heart to heart then church to church, soon causing upheavals even in Episcopalian, Lutheran and Catholic churches.

Services at Northside Baptist lasted nearly an hour longer than normal. Pastor Holmes had so many "decisions" to read after his altar call, he finally ended the meeting with a tearful prayer then asked everyone to return for evening services at 6 p.m.

Josh and Joy drove into Fayetteville for lunch at a favorite Italian restaurant, but both of them were too excited to enjoy their meal. It wasn't that their Spaghetti Bolognese was anything less than authentic Northern Italian. It was great as usual, which was probably why the restaurant had managed to stay in business when so many others had failed in recent years. Today, Josh and Joy were hungrier for spiritual food than spaghetti, so they ended up taking home to-go boxes.

Each of them had been among the hundreds who came to Northside's altar during morning services. Joy prayed to see her kids again soon. Josh prayed for forgiveness, having now killed *five* men. It bothered him that he was less bothered this time for having killed another human being. Neither told the other what was on his heart though the intenseness of what they'd experience was shared spiritually.

When they got home, Joy turned on the TV and both saw where the experience they'd had at Northside was being replicated around the country and the world. The news media called it a *"fear-induced hysteria,"* claiming the hundreds of millions of worshipers had been tricked into *"acting like scared children"* by Baptists and radical fundamentalists who were little more than *"terrorists of the mind,"* who wanted to *"rule the hearts of the people by making them afraid,"* teaching them a litany of *"doomsday"* lies.

It was almost startling to watch and listen to so-called professional journalists so openly criticize anyone who dared believe the Bible. How dare these millions of believers choose God over the media's *unbiased* opinions!

Presidential candidate Chuck Hampton was caught on camera as he left his home church near Dallas and asked to explain the revival spirit that was suddenly sweeping the planet. The reporter had stuffed the microphone in Hampton's face, hoping he'd say something he could use in the live broadcast that would show the fanatic worshippers the source of their fear was subversives like the American Party.

"What do you want me to explain?" Hampton asked, turning back toward the inside of his church, pointing at the altar where a dozen people were still on their knees in prayer. "For more than 150 years, the world has been poisoned with *neo-Gnostic*, humanist preaching and socialist doctrines.

"Folks like Mann, Hegel, Peabody, Marx, Engels, Freud, Darwin…Westcott and Hort, Wundt…oh, and Dewey wanted to control knowledge, *all* knowledge – *academic and biblical knowledge* – so they forced our children into public schools, took away our King James

Bible and brainwashed the next four generations with their socialist-humanist propaganda.

"Though we were better than 94 percent literate 150 years ago, we're less than 50 percent literate today. Though we were a *Christian* nation in 1860, we're little more than *religious heathens* today! At least *your* president got that much right.

"This *revival* you're witnessing is not my doing and not something you can lay to the blame or credit of the American Party. This strange outpouring of spiritual fervor is nothing but the work of *God the Holy Spirit*, that part of the Holy Trinity you faithless devils pretend doesn't exist. Look around you now and see God saving the souls of millions! Open your eyes, *liberal*. Open your mind!"

The reporter tried several times to stop the interview, but Hampton grabbed his wrist and finished saying what he felt led to say. Then the reporter tried to get his sound man to stop recording, but he couldn't get eye contact with him, so Hampton's entire statement went live – *worldwide*.

Pundits on every network were trying to explain away what he'd said, but their best spin wasn't going anywhere. Hampton was too popular, now holding the support of 60 percent of likely voters. He was also popular with foreign nationals, though their leaders feared and hated him, as did U.S. leaders, elected and *unelected*.

Through it all, Washington was silent, partly because it was still seething from yesterday's news fiasco about what was now officially being called *"loose cannon"* Homeland Security agents. The president's handlers were not ready to take on tens of millions of Bible-believing Christians. *One crisis at a time.*

By 3 p.m., it was past time for Josh's Sunday afternoon nap. He excused himself to his study, where Nathan's old bunk bed waited for him. Josh had been taking naps on Sunday as far back as he could remember. It was a tradition Papa had taught him well. Sunday was a day of rest, and taking a nap on Sunday was the best way a fellah could get his rest.

On those rare occasions he didn't get his Sunday nap, Josh felt tired and listless all week. Though she always teased her *"little boy"* for having to take his nap, Joy appreciated his Sunday naps as a time she could clean the house, grade papers or read her *Southern Living*, *World* and *Our State* magazines.

It was hard to fall asleep today though. The stitched wounds in his arm and shoulder throbbed, particularly when he rolled onto his left side or laid his head on his right forearm. Besides, too much was going on in his soul and spirit to get his body to rest, so Josh prayed.

He praised God for the revival he experienced in person and saw on TV. Was it a sign of something bigger to come? No, he wouldn't ask that. He didn't need to see signs. That was testing God and he wouldn't do that.

He did want to know how long the revival would last and how far it would reach. Would it be remembered like the *Great Awakening* or even the *Sandy Creek Revival*? How many souls would be saved? Would this revival finally take the gospel to every creature willing to hear it – in every part of the world? And if it did, wouldn't the Lord come for his church now? *What was next?*

He asked question after question, believing he'd get some kind of answer. To pray, not believing was talking to the wind. When Josh prayed, he talked to God, expecting not only for the Lord to hear him but to respond to him in some spiritually discernable way. When he prayed this hard though, he grew tired quickly, which was part of his objective. He finally fell asleep, or he thought he did.

He heard his own voice asking how long the revival would last then he heard what sounded like his own voice answering back that it would only be a *one-week revival*, the shortest in Christian history. But its effects would exceed all other revivals, for it would reach *every living soul willing to hear and respond to the gospel.*

Then as quickly as it started, the revival would end. Though he was sure he was dreaming, Josh wondered why he was asking and answering his own questions? And where did he get this information to give the answers?

Josh then found himself looking deep into space. In fact, he was out in space, seemingly floating there. His dreaming of outer space was unusual as he wasn't really interested in astronomy and didn't care for space adventure movies. Star Trek, Star Wars, Star *squat* – he didn't care.

Give him a western or a war movie or Shakespearean play, or let him read a book. But now he could see stars by the millions, some brighter than others, and he could see gray objects moving through space, many of them in small clusters like the pellets fired from a shotgun as seen in slow motion photography.

A very large, rocklike object coming from his right appeared like it would pass in front on him, but a cluster of smaller rocks coming directly at him intersected with the bigger rock, the impact causing it split into several smaller pieces that tumbled and spun off to his left.

His eyes followed these smaller rocks as they headed for what looked like a planet. As he drew closer, that planet looked just like the old Apollo mission footage he'd watched of earth as seen from the moon. It *was* earth! This realization caused him to gasp and flinch in his sleep.

As these rocks continued on their track toward the earth, he helplessly followed along with them, just above them. The closer the cluster of rocks got to the earth, the more he could make out about his own planet. He could make out Europe and Asia with Africa as this blue marble rotated slowly in a counter-clockwise direction. Now he could see the Atlantic Ocean, North and South America then United States, all the way from the east coast to the west coast.

As he and the rock objects his eyes were following entered the earth's atmosphere, they began to burn a fiery red. He didn't. Two smaller rocks way ahead of all the others soared across the sky as balls of fire, barely clearing the magnificent Rocky Mountains. One exploded several miles above the city of Portland; the other slammed into the green mountain forests just north of San Francisco.

Another much smaller rock drifted well south of these two and slammed into the mountains just north of Las Vegas. As if adjusting indirect fire, a much larger one followed on its heels, exploding several miles above Sin City itself. Josh trembled as he watched these explosions taking place all over the country.

He was disgusted with the corrupt moral values of his country and the world as a whole and wondered why God endured so long. But now as he was seeing what appeared to be God's judgment against an ungrateful, godless nation, Josh could identify with the prophet Habakkuk, feeling a sort of rottenness in his bones.

Still forced to observe the devastation in front of him, he watched a huge explosion obliterate what used to be the city of Chicago, another Detroit and still another St. Louis. Two final explosions were more than he could bear to see. The largest of all rocks exploded a mile above the city of Arlington, turning Washington, D.C. into a lake of fire. Though smaller, the last rock exploded just south of and less than a mile above the city of Raleigh.

"**No!**" Josh awoke in a sweat, his heart pounding in his chest. He was dreaming, he told himself. *"Lord, please tell me it was all a dream, a nightmare."*

There was no response. He knew why. It was more than a dream; *it was a vision. He had dared to ask what was next!* He sat up, breathing heavily as he reached for his glasses. Nobody would believe him, but he had to warn Joy and the kids! He had to tell his family and friends, the *world.* There were souls to save. He swung his legs around and slid to the edge of the bed, but as he tried to stand up, he heard a voice much like his own saying, "**No!**"

The floor was suddenly like the deck of a fishing boat, three hours off shore. Josh was unsteady on his feet, and he saw huge black spots that moved around the room. He leaned against the bedpost with one hand and flipped on the light switch with the other. The spots were still there. The dizziness was worse.

He felt lightheaded now and a little disoriented. *He was having the stroke his doctors had warned him about for years!* All that blood pressure and cholesterol medicine, fish oil pills, a low-dose aspirin a day, every day, *and what had it done for him?!*

He tried to sit back on the bed but missed it, hitting the floor hard with all his weight. Josh felt faint, unsure which way was up, so it didn't surprise him that he found himself laying on his side, looking into the carpet. He tried to call his wife.

"*Joy*," he muttered, with much effort to mouth her name.

If he was going to die, Josh wanted to see Joy's face just one more time. But all he could see was a steady rotation of large, black spots on the floor in front of him.

Chapter Six

"Same old song; just a drop of water in an endless sea;
All we do crumbles to the ground, though we refuse to see.
Dust in the wind. All we are is dust in the wind."
Kerry Livgren (*Kansas*), "Dust in the Wind"

"Josh," Joy was calling to him, waving her hand in front of his face. "Josh, can you see me? Can you hear me?"

Josh blinked his eyes to get them to focus. He could see her faintly and hear her fine. In fact, his hearing seemed to be extra sensitive, like the volume on everything was turned up from *loud* to *blaring*. He was in bed, but it wasn't his bed. Where was he?

"*My glasses?*" he whispered. "Where're my glasses and where am I?"

"You're at Womack," she told him, referring to Fort Bragg's Army Medical Center. "You've been out for over 15 hours, Josh. You had a stroke. *I thought I'd lost you!*"

Clearly, Joy had been crying, and she began crying as she leaned over him on the bed, holding him by his right hand. She was half seated in a chair next to the bed, where she'd stayed all night. Josh's left arm was strapped to the bed rail with I.V. tubes running from the back of his hand up to plastic bottles hanging over his head.

Several thin wires came out of the neck of his hospital gown and connected to an electronic monitor that beeped annoyingly every so often. To his far left was another bed, but it was empty. No roommate, at least. Yeah, he was in the hospital alright. Josh hated hospitals.

"It's alright, *Muffin*," he told her, calling her by the pet name he'd given her some 35 years ago when they began dating. He gently stroked her soft hair down its length onto her shoulders, which he began massaging. "I'm not leaving ya. *We're gonna leave this world together*."

A mild ache in the left center of his head caused him to remember the last thing he'd seen before blacking out. It was the carpet. The mental image made him realize he wasn't to mention his vision of their near future or why he was so certain they'd leave this world together.

"Do ya promise?" she asked, still sobbing.

"Promise," he sighed and looked up at the ceiling.

"Goo' mo'ning," the heavy set nurse's aide said as she marched in the room unannounced. "I sees he's 'wake. Ya feel like ya can eat some brake'fas?"

"Coffee, for sure," Josh told her then realized his stomach was talking to him. "Some grits and eggs with three or four slices of bacon would be good too."

"*Nah, sir*," she laughed, which caused her huge tummy to bounce. "I don't thank 'day gon' let you 'ave no bacon fur long time."

As soon as she cleared the doorway, Joy chewed his ear about all the BBQ, steaks and hamburgers he'd put away over the years.

"Yeah, but I washed it all down with fried chicken, fried fish, fried okra, fried corn bread, fried…" he tried joking with her.

"*It's not funny, Josh*," she tried to stay angry with him but blushed when he gave her that boyish look. "Ya know, they gave you some kind of clot dissolving drug as soon as they got you here yesterday. Dr. Dahl said that's what saved ya. He said you may not even have any bad side effects. *How ya feeling, anyway?"*

"I don't know," he admitted, not asking the identity of Dr. Dahl. "I feel kinda fuzzy. Everything's blurry too. Oh, you wanna give me my glasses. That might help."

Josh didn't know how to be serious about his own health. He'd joked around with her like this when she first saw him in the recovering room after his jump injuries that nearly killed him. He'd told her that if he continued having hard landings like that one, he'd have start wearing a parachute like all those other sissies.

He made her worry, but he kept her laughing. He was the father of her children and the only man she'd ever loved, the only man she'd ever known. Had she lost him, Joy was sure she'd have grieved herself to death.

After a breakfast of black coffee, pulp-free orange juice and unbuttered, whole wheat toast with a bowl of tasteless fruit, Josh was still hungry. He wished he had one of his mama's homemade, cathead biscuits smothered in Georgia cane syrup. He was craving something sweet.

Last night's on-call physician, Dr. Dahl, came by his room and performed a few motor skill tests on him, checking to see if he had any paralysis or numbness anywhere. He shined a tiny flashlight into his eyes after making him remove his glasses then reported Josh seemed to be recovering fine, that he'd allow him to go home as soon as they could get all the paperwork done to release him.

"You're a very lucky man," he told Josh. "We'll do some more tests next week, but I think you've gotten through this stroke remarkably well. You may experience some short term memory problems for a while or suffer from verbal problems, like dyslexia, particularly when you're writing.

"That's because the clot we dissolved had formed on the left side of your brain. I don't think there's a lot of damage there though, but we'll get another MRI on it next week to be sure. We'll let ya rest a while first."

"You mean, you already did an MRI?" Josh asked.

"Yes, sir," Dahl said. "We did one last night."

"And it showed a blood clot on the left side of my brain?" he continued.

"Yes, sir. A small one," the doctor explained.

"A small brain or small clot?" Josh joked.

The doctor chuckled and told Joy her husband was going to recover fine. He'd obviously recovered his sense of humor. Joy smiled and thanked him as he left her and Josh alone again. She saw no reason to tell Dahl that Josh was the kind of man who'd find humor in just about every situation. It was what attracted her to him, even before he knew she existed.

Josh had come by their high school to visit some of his former teachers shortly after he graduated from Ranger School. Joy was still a student at the time. She remembered thinking how heroic he looked in his dress greens with his jump boots bloused and shiny, his bold, black Ranger beret, his black and yellow Ranger tab on his shoulder and sparkling silver jump wings on his chest.

Although he knew her, he didn't really *notice* her for the first time until she *happened* to be home from college the same weekend he *happened* to be home on leave. Apparently, he noticed her *a lot*. She'd never have believed she'd become an Army wife, but it was a life she loved almost as much as she loved her soldier.

"Do you mind if we come in?" a lady's voice with a strong northern accent called from the doorway. It was Kathy with her new "friend," John, the widower from Back Swamp Baptist. "I heard about your stroke at church last night when Brother Lopez asked for prayer for his friend. I couldn't believe it was your name he was saying.

"Anyway, I asked Brother Cunningham if I could leave for a few hours this morning to visit you. *Oh…ah*, this is *John Pinckney*. He's ah…a *friend* of mine. John's retired from the Air Force, so I called him to see if he could help me get on the base to see you."

Kathy blushed a little when introducing John, who blushed some himself. They were indeed friends, but their friendship was growing. They'd both found someone to fill a big void in their lives. Kathy already loved his grandchildren like they were her own. He appreciated having an adult to talk with and spend time together. There was little doubt they would continue to grow closer.

Josh and Joy said 'hello' to John and asked the usual *'how ya doing'* questions that no one really expects a truthful answer to. John surprised them and caused Kathy to blush again when he said he was *"much better now,"* seeing that Josh was *"way too ugly"* to leave his *"pretty wife"* and *"try to take Kathy away"* from him.

"John!" Kathy scolded him.

"Joy's not only pretty, she's mean," Josh told him, smiling. "I wouldn't wanna cross her by chasing another woman. And besides, I've seen what Kathy can do with a taser. You could be in for a real *shock*."

"Ha ha," Joy said. "Very funny."

"Really," Kathy added. "I can see you two ought to get along just fine. It must be a military thing."

"Maybe," Joy agreed. "More likely a *man* thing. We wouldn't understand."

"You're not s'pose to understand us," John chuckled. "*Just love us*."

"*Amen*, brother," Josh added.

Having three people gathered around his bed made Josh uncomfortable, but he did a good job of hiding it. He answered the expected questions about how he was feeling. Joy explained how she'd found him and what happened when they got him to the hospital.

Speaking mostly to Kathy, Joy said she'd heard a loud noise when Josh fell. She was already walking toward his study when she heard him call her name. She knew by the sound of his voice that something was *very* wrong.

After a few minutes, the two women stepped out in the hallway while Josh and John compared life in the Army with life in the Air Force. John was originally from a little town just east of Lake City, Fla. He was stationed at Pope Air Force Base during the last eight years before retiring there.

He and his wife had bought a small horse farm there over in Benton County. They only had one child, a boy who loved horses and the outdoors, especially hunting and fishing. Instead of following his father into the Air Force or even going to college, his adventure-loving boy just *had* to be a paratrooper. He was killed in Afghanistan shortly after being promoted to staff sergeant. His wife and their two children moved in with John and his wife.

"I was watching the kids one day while Becky and Leah went on base to the commissary and BX," John said, staring out the window at the parking lot 10 floors below. "A few hours after they left, I got a call from the Fayetteville Police Department. They were passing a tractor trailer truck on the All-American when a tire blew out on the truck. A large chunk of it went flying into their windshield. Becky must have lost control of the wheel. The car flipped and rolled several times."

"I'm sorry, John," Josh told him, watching his eyes go lifeless for just a moment. "You've had some hard losses."

"Yeah," he sighed then turned and looked at Josh. "I thought I'd lost my faith too. I was so bitter. First, he took my son then he took the wife of my youth and my grandbabies' mama. Until I met Kathy, I was just going through the motions for the kids' sake. She's had some hard losses too."

"Yeah, I know." Josh said, himself sighing, "You know it's no accident that y'all are together."

John just shook his head in agreement. Part of him still hurt for what he'd lost, but he was so grateful for Kathy. Josh closed his eyes and without speaking thanked God for bringing two broken hearts together. It was his burden now not to tell them how little time they would have together.

Out in the hallway, Joy and Kathy's conversation went pretty much the same. Joy told Kathy how *blessed* she was being at Kathy's baptism. On hearing her refer to members of her church as "brother" made Joy all the more convinced that Kathy was not only genuinely saved, she was a *Baptist*.

"That's not a good thing to some people," Kathy said, looking at the floor. "I tried calling my kids in New Jersey to tell them that I've changed. I told them about the experience at the store then the mess I made at the school board meeting. Neither Kirk nor Katie had much to say. Then I told them I got saved.

"I heard my ex-husband swearing in the background when I said that. He got on the phone and asked me what I was talking about. I told him that I had gotten saved, that I'd accepted Jesus as my personal Lord and Savior, and that I was recently baptized at Back Swamp Baptist Church where I now taught at the academy. He cursed me in front of my kids. *Told me they would find it a lot easier to forgive me for my lies and adultery than for becoming a Baptist!* Then he hung up on me."

There was a silence. Kathy continued looking at the floor as Joy tried looking her in the face. She was close to crying. Kathy whispered that she'd always been taught to look down on Baptists, but she never really thought she *hated* them. Now that she was feeling that hate directed toward her, she felt guilty for all the years she'd passed judgment on others.

"There is another way to look at it," Joy told her, holding Kathy by both shoulders and looking her in the eyes. "You know the world hated Christ so much they crucified him. They hated the first Christians so much, they beat, tortured and murdered them. Jesus didn't stay dead, so the world still hates him.

"And those of us who love him and try to serve him the way the Bible *teaches* us and Holy Spirit *leads* us are just as hated now as we were back then. The fact that you realize you're hated for what you believe should give you some sense of consolation. You're part of a pretty special group of people. *You're a Christian!*"

The two ladies hugged and cried on each other's shoulders. Not so many years ago, Joy wanted to slap

Kathy's face for forcing her husband out of a job. But it was God's hand in it, more so than Kathy. She meant it for evil, but God meant it for good. They came back in Josh's room to find the two men watching the news.

The unprecedented revival was still going strong around the planet. People were still flocking to churches everywhere, crying before altars that had not heard a Bible sermon preached in over 100 years.

The Vatican issued a statement praising the *"movement,"* as it was now being called, for its *"sincerity"* but warned of *"misguiding spirits"* who might lead the *"foolish to accept heretical doctrines and violate the teachings of the Church."* The Church of England issued a similar statement as did every mainline protestant denomination.

Baptists, fundamentalists and evangelicals, however, continued to encourage the spirits of those seeking God. Christian academies like Northside and Back Swamp closed off their sanctuaries from school business during the day, so people could come in off the street to pray.

The situation was apparently quite a bother to many local governments and police departments for the traffic headaches it caused. Most national governments, however, remained silent – except in Islamic countries where public worship of any god but Allah was forbidden. Still, despite beatings, stonings and even beheadings, the spirit that moved among believers and those wanting to be saved could not be quenched.

"That reminds me," Joy blurted out, turning everyone's attention away from the screen hanging on the wall across from Josh's bed. "Are y'all coming to the joint services this Sunday? We've heard this Rabbi Nydel before. He's a really good preacher."

"We'll be there," John answered for Kathy, smiling at her. "I've heard about him. He's a Messianic Jewish missionary or something like that, right?"

"Something like that," Josh agreed. "Pastor Holmes said Nydel was going to speak on Jewish holy days and how they relate to New Testament prophesy. Ya know, Yom Kippur is coming up in a few weeks. The 27th, I think. I remember some 40 or so years ago, World War III almost started during that particular holy day."

"Oh, I remember," John said. "I was on alert at a special little base out west where they keep some really big stuff we're not s'pose to talk about. I'm just glad we didn't have to use any of it."

Everyone agreed as John and Kathy said their *'goodbyes'* and excused themselves. Joy watched them leave then walked to the door to make sure they were gone. She then told Josh about Kathy's rejection by her family, first because she was *"so wicked,"* now because she was *"so saved."* Josh thought about what she'd said a moment then said they needed to pray for her and John, that they seemed to be just what the other needed.

While they were praying, a nurse suddenly entered the room and said she was going to start disconnecting all his tubes and wires, so he could get ready to go home. As she started with his I.V., someone forcefully knocked on the doorpost.

"Anybody in here know where I can get some really great BBQ?" Westin asked as he came on in the room. Joy knew his sense of humor was a lot like Josh's. "How ya doin', old fellah?"

"I've felt worse," Josh told him. "Good morning, Dave. Benton County running alright without you guarding the fort?"

"I s'pect it'll get along okay without me for a few hours," he told him. "Mind if I pull up a chair?"

Since he was about to stay a while, Joy excused herself, saying she was going down to the cafeteria to get something to eat. The nurse finished unhooking the I.V. and E.K.G. and left the two men alone to talk.

After ensuring Josh was in his right mind, Westin thought he'd bring him up to date on local news and events. He began by telling him Barefoot had disappeared Saturday evening, shortly after giving his statement to Johnson County detectives and the FBI. Josh wasn't surprised. Ballard gave law officials a factual statement for once in his life then refused to talk with reporters, saying he didn't trust them to report the truth. That was a surprise.

Sunday evening, the wife of a Johnson County man found him dead when she got home from church. He was sitting in a rocking chair on the back porch of his doublewide. They lived on a large wooded lot in a remote area of the county. He didn't have a mark on him, but an initial coroner's report suggested his neck had been broken. His name was Hollis.

Hollis supposedly had connections with the Klan, but local law enforcement suspected he worked for the feds. It was certain he had been a Klansman prior to going to federal prison five years ago for drug and weapons violations. But his sudden parole two years ago and having an ample supply of cash to buy land and a doublewide made quite a few folks suspicious.

"*Jake*," Josh muttered. "I heard him telling that agent Brown he knew the feds had moles inside the Klan. Somehow, I can imagine this Hollis fellah was the culprit that helped Brown and Garrison catch Jake."

"That's what I'm thinkin' too," Westin said. "If it turns out a broken neck is this guy's the cause of death, Jake's the man to have done it. Breaking necks and poison injections were his specialties. Ya know, I almost can't blame him for taking care of a rat like that, even though he's left a wife and three hungry kids with no daddy."

"I know what you mean," Josh agreed. Jake's a hard one to figure. Bet ya didn't know he was Jewish."

"*What?!*" Westin asked, "*What are you talkin' about?* **He's a Klansman!** How could he be Jewish? Besides, I've known the man for over 25 years, and I didn't know that."

"Yeah, well, I've known him for over 30 years," Josh said, matter-of-factly. "I carried him out of the jungle back in '82, his leg broke and running a high fever, high enough to have him talking out of his head. He was speaking *Yiddish.*"

"Yiddish?" Westin repeated. "You're kiddin' me. Where did he learn to speak Yiddish?"

"His grandparents," Josh answered. "They and his mother escaped Hungary in the mid-1930's just before the Nazis took over. I think their last name was Buber, or something like that, but they changed it to Barber, which made it easier for them to immigrate to this country. I know all this because I grilled him on it later.

"Jake's fever broke the day after I got him back to base camp. I asked him to explain why he was speaking Yiddish. At first he tried to deny it then he said he might as well '*tell somebody the truth.*' Even his wife didn't know it. He said his family came to New York first then moved around a lot, his grandfather looking for work as a jeweler. They ended up settling over the state line in Connecticut.

"I don't remember how he said his father met his mother, but I do remember he was a soldier and an *agnostic*. When Jake – or I should say, *Jacob*, their second child – was about seven, the family moved here. The grandmother came with them, his grandfather having died by then. I think he said his father was stationed here at Bragg. Either way, it worked out for them since the name Barefoot's common in this area."

"Jacob, huh?" Westin shook his head. "Was he raised Jewish?"

"He says not," Josh answered, shrugging his shoulder. "But then, Obami says he wasn't raised a Muslim either. I don't put much stock in what some folks say. When I asked Jake how he could to speak Yiddish so well, he asked me how I was so sure he was speaking it that well. He had me there.

"Apparently though, his grandmother had a strong influence on his early life. I think he learned more than just the language of Eastern European Jews. When we had our *Biblical* discussions – *and we had many* – I figured out right away, he knew the Law and the Prophets as well or better than I did. He knows more than a little bit of the New Testament too.

"But it's only head knowledge, as far as I can tell. Not only does he not believe Jesus is the Messiah, he told me he's not so sure there is a God at all, that if there was, he wouldn't have allowed the Holocaust to happen. I remember though, he paused to think a minute when I told him about the 50 million Baptist-like Christians who were murdered by their supposed fellow Christians between 400 and 1700 A.D."

"*Uhmp*," Westin grunted, listening but saying nothing. He'd read *Trail of Blood* and other books that traced the bloody history of persecuted Baptists, so he knew what Josh was talking about. There had indeed been other Holocausts.

"Jake said the fact that Baptists have been hated and persecuted for 2,000 years only supported his belief that there must not be a God," Josh continued. "So I told him that suffering and persecution tend to bring about change and revival, that Baptist Christians continued to be persecuted, even after the Reformation and up to the time of the Great Awakening and Sandy Creek Revival. But by the mid-19th century, Bible-believing Christians finally out-numbered the pseudo-Christians and heathens, so the worst persecution stopped. I told him that's when the church stopped growing."

"That's true," Westin agreed.

"I told him there hasn't been a major revival in over 100 years," Josh said, watching with some interest a news report about thousands of "*fanatic worshipers*" in the streets of London, Edinburg, Geneva, Canterbury, Wittenberg and Rome, all singing hymns about Jesus. He smiled and continued. "Then I reminded him that following the Jewish Holocaust, the nation of Israel was re-born and returned to Palestine. I could tell I'd stumped him on that debate.

"Now I wonder if he was referring back to that discussion the other day when he alluded to what would happen if the government stopped allowing us '*Bible thumpers*' to worship at all. What do ya think he thinks of this worldwide revival?"

"Good question," Westin said, shaking his head again. "That is something to think about, but I'm still stuck on him being in the Klan in the first place. I don't know much about the Klan, but it looks like they'd know a little bit about their people before they took 'em in. I realize they probably don't do FBI-type background investigations, but they gotta do something to check the pedigree of their members."

"In his case, there's not a lot to check," Josh said. "Jake had an older brother who was killed in Vietnam. No other siblings, nieces or nephews. His grandmother and parents are dead, and he believes all his relatives left behind in Hungary ended up dying in concentration camps. And as I said, since his daddy's last name is a common name in this neck of the woods, I s'pect the Klan was just more than happy to get a man with his military capabilities and without a whole lot of questions asked."

Westin agreed and sat there in silence a moment, something bothering him about the information he'd just received. A male nurse came in the room with some release forms for Josh to sign. As he signed them, Westin stood and began pacing in front of Josh's bed. The male nurse then left the room, giving Josh permission to get dressed as he closed the door behind him. Josh's personal things were in the closet.

"Josh, has it ever occurred to you that Jake might feel just a little bit vulnerable with you having this information about him?" Westin asked, stopping at the foot of the bed as Josh pulled back the sheets and started getting up.

"If you're thinking he might want to keep me quiet, yeah, I've considered it," Josh admitted, standing up and looking around the room with a different perspective. "When he revealed his family heritage to me 30 years ago, he wasn't in the Klan. But if he'd wanted to silence me, I s'pect he'd have done so before now."

"So, you trust him?" Westin asked, turning away as Josh slipped on his trousers then removed his hospital gown.

"Not really," Josh said, grinning somewhat as he buttoned his shirt. "I trust the Lord, Joy, my kids, you and Koz. Everybody else gets the third degree."

Westin laughed and thanked him for his trust then told him to take the next two weeks off and rest. He'd already talked with Dr. Dahl before coming by to visit. Looking at his watch, he said he had to get going, that he'd told McPhall he'd meet one of her in-laws around 11 o'clock at a trailer park near Overhills about a possible deputy's job.

Before leaving, he told Josh he'd have McNeilly bring his Model 700 by his house this week. He didn't realize he'd kept it that long. As for his "buffalo rifle," Johnson County folks had that one. He couldn't say when Josh would get it back.

The two men separated with a handshake then a prayer. Westin thanked God for sparing his *"best friend"* and subordinate and asked him to watch over him always.

****

"Take off that Ranger beret, *ya dirty leg*," Westin mumbled out loud as he waited for a military doctor to cross the parking lot in front of his Challenger.

With his brief case in hand, the light colonel was wearing his Class B uniform with shiny low quarters and a black "Army" beret, standard headgear now for non-airborne soldiers but not back in Westin's day. The

Rangers were snubbed over 10 years ago with a political decision to enhance morale and enlistment in the all-volunteer Army. Non-airborne personnel, a.k.a., *legs*, were issued the famous black beret and the elite Rangers were issued a faded dust cover!

It made Westin sick every time he saw legs wearing a beret they never earned. Berets were supposed to be for Special Ops soldiers only, and there was nothing special about being a leg. It was part of the reason he seldom came on post, despite his military benefits as a retired sergeant major.

But there were other reasons he avoided the base. Soldiers were supposed to protect and defend the Constitution, but since the *Defense Authorization Act of 2006*, the federal government was using federal troops to enforce its *unconstitutional* power over states and municipalities.

A division-size contingent of separate active duty brigades from Forts Bragg, Drum, Stewart, Hood and Lewis had been given a special mission as *"emergency"* forces, supposedly to fill the role National Guard units had always filled during natural disasters or attacks like 9/11.

As part of NORTHCOM, the excuse for creating these units that Guard units were being used to support the War on Terrorism in Iraq and Afghanistan. But now that half the states were refusing to release their Guard units for federal service, hostilities between the active Army and Guard was a real possibility.

The gas riots were a test for using these federal troops to secure large urban areas. He knew from his SOCOM connections, it didn't go as well as the media reported it. In fact, it went rather badly.

Innocent civilians were arrested and mistreated by troops under orders to confiscate privately owned weapons, with a mission to disarm entire cities. Home owners who dared resist military authority found their doors kicked in and houses ransacked by soldiers looking for firearms. Men and women, even children and senior citizens were thrown to the floor and their hands tie-wrapped like common criminals if they so much as mentioned their 2nd amendment rights. It was shameful that any American soldier would dare treat a fellow American that way!

Westin's personal knowledge about containment camps that were now on every federal installation in the country only added to his concern. He prayed Chuck Hampton would be able to undo all that had been done, but there were so many *unelected* powers to overcome, he wasn't sure he could do it in two terms or even if those powers would allow Hampton to win. Brown and Garrison were proof as far as he was concerned; the feds were not above murder and arson to accomplish their agenda. Assassination was probably a viable option.

It grieved Westin that the Army he'd served and loved wasn't the same, now that *presidentially-protected* perverts had run most of the real soldiers into the Guard. Now America's active duty military had become much like Germany's Wehrmacht in the late 1930's – hundreds of thousands of foul-mouthed, functionally illiterate proles willingly put on a uniform for the sake of a job. Most of these *so-called* soldiers were little more than blindly obedient worshipers of the new Fuehrer.

Su still liked to come on post, but he never let her come by herself or after dark. Their daughter, daughter-in-law or one of her friends would always go with her to the commissary, PX or medical clinics. Westin preferred Wal-Mart for buying groceries and the local pharmacy if he needed to self-medicate. But he almost never got sick and at 67, he was in great health. Well, maybe not *great* health. Every joint in his body ached from nearly 500 parachute jumps, not counting HALO jumps.

Age and weight problems had brought on diabetes and blood pressure problems too, but he got them both under control by changing his diet. At least he didn't have the injuries Josh had. God had been good to Westin. He hadn't told Su, but he had decided after this election, he wouldn't run again in 2016. He'd let those younger guys like Dinkins fight the politicians, drug pushers and gang members.

Westin was deep in his thoughts. Actually, he was daydreaming about a time when he and Su would buy an RV and travel around the country before travel by private citizens was restricted by the all-mighty feds, as if the price of gas hadn't already done that. His thoughts were interrupted by a call from McPhall. She wanted to know his location, if he was going to be able to meet with her ex-husband's cousin at 11 a.m. He assured her he'd be there, maybe a few minutes late, but he'd be there.

He guessed this ex-husband's cousin must be her current fellah. All in the family, he thought. She changed boyfriends every three or four weeks, had four kids, all with different fathers. Westin had no idea what sort of education, training or possible criminal background her new flame might have.

He didn't even know his name. But she asked him for a favor, and, like King Herod, he foolishly agreed before asking what she wanted. He wouldn't make that mistake again. But he only agreed to talk with the guy. He didn't agree to hire him.

When he stopped at the last traffic light in Spring Lake, a Braxton County deputy slowed down as he drove by him. He was checking out the Challenger, a hot red sports car with a big ol' Hemi. The young deputy was probably thinking this was somebody he might need to follow. He was sure he'd catch Westin speeding. Red sports cars had that reputation.

But as the deputy made eye contact with the Challenger's driver, he recognized it was the Benton County Sheriff. Westin could see the deputy's face blush a red that matched his Challenger. The two men then nodded toward each other in passing.

The Challenger did push the speed limit just a little when Westin got beyond the Spring Lake city limits and especially after he crossed the county line. The big engine rumbled then purred like a big kitten when he slowed down then roared like a lion when he sped up. Westin turned off NC 210 on to Ray Road then another paved road, which led toward the trailer park and his appointment.

Piney woods lined both sides of the road like a thick, green wall, and there was almost no shoulder next to the pavement. As he slowed down for the stop sign ahead, the hair on the back of his neck stood up on seeing a Chevy sedan stopped on the other side of the intersection, perpendicular to him. A soldier's instinct made him hit the brakes, still 40 yards from the intersection. Too late though.

Front and back driver's side windows were already lowered on the sedan, and the muzzles of two M-4's could be seen. It was like something from a bad movie.

Who'd be stupid enough to ambush a county sheriff?! He wondered if they were gangbangers getting even for a drug bust his men had made earlier in the summer, or if this was how the feds had decided to get rid of him after Winslow lost all chances for winning the election.

He could see the flash from the weapons' muzzle then rounds began hitting his windshield. One round hit him in the right shoulder. Another caught the right corner of his jaw, knocking his head back against the head rest. It was too late to back up and the road was too narrow to turn around.

Since this was a classic *near ambush*, Westin did what he was trained to do. He *attacked*. He didn't even feel the round that chipped glass in his face and dug into his left collarbone. He stomped the gas pedal and let the Challenger's Hemi gather up all the speed she could gather in that short, 40 yard stretch.

Rounds continued flying through the window. At least his glasses protected his eyes. But one round took a chunk out of his forehead while another hit a vital spot in the center of his chest. It wasn't enough to stop him though.

The Challenger was doing close to 50 mph when it collided broadside with his attackers' vehicle. The impact knocked the little sedan into a deep ditch, but its passengers were splattered against the inside, either dead or dying. Blood poured down Westin's face as he turned off the ignition and released his seat belt. Pain shot through his shoulder as he moved his right arm.

Westin tried to open his door, but it was stuck. He bumped it with his left shoulder then realized he had been shot in that shoulder too. He bumped it again anyway and it opened, allowing him to roll out onto the ground. He tried to get up but couldn't, so he crawled a few yards from the driver's door before finally collapsing. He needed to make the arrest, but he couldn't get up.

It was then that it occurred to Westin he was dying. He could hear a hissing sound coming from his chest. He hadn't thought much about dying since leaving the Army. Figured he'd live till the Lord come. Should have known this line of work had its risks though. Blood dripped into a pool in front of his face on the hot pavement where he laid his bald head.

He watched his own blood form up and spread out, filling the cracks in the asphalt. It was redder than his Challenger – his *change of life* sports car, as his son called it. *Sweet deal*, his daughter called it. It was a 2009.

He'd bought it new in 2010 on a car lot where it had sat unsold for 18 months. Got it for half price too. Yes, it was something he'd coveted since '71 when he fell in love with the first line of Challengers. But he and Su and the baby were barely able to get by on a buck sergeant's pay. They didn't need a sports car. He didn't need it now either.

"I'm sorry, Lord," he whispered. "I should've come clean with ya about this car a long time ago. *Please forgive me.*"

Westin tried one more time to raise himself, only to drop back to the pavement, knocking out what little wind he had left in him. Now he couldn't breathe. At least the pavement didn't seem so hot anymore.

"*Watch over Su for me, Jesus,*" he thought then closed his eyes. He was so sleepy. Thought he'd rest his eyes a little while.

****

"Three rib-eye sandwiches," Koz told the girl at the counter. "And let me have two large orders of fries and three sweet teas."

The girl rang up his order then took the debit card he was holding out for her. A minute later he was signing the receipt then standing around impatiently waiting for his order. Koz was irritated. McPhall was acting goofy, not that she was ever all there. First, she called him and Watie and asked them to come by the courthouse during lunch, that she had some paperwork they needed to fill out. Then she calls again and tells them to come by around 11 a.m.

She did the same thing to Massey and his partner and later she sends both Nichols and Harriman on a wild goose chase to investigate a suspicious car way out at Buffalo Lake. It was a long way to Millingham from the Anderson Creek annex and Overhills area where both Task Force teams were patrolling, and with them gone, Nichols and Harriman needed to stay on patrol. They couldn't be in two places at the same time. Besides, did she think she could give orders just because Sheriff Westin had gone to Bragg and Maj. Dinkins had gone to Johnson County? Her new admin officer position was going to her head.

This evening, he and Watie and several of the other fellahs were planning to go see how Josh was doing; that is, if Sheriff Westin thought he was up to it. Maybe they'd see him there at the courthouse when Koz got back with lunch.

When he and Watie got to the courthouse earlier, McPhall had several administrative forms for everybody but Koz. He was *"all caught up on his stuff,"* she'd said. But since he had to wait for his partner, she asked Koz if he'd mind picking up lunch for her. Then she started singing the praises of Ribby's Steakhouse in downtown Millingham.

He didn't have anything better to do, and it wasn't like him to turn down a steak, whether it was on a bun or hot off the grill. She knew that though; she just seemed to want to get him out of her office, and he wondered why.

Traffic was light, not that Millingham ever had a traffic problem. It was the county seat, but its population was just over 3,000. Most of the buildings in the downtown area were over 100 years old, including Ribby's. He and Sharon had been here before, their anniversary, he thought. It wasn't a fancy place, but they served great steaks. He was curious to see how their rib-eyes tasted as a sandwich.

Always the observant SEAL, Koz couldn't help noticing two men sitting in the front seat of a Chevy sedan that was parked in front of Ribby's. The driver's side window was open, but the sun visor was down, so Koz couldn't see the driver's face when he walked in front of his car.

The passenger was a non-descript, short haired Hispanic man, casually dressed. He seemed to be watching Koz as he walked by, which annoyed him. Koz had parked across the street and had the feeling someone was watching him as he walked to the restaurant.

He left the restaurant with a white paper bag filled with steak sandwiches and fries and a cardboard tray holding three sweet teas. As he passed in front of the sedan, Koz noticed the driver lifting the sun visor. It was only a glimpse, but as he went by, Koz thought the driver's face looked familiar.

Half way across the street, it occurred to him the familiar face was *Sherman*. It was then he heard the distinct sound of a shotgun's safety being pressed to the *Off* position. He swallowed hard, dropped his lunch and reached for his pistol. Too late though.

The shotgun blast hit Koz between the shoulder blades in a 9-inch diameter pattern. The big man was pushed forward by the impact. He came down hard on both knees then skidded forward onto his face. He felt nothing. His spinal cord was severed in six places by the buckshot and both his lungs were collapsed. As he lay there fading into eternity, he could hear a car start up and speed away.

Why would Sherman want to murder him? Watie was the one who'd kicked his butt. Now what was Sharon going to do without him? How would their sons remember him? He'd tried to be a good husband and father, especially these last few months. Koz tried to whisper a prayer for mercy for his family, but there was no air coming from his lips. All those years he'd wasted as a husband, as a father and as a *Christian!* Though he regretted those lost years, he died peacefully, knowing he'd finally got it right before he was called out of this world.

****

"Josh, don't eat anymore donuts," Joy admonished him as he dug into the box of Krispy Kreme donuts on the console between them. Joy was driving her Stratus. "You've already had three. You're gonna make yourself sick."

Josh had been released from the hospital over an hour ago, but the craving he had for something sweet was insatiable. He pleaded like a little boy to his mommy to make a major detour into Fayetteville to the local Krispy Kreme bakery. It was one of the few left in operation, the company having closed many of its stores in most cities, especially outside North Carolina. Josh had bought a dozen fresh, *hot* glazed for himself and a half dozen chocolate-covered glazed for Joy. So far, she'd only had one.

"Come on and have another one," he told her. "They'll sweeten your disposition."

She laughed but not much. She had a surprise she'd been putting off telling him all morning and was looking for a way to tell him. She'd even turned off her cell phone, so they wouldn't be disturbed by Josh's endless well-wishers. Still, she hadn't found the right way to bring up her surprise.

"Muffin," Josh said, seemingly musing as he licked the glazed coating off his fingers. "That Dr. Dahl told me to rest for a couple weeks, and Dave even told me to take a couple weeks off."

"Yeah, and you *need* to rest," she told him, interrupting.

"I was thinking though, *why don't we get away this weekend?*" he turned to her, almost excited. "Let's go home to Barney. We could invite Kathy and that new boyfriend of hers and his grandyounguns. I wouldn't mind having Koz and his family come join us. Dave and Su too. Watie and Lopez with their families too. Yeah, and Nichols, Harriman and Hooper."

"Josh, *are you crazy?*" she asked, not really meaning to question his sanity but wondering if he was showing some strange side-effect from his stroke. "Our families aren't gonna put up that many people. Do you think they run motels? And there aren't any motels in Barney. Besides, we can't be gone this weekend. We'd miss hearing Rabi Nydel."

"Yeah, I know," he admitted. "But we've heard him before, and I just felt like going home to Georgia."

"Me too," she admitted, though not everything. "But we can't go this weekend. *Our kids are coming to see you!*"

"*What?!*" Josh asked, more saddened by this news than she'd ever understand. He had re-lived the vision over and over in his mind and had not recalled any meteors or asteroid fragments or whatever it was he was shown hitting Oklahoma, Western North Carolina or Coastal South Carolina. His kids were safe – *until now.*

"Did you think I wouldn't call them about their daddy having a stroke?" she asked, annoyed that this was how she had to spring her surprise. A nagging thought in the back of her mind said her special prayer Sunday morning was indirectly responsible for his stroke. She had wanted to see her kids again *soon.* "Abigail and Joel will be here Friday night. Nathan and Jenny will be here around lunchtime on Saturday. Rachel and Phillip should get here in time for supper.

"They were worried about you and all wanted to come see you last night. I told them to wait till I called this morning. While you were talking to Dave, I called each of them and asked them to make plans to see you this weekend. *We're gonna have a full house again.*"

Josh had tears in his eyes and she could see it, only she misinterpreted the tears for happiness in knowing his children wanted to see him. She couldn't know the truth behind these tears. The *full house* she was looking forward to spelled the end to the *House of Athol*. The whole family would leave this world together.

"*Oh no*," Joy said, slowing down as a reaction to seeing blue lights in her rear view mirror. "What did I do? I didn't think I was speeding."

She pulled over onto the shoulder of the road and turned off the ignition. A deputy's patrol car pulled in behind her and a Task Force SUV pulled around in front of her, blocking her escape. Josh immediately recognized Hooper approaching in his side mirror and Watie leaving the driver's door of the SUV. They both came to the passenger side of the Stratus.

"Hey, Josh," Hooper said, his voice deep and solemn.

"Hey, Hoop," he answered. "How's it going, Brother Watie?"

"I s'pose you know why we stopped ya," Watie said, a serious look on his face.

Josh took a deep breath, looked at Joy then at the Krispy Kreme boxes on the console between them. A boyish smile appeared on his face.

"*You smelled the donuts?*" he asked with a chuckle.

"*What?!*" Hooper responded with another question. "Man, you mean you don't know about Sheriff Westin?"

"Know what?" Josh asked, his own expression turning serious. A sick feeling filled the pit of his stomach.

The two officers looked at each other then the ground. Hooper's eyes welled up with tears as he tried to look away.

"We tried to call your cell phone then Joy's then we called Womack," Watie told him, apologetically. "They said you'd been released an hour ago.   Josh, *Sheriff Westin's been murdered.*"

Josh didn't answer. He'd just been gutted. To hear your best friend has died is an awful thing. To hear that he's been murdered makes a man want to scream out in rage and shake down the world to find his killer. As his anger built, he noticed Hooper was actually crying and Watie was close to it. There was something else.

"There's something else, ain't there?" he had to ask.

They shook their heads affirmative. Joy had begun to cry, calling out Su's name and the names of their children and asking who would kill a good man like Dave.

"Koz," Hooper blubbered out like a broken hearted child. *"Some son-of-a-female dog done shot 'em in d'back wid' a shotgun!"*

"Not Koz!" Josh shouted, "**No!**"

Koz was only 10 years older than Nathan. He was like a second son to Josh. Losing his two best friends in a single moment of time was more than he could bear. He opened the car door and leaped outside so he could stomp the ground and howl like a wild man. Cars passing by slowed to a careful crawl around them, seeing the stopped Stratus pinned between two patrol vehicles with lights flickering, especially seeing Josh on a tirade of pure anger, screaming at the Carolina pines he was facing.

Swearing was a habit he'd broken when Rachel was a toddler. She'd repeated some special words he'd had for a long traffic light one morning when he was taking her with him to get a few things at Winn Dixie. Hearing her parrot him caused him to re-think everything he said and did and the example he was going to set for his children. He'd prayed for help in controlling his tongue and over a period of several months, he was able to stop cussing.

Even now as emotion burst like a dam inside him, his tongue was selective with its words of anger. He'd lost his two best friends in the whole world just days before they were all going to be killed by an act of God meant as punishment for a godless nation. *My God! Why?!*

"Sheriff Westin was ambushed," Watie told Josh, trying to calm him down with details. "Nobody even knew where he was then these kids called the dispatcher about a shooting outside a trailer park near Overhills. None of our guys were patrolling the area at the time, so Hoop went out to check on it himself."

"I rec'nized d'Shurf's red Challen'ga quarta mile from it," Hooper said, taking a deep breath and clearing his throat. "He'd plowed into d'side of a Chevy and wuz laying on d'road by d'do' of his car. He wuz already dead. I jest don't un'erstan' what he wuz doin' d'are."

"When he left the hospital, Dave told me he was going to meet some in-law of McPhall's about a deputy's job," Josh spoke up. *"Did she forget?* He even told me the time he was to be there: *11 a.m.* And why wasn't there any of our guys on patrol? Watie, where were you and Koz? Where was Massey and Martinez, Nichols and Harriman?"

Watie started cussing and kicking the ground. Hooper had a few choice words of his own as he rushed back to his patrol car. Josh told Joy to stay in the car then followed Hooper to his vehicle. She barely heard him. She was calling both Su and Sharon's names over and over. Hooper was already on the horn calling for Dinkins. He got him a few seconds later.

"Maj. Dinkins," Hooper said, nearly shouting into the radio handset. *"Is McPhall still d'are?"*

"Why?" came the answer. Dinkins' patience sounded worn. "We got too much going on 'round here for private conversations."

"I don't wanna talk to her," Hooper continued to shout. *"I wanna choke her!* She knew Sheriff Westin wuz going to d'at trailer park 'cuz she set 'em up to go meet somebody d'are. She's also d'one who called two Task Force teams off d'road to be at d'partment headquartas at 11 'clock and sent Nichols and Harriman to look fo' a car out at Buffalo Lake d'at wasn't even d'are. *And she's d'one who put Koz up to going to d'at steakhouse to get her lunch!"*

"Oh, my God!" came Dinkins' response. *"She's also the one who set up my meeting with my Johnson County counterpart.* And I let her take the afternoon off 'cause she said she was too upset over Dave and Koz!"

"Just ask 'em where she lives," Watie told him, calmly but with venom in his deep voice. Josh never heard him approach and here he was standing beside him. *"I'll go get her myself!"*

"No," Dinkins shouted on the radio. "Take a minute and calm down. *Be professional!* I want you both to go get her and bring her in. Try not to let on you s'pect anything. I'll see if I can get more patrols out there to find Capt. Athol."

Hooper let Dinkins know Josh was standing there next to him, that they'd stopped them on their way home. Dinkins thanked God then asked to speak with him, so Hooper gave him the handset. Their greetings were cordial and brief. Dinkins came straight to the point.

He suspected that the two men who'd killed Sheriff Westin and whoever shot Koz in the back might have been feds. Dodds already had a Homeland Security team in there telling SBI agents and his detectives what to do, who and how to investigate both murders. He claimed these were Klan hits, that Barefoot was trying to eliminate those he considered a threat to his organization or him personally. Dinkins wasn't buying it and had already contacted the FBI.

"Something else, Josh," he added. "I'd like for you to let us put you and Joy in protective custody. I think this mess has something to do with those two Homeland Security agents you and Koz brought down. Whoever killed Dave and Koz probably has their sights on you. Before Inspector Watie and Cpl. Hooper go after McPhall, I want you to let 'em follow you home. Let 'em check your house out before y'all go in. I'll send a couple deputies over as soon as I can."

Josh wanted to protest the special protection, but for Joy's sake, he acquiesced. He needed to get home first and get armed. His two big game rifles were gone. All he had left were squirrel rifles, a 20 gauge and a 12 gauge and his .327 magnum. He was worried though about Joy being caught in the crossfire. He'd have to send her to visit somebody. Su had her kids nearby to stay with her, but Sharon was alone with three young boys. Yeah, that would work.

****

"Two deputies will be here in just a few minutes," Josh reminded Joy, pleading with her to go stay with Sharon, whom she'd called and cried with on the phone.

She had packed an overnight bag but was mothering him to death about what he could eat for supper and whether it was even right for her to leave him there alone.

As she emptied the refrigerator of yesterday's Italian lunch leftovers he would be allowed to heat up in *her* microwave, Josh retrieved his pistol from the master bedroom and checked it to make sure it was loaded. It was, of course. He slipped it back in its holster, clipped it on the left front side of his belt then pulled out his shirttail to cover it up, so Joy couldn't see it.

"Are you sure you're gonna be alright?" she asked as she entered the living room where Josh stood, eating another donut. "Oh, *please don't eat anymore donuts!*"

He started to complain about being treated like a kid, but his still sensitive hearing picked up the sound of a car pulling in their driveway. That would be the two deputies Dinkins promised, he thought. He wondered though why they didn't have on their headlights. It was almost dark.

"See, you don't have to worry about leaving me alone," he told her, pointing his finger at their living room's plantation blinds in the direction of their driveway. "The guys will keep me company."

He picked up her overnight bag by the doorway and opened the door for her as she began scolding him about *"the guys"* not leaving *her* kitchen a mess. He was only half way listening to her when he noticed the car in the driveway was not a patrol car but a Chevy sedan. Joy was still rattling on about *"a bunch of men"* in *her* house while descending the porch steps when Josh noticed an Hispanic-looking man getting out of the driver's side with what appeared to be a shotgun.

Josh immediately shoved Joy off the steps into the azaleas where she landed hard enough to knock the wind out of her. He then plucked his pistol from under his shirttail as the shotgun wielding, would-be assailant pumped a round in the chamber and raised the gun to his shoulder. Josh fired first, three times, in fact.

All three shots hit their mark, center of mass. The gunman fell backward against the car then onto the concrete driveway. Then a shotgun blast exploded from the wooded area on the opposite side of the sedan; Josh was sure he was a dead man. He leaped into the azaleas with Joy, partly to check on her and partly to avoid the second gunman improving his aim.

No other shots were fired though. Moments later, a car could be heard speeding away further down the block. Lying atop of his wife, her face filled with tears and terror, Josh kissed her and whispered it was going to be alright. She didn't believe him, but she had at least gotten her breath back enough to cry out.

"*Shhhhhh,*" he told her, putting his hand over her mouth.

A set of headlights turned into the driveway behind the sedan. This time, it was a patrol car. Seeing two bodies laying next to the sedan with shotguns beside them, the deputies turned on their patrol lights then leaped from the vehicle, pistols drawn. One deputy took a position behind the sedan, the other at the rear of their patrol car. The tall one was Harriman. Although he couldn't see him, Josh was pretty sure the shorter, blond-haired deputy was Nichols.

"*We're alright, fellahs!*" Josh yelled, still hugging his wife. "We're over here."

He stood up slowly and raised his pistol in the air. Harriman stepped out from behind the vehicle and approached carefully. Seeing Josh in the light, he put his pistol away and called for Nichols.

"Wow! How did you get both these guys?" Harriman asked.

"I didn't," Josh answered, shoving his pistol back in its holster as he helped Joy onto her feet. "I never even saw the other guy though I heard a shotgun go off from inside that patch of woods over there. A minute or so later, I heard a car take off, a piece from here."

"*Hey y'all!*" Nichols called from the opposite side of the sedan. "Ya may wanna come see who this one is."

Josh allowed Joy to sink back to the ground in a yoga position by the front steps then he and Harriman rushed over to Nichols where they found their former rat and colleague, Sherman. He was laying face up on the pavement – *that is*, what part of his face was left.

The shotgun blast hit the right side of his face and head, removing a good part of both. Nichols slipped on a pair of surgical gloves and picked up Sherman's shotgun, opening the breach to sniff the chamber. It had recently been fired but not in the last five minutes. Sherman didn't accidentally shoot himself.

As Nichols and Harriman called in CSI and relayed information about the shootings to Dinkins, Josh carried Joy back inside the house. She seemed to be going into shock. Just as he got her seated on the coach, the phone rang. He let it ring several times before answering it.

"Hello, *preacher*," a deep voice on the other end responded when Josh finally answered. "I'm sorry my man was a little late. At least he got one of 'em for ya."

"*Jake?!*" Josh asked, "Where are ya?"

"Oh, I can't tell ya that," he chuckled. "And please don't try to trace this call. I just wanted you to know I had nothing to do with Dave's murder. I respected that man like the father I wish my daddy had been. And you know how much I was impressed with Koznowski. Besides, *the man saved my life*. That means a lot to me. You should know that.

"I heard what happened to them this morning and figured you were probably next. How ya getting along with that stroke, by the way? Sounds like your aim's a bit off. I heard it took ya three shots to bring down that amateur assassin."

"My aim's fine," he told him. "All three shots hit their mark. Just felt like one wasn't enough for a fellah willing to shoot my wife just to get to me."

"That's the spirit, lad," Jake said. "I understand you had a Judas in your department that set up Dave and Koznowski. You're gonna eventually find out McPhall was a reservist in the president's *civilian army*. Your men won't find her at home though. She dumped her pile of younguns off with an aunt then tried to make it to the safety of D.C. Ya might wanna have somebody check the last stall in the lady's room at that rest stop just north of Smithfield."

"*Why ya doing this, Jake?*" Josh asked, his voice calm and concerned. "Ya know ya can't keep getting away with this."

Jake reminded him he was indebted to Josh twice over, but that he was probably right. He'd *"catch a bullet"* someday *"but not today."* If Josh was referring to his *"pedigree"* though, he was fairly sure the folks at the top of his organization were aware of it. They *"acquired"* him for his skills as a trainer of killers, not his ethnic background. All that racism stuff was just a façade anyway, he said.

He then reminded Josh the list of books he'd challenged him to read 30 years ago, books by Orwell,

Bradbury and others. He'd read them all and hundreds more, even read the KJV Bible through a couple times. But Jake came to a different conclusion than Josh. If there was a God, he seemed to be content to let a few very powerful people control everything and everybody, and not do anything about it.

"It sounds to me like you didn't finish your homework," Josh told him. "You left off right in the middle of your assignment. Those few powerful people you speak of, past and present – *Gnostics, Rosicrucians, Illuminati, Blue Masons, the Mafia, the Klan, Nazis, Bilderbergers, Bohemian Grove's 'art club,' the Tri-Lateral Commission, Skull and Bones, the Council on Foreign Relations* – they're all nothing more than denominations of the same religion."

"*Really?*" Jake said, his photographic mind taking in every name listed. He'd do a second check on each one but not let on to Josh. "*And what religion is that?*"

"*Mystery Babylon,*" Josh told him. "Go back to your KJV. Then Google *Adam Weishaupt, Giuseppe Mazzini, Albert Pike, Madame Blavatsky* and *Aleister Crowley*. All these groups and all these people are connected like segments of a spider's web – *and you work for 'em. Think about it, Jake. Think about it!*"

There was a short silence on the phone. He was thinking about it and would continue to do so. After a long pause, Jake thanked the *preacher* for his latest sermon and promised to think about it in the future.

"*In the meantime,*" he asked Josh to "*keep* [his] *head down until the smoke cleared from this mess with the feds.*" He then jokingly told Josh to be careful about believing all those "*crazy conspiracy theories,*" that somebody might think he was a nut case.

"Take care, old man," Jake said, giving what he was sure was his final goodbye to a friend, the only real friend he'd ever had. Josh was the only man who genuinely cared for his soul. "Oh, *please try to stay out of the way when the Invisible Army starts to march.*"

Chapter Seven

"This is my Father's world. O let me ne'er forget,
That though the wrong seem oft so strong, God is the ruler yet.
Maltbie D. Babcock, "This is My Father's World"

Jake was right. State troopers found McPhall in the last stall in the lady's room at the rest stop on I-95, just north of Smithfield, N.C. She wasn't hanging out there because she had a bowel problem either. She was dead. Just hearing there wasn't a mark on her made Josh assume her neck was broken. *Jake*.

Tuesday proved Benton County wasn't the only county with wanna-be assassins. The Johnson County Sheriff and the detective that investigated Saturday's shooting were ambushed Tuesday morning while walking out of a local coffee shop. Both lawmen were wounded, but they survived, thanks to the help of two deer hunters.

The two assailants opened fire from the driver's side window and door of a mini-van parked across the street from the coffee shop. The hunters were just getting into their pickup when the sound of automatic weapons made them drop. After seeing where the shots were coming from and to whom they were directed, they decided to return fire with their .50 caliber, black powder muzzleloaders.

There were now six dead would-be murderers, five of which mysteriously had no connection to any organization, including the Klan. But that was not what Dodds and Regional Director Hershberger were telling the media.

They continued to assert the killings and the killers were Klan-related, even claiming Sherman had been dismissed from their department after it was determined he had a *"close friendship with a Klansman."* That Klansman's name was Hollis, which, to Josh, didn't support their assertion at all. Like Sherman, Hollis was a federal informant.

McNeilly obtained some inside information that all three assailant vehicles had been purchased by the U.S. government. His source was Peyton, who it turned out was more than a little sympathetic to what had happened to Westin and Koz. He dropped a document on McNeilly's desk with vehicle identification numbers matching the vehicles found at Westin's murder scene, in Josh's driveway and at the attempted murder of the Johnson County's sheriff and his detective.

McNeilly passed the document on to Dinkins, who withheld it from Dodds and Hershberger until FBI agents Messner and Murphy arrived just before noon. How McNeilly obtained the documents wasn't revealed even to the FBI. But Messner and Murphy's very presence at the courthouse put the Homeland Security team into a whirlwind. Hershberger demanded to know why they were there. *How dare the FBI try to upstage the Department of Homeland Security!*

Hershberger tried to order the FBI agents to stop their investigation and return to their Greensboro office. He said his department was handling these murders because they involved a domestic terrorist organization, the Ku Klux Klan.

Messner simply handed him his authorization from the Bureau's D.C. office. The authorization included a recommendation that the ATF conduct its own investigation of the firearms used during the murders and attempted murders.

"You're going to ruin everything," Hershberger protested. "We know what's going on here. We have a handle on this."

"Sir, we don't know if you have a handle *on* it or a hand *in* it," Murphy interrupted. "We're here to do our job. I s'pose you can go on doing whatever it is you do. We'll try not to get in your way and would appreciate it if your people would stay out of our way."

Hershberger was apparently too caught up in himself and his assumed authority to note Murphy's comment about his department's possible involvement with the murder of two local law enforcement officers. Dodds picked up on it though and explained as much to Hershberger as the two FBI agents left with Massey and Martinez to visit the site of the two murders.

"What do you mean *'a hand in it'*?" Hershberger shouted but too late. They were gone. Courthouse employees stopped what they were doing to take note of this tall, thin, goofy-looking man yelling down the hallway.

Hershberger fumed with anger, his narrow face burning red. He marched into Westin's old office where he'd set up his temporary headquarters, his penny loafers clacking on the tile floor like the tapping of a woodpecker. He snatched up the phone and started dialing then quit and started over. Again, he realized he was dialing the wrong number and cursed himself as he quit then started dialing again.

****

Late Tuesday afternoon, Ballard returned from work to his upscale home in the low rent section of Fayetteville. But before he entered his house, he got a phone call. His wife handed him the phone when he came in the door. He'd had a couple of hard days, almost skipped work this morning because of last night's news about what had happened in Benton County yesterday. Then he heard on the radio this afternoon that someone had tried to kill Johnson County's sheriff and the detective who took his sworn statement.

The only two people directly connected to Brown and Garrison who hadn't been shot at or killed was himself and Barefoot. Ballard tended to agree with Homeland Security's theory being promoted by the press, that all the killings and near-killings had a Klan connection. *It had to be the Klan.*

"*Hello, Ballard,*" a deep voice saluted him on the phone. "I 'magine 'bout now you're thinkin' I'm out to get ya 'cause you probably believe that crap put out by the feds through their public relations folks. Well, *it ain't true.*"

"***Barefoot?!***" Ballard asked then called the marital status of Jake's parents into question. "No need to lie to me. *I know it's you.* And let me tell ya right now, you come after me, I got somethin' fur ya."

"*Good,*" Jake laughed. "It's time you stopped being a wuss, 'cause you're gonna need that kind of spirit. I say again though, I ain't the one comin' after ya. I was even gonna put a couple of my fellahs out by your house to guard ya, but my people would tend to stand out in your neighborhood, *if ya know what I mean.*

"I highly recommend ya get your wife out of the house this evening and get as many of your home boys over there with ya. *And have 'em armed to the teeth.*"

"Why you tellin' me dis?" Ballard demanded. "I know you ain't sud'enly taken a liken to black folks."

"Nor any other race of humans, for that matter," Jake answered with a rare breath of pure honesty. "But I figure if Josh Athol can judge your life worth sparing two times, the least I can do is warn ya that the feds are comin' after ya."

"*The feds?*" Ballard asked, "Why ya say the feds?"

There was no answer. Jake was gone. Ballard held the receiver in his hand a few seconds then called his wife. He wanted her to go visit her sister – *right now*, no lip. At first, she looked at him like he was crazy, something she'd done on more than one other occasion. But she knew enough about what was going on to see what he was trying to do. She asked him if he was going to be alright, and he assured her that he was. As she went back in the bedroom to pack a bag, Ballard called a few friends.

Later that night, a home invasion at the Ballard home went terribly bad for the intruders who were met with shotgun and pistol fire. Two of the three gunmen died in the doorway they kicked in, thinking to surprise the homeowner. A third man tried to make it back to the getaway car. He didn't make it.

****

"Did ya hear Fort Bragg's CBRNE brigade has been alerted?" Dinkins whispered to Josh as the combined, outdoor funeral service for Dave and Koz slowly got underway. The governor had appointed him as sheriff, at least until after the election. Dinkins was a Republican.

Scores of mourners were still viewing the bodies, which lay in caskets, side-by-side in the middle of Millingham High School's football field. It was the only place large enough to hold the more than 1,400 people who'd showed up to pay their last respects to Dave and Koz. Josh refused to look at either of his old friends. He preferred to remember them alive. Figured to join them in a few days.

"No," Josh admitted, returning the whisper. "What fabulous emergency have the feds invented to deploy federal troops in North Carolina again?"

"*Us*," Dinkins said, a little too loud. "It's Hershberger's doings. He wants to deploy the CBRNE in Braxton, Benton and Johnson counties. He plans to use active duty troops to confiscate all personally-owned firearms in every household in all three counties. *Claims that's the best way to stop this current wave of shootin's.*"

A light breeze ruffled Josh's silver hair, reminding him he needed a haircut. He sighed, looked up at the cloudless blue sky then he sighed again. He had no doubt the feds were behind both murders and the attempts on his life. Sherman's dead body near the body of the man that tried to kill him and Joy was evidence enough. *If only God would let him.....*

Those SS liars hadn't dismissed Sherman; he'd just been *reassigned.* Besides, a preliminary fingerprint check of all six shooters found them to be former soldiers or Marines. None were Special Ops at least. Most had less than stellar military records. So far though, except for Sherman, there wasn't a *direct* connection to America's KGB. *If only there was!*

"So what's stopping him?" Josh asked, watching Joy raise her finger to her lips, telling him to "*shhhhh.*"

"Believe it or not, *the gov'ner*," Dinkins answered, back to a whisper. "She's even told the president if Homeland Security orders a deployment of federal troops in *her* state again, she'll call out *her* National Guard. The last time left Charlotte-Mecklenburg County with a worse crime problem than ever before, probably because honest cit'zens were the ones they disarmed. She's a liberal, but she knows just how far she can push the *God 'n Gun* Democrats that helped put her in office."

"*Politicians!*" Josh whispered, shaking his head.

"That ain't all," Dinkins continued, still trying to whisper. "The gov'ners of South Carolina and Georgia have said if the president deploys federal troops inside North Carolina, they'll call out their Guard units to su'port their sister state. And I heard just a few minutes ago a bunch of other states are promisin' the same su'port.

"Anyway, the Sec'tary Defense just ordered that CBRNE brigade to stand down – *after* he got a personal phone call from Chuck Hampton, who's promising to try to defuse the situation. He's s'pose to land in Raleigh at 3 o'clock to speak with the gov'ner. Then he's gonna come down here to see us."

"*Us?*" Josh repeated, too loud again, so that he got that look from Joy again. Returning to a whisper, he asked, "He's coming *here?*"

"Yep," Dinkins said, almost grinning. "Says he wants to meet you *personally*. In fact, I invited him to go to your church this evening. Hope ya don't mind."

Josh sighed and shook his head. Chuck Hampton *himself*. He'd had a chance to meet the current wanna-be king when he visited Fort Bragg earlier in the year during one of his campaign stops. Josh declined the opportunity and opted out of the assignment to provide additional security with Braxton County's Task Force. Dave understood and assigned the job to a couple of his majesty's disciples.

Hampton's 62 percent standing in this morning's polls made him about the closest thing to a president that Josh ever cared to meet. He did wonder though why Hampton would want to meet him. He also wondered what he intended to do to defuse the current situation.

The governor's unexpected move created a Mexican stand-off and maybe bought the families of her state a few more days of peace until devastation she didn't know about rained down from heaven itself. Had such a hostile deployment of active duty and Guard troops taken place, there would have been war. Besides, local gun owners would never willingly hand over their guns without a fight. Yeah, it would mean war.

About 150 years ago, a self-serving, egotistical president started a similar war that destroyed nearly one million American lives when he stubbornly moved federal troops onto an abandoned fort belonging to the sovereign state of South Carolina. He'd hoped to intimidate Southern states to submit to his concept of an *indivisible* Union and, most importantly, force Southerners to continue to pay high federal tariffs. Josh hoped today's self-serving, egotistical president wasn't as stupid.

He looked around at the crowds gathered in the bleachers on both sides of the football field. Along with Dave and Koz' family members, he, Dinkins, their wives and most of the Benton County Sheriff's Department were seated in folding chairs on the field. In front of him were the pallbearers, mostly deputies, detectives and Task Forces inspectors but also a few officers with the Millingham Police Department, including Don Rushton, the *"friend of a friend"* who'd gotten word to Koz several years ago about a deputy's position in Benton County.

Rushton and Koz had served in the Navy together, though Rushton never joined the SEALs. He was an MP who'd picked Koz up once for public drunkenness and fighting in an off-limits bar near Virginia Beach.

They were both from Maryland and struck up a casual friendship that included another MP who later did join Koz' SEAL team, but their mutual friend was killed a couple years ago in a training accident. As soon as Koz took the job here in Benton County, Rushton invited his family to join his church. Until a few months ago though, Koz hadn't been a very good church member.

Anderson Creek Holiness Church and Doone Pentecostal Free Will Baptist Church had agreed to a joint service for Koz and Dave's families' sake. Josh figured the entire congregations of both churches were there, along with most of the congregation of his own church and Back Swamp Baptist.

He knew several city and county officials attending were members of the Eastside Methodist Church, and he'd spotted a few others that he knew were members of Smoky Creek Presbyterian Church. Most folks though were just concerned members of the community who supported their law enforcement officers.

He'd even spotted FBI agents Messner and Murphy in the bleachers before the crowds started to gather. Homeland Security agent Tim Peyton was there too, which surprised Josh. He was a peculiar one for Josh. Hard to figure. He certainly had a different spirit about him. Was he one of them or not? Josh wasn't sure. At least no other SS henchmen attended.

Pastor Benjamin Clarke's words were comforting to the families and friends, but not to Josh, who selfishly missed his friends. Knowing what he'd been shown about the near future, he couldn't stop wondering why they had to have their lives shortened by these few days. Sunday's vision was more like a dream now; it was as clear as a window into tomorrow. At least Su and Sharon and their children would only be separated from Dave and Koz a little longer.

"*And this gospel of the kingdom shall be preached in all the world for a witness unto all nations; and then shall the end come,*" Clarke said, quoting Matthew 24:14 and finally drawing Josh's attention to his sermon. "Look around you now, Christians. This *worldwide revival* is no accident. It's prophecy being fulfilled. The entire world is hearing the gospel for the first and probably the *last* time. ***The Lord is coming!***"

Josh studied Clarke's dark, leathery face. He was a big man, not so much tall or heavy set but muscular. He had some facial hair on his lip and chin that partly concealed a childhood scar that followed the outline of his mouth. He looked like he'd kissed a dashboard at 55 mph. Koz had told him a little about his pastor but not everything. He knew Clarke was a part time farmer, which explained his weather-beaten appearance.

Although he didn't get overly emotional like most Baptist pastors tend to do, Clarke obviously loved the Lord and sorely missed the young man who'd finally started being the husband, father – *Christian* – that God meant him to be. Dave's son-in-law and his son had both deferred to the elder pastor for today's sermon, mostly because their grief was too heavy to preach today. Clarke's grief was evident as well.

Josh repeated the scripture verse that Clarke had just quoted and thought long and hard about it, trying to remember the rest of the chapter. He could read each verse in his mind's eye, smiling to himself when he *read* verse 37.

"But as in the days of No'e," Josh whispered to himself and reflected. Maybe there was more to his vision than he realized. Maybe he shouldn't grieve as those who have no hope.

****

Massey went home sick after the funeral, so Josh agreed to work his shift. So much for getting the rest he needed. During the funeral services, he'd figured something was wrong with Massey, seeing him sitting in the seat in front of him pulling at this right ear lobe, which appeared red and slightly swollen. Josh told him it looked like he'd been bitten by a spider. Told him to go to the doctor. A man of few words, Massey thanked him for his concern and said he'd let his wife look at it first. She used to be a nurse.

After the funeral, Josh took a moment to inspect the dozens of wreaths displayed around the two caskets. Just as he was about to leave, he noticed a wreath with Ballard's name on the sender's card. A small card offered his *"sincere condolences"* to their wives and their children and thanked the Benton County Sheriff's Department for the sacrifices it made for the community.

As he was about to walk away, Josh noticed the receipt from the flower shop was stuck to the back of the card.   He unfolded it and saw where the flower arrangement from Ballard was actually paid for by the Fayetteville city council.   Even in his rare moment of gratitude, Ballard arranged to have tax-payers foot the bill.

Because he was on the road with the Task Force in Massey's place, Josh missed the fireworks when Hampton's motorcade arrived from Raleigh, complete with an escort by the North Carolina Highway Patrol *and* the National Guard. The governor was concerned about threats against Hampton's life and refused to let anything happen to him on *her* watch in *her* state.

At the courthouse, Hampton met behind closed doors with Dinkins, Hershberger and a representative from the governor's office.   His powers of persuasion were apparently pretty good. Hershberger agreed to withdraw his request for federal troops. The stalemate was over – *for now*. But Josh was sure America's Gestapo had a follow-up plan already in the works. He didn't care, so long as they didn't try to implement it for at least four more days.

Church services at Northside that evening were different. The global revival was at its peak now, causing the tiny church to fill up quickly. Then Chuck Hampton's motorcade of State Patrol cruisers and National Guard hummers arrived.

Since it was a clear, warm evening, the men of the church gathered all the chairs from the academy classrooms and sat them up outside. The sound man rigged up the extra speakers used during Sunday dinners-on-the-ground, and pretty soon even the strangers wanting to take part in their Wednesday evening prayer service were accommodated.

Pastor Holmes was not one to make his church services a political forum, but he did invite Hampton to begin the meeting with prayer. Hampton first asked for God's grace for Dave and Koz' families then graciously thanked the Lord for the phenomenal revival and for the millions of souls hearing the gospel for the first time and especially those responding to it.

He especially thanked God for awakening the hearts and minds of Christian Americans about what they had *allowed* to happen in this country and asked him not make those who believed the Bible and supported the Constitution – *the last Americans* – watch the destruction soon to come.

"*Even so, come, Lord Jesus,*" he said, his otherwise deep, masculine voice quivering as he ended his prayer. The man almost sounded as though he might cry.

There was an unexpected short silence then several "*Amens*" given inside and outside the church. Hampton prayed like a man who believed he was speaking to God, not simply participating in a religious ritual. Josh reflected not only on Hampton's request for the promised rapture but his apparent belief in a coming destruction.

After the prayer meeting, Hampton talked with Holmes and several church members, all of whom told him they were voting for him. He thanked them and smiled, almost as though winning the election didn't really matter that much anymore. He seemed to know something he wasn't telling.

When Josh got his chance to talk with Hampton, the thousands of things he wanted to say disappeared from his mind. Without realizing why, he started talking about Northside services this Sunday, telling him about their special guest speaker. Hampton had not only heard of

Rabbi Nydel, he'd listened to him preach. He'd even read a couple of his books.

"You know, Yom Kippur starts in a few weeks," he told Josh as the two men stood near the sanctuary doorway surrounded by Secret Service agents, State Troopers and Guardsmen. "In fact, Sunday will start *Rosh Hashanah* or *Yom Teruah*, whichever you prefer. It's a very symbolic feast that begins with the blowing of a trumpet and follows with a seven-day period of atonement. *Hmmmm.* Anyway, I'm sure Dr. Nydel will tell y'all about it. I wish I could be here, but I've got to go to a campaign rally in Georgia tomorrow then Florida on Friday."

"Where in Georgia?" Josh had to ask, as if he knew the location of every town and city on hearing its name.

"Savannah," he told him. "Oh yeah, Maj. Dinkins told me you were from Georgia. He told me quite a bit about you. Where're ya from in Georgia?"

"Oh, it's a little bitty town called *Barney*," Josh shrugged, almost blushing that Dinkins had been talking about him. "We're known for peaches and pecans."

"I've heard of it. It's not far from Valdosta, if I remember right," Hampton responded. "A preacher friend of mine's from another little town close to it. Ever heard of *Hahira*?"

"Oh, yeah," Josh responded eagerly. He wished they could spend some time talking about his favorite fishing holes and hunting areas.

"I've been trying for six months to help him get his church building and Christian academy back from the feds," Hampton smiled then his expression quickly went sour. "They meet under a large tent on the empty lot next door to the church right now. *Hump!* These humanist morons just don't get it! They can close the doors on every church in this country, but *the buildings aren't the church.* I tell ya it's gonna take the Lord himself to fix this mess.

"Three *times* in *three* years, we've voted for UN sanctions against Israel. You don't do that without divine repercussions. It all goes back to when they had a so-called *gay* minister pray at That One's *coronation.*

"The whole country should've realized we were heading for destruction. The Bible clearly says homosexuality is *an abomination to God.* I s'spect the *unrepentant* prayers of a homosexual are also *an abomination to the Lord. And since he prayed on behalf of this nation, I believe America has become an abomination to God.*"

There was a moment neither man spoke. Josh could not disagree with Hampton and could think of nothing to add to his assessment of the situation.

"It doesn't matter how well I'm doing in the polls. The powers that really control this country can't let the likes of me win the election," Hampton continued, sighing. "They know I'll push for a repeal of the Patriot Act, the Veterans Disarmament Act, the National Defense Authorization Act, the Hate Crimes Protection Act and the Fairness Doctrine. They know I'd dismantle then close the Department of Education, Homeland Security and ultimately the IRS.

"They can't let that happen. But if they don't like me, they'll hate my running mate. Nobody knows much about 'Big Joe 'cept that he's a former Congressman and former University of Oklahoma football star."

"I know 'bout him," Josh told him, almost smiling. "He's the only member of the Congressional Black

Caucus to be asked to leave the Congressional Black Caucus. By the way, Dinkins said something about you receiving death threats. Is that the first time?"

"No," he answered, looking at the floor. "Threats are a daily thing. But this last one wasn't a threat so much as a promise. Your governor's protecting me with her State Troopers and Guardsmen because she doesn't want anything to happen to me while I'm here. Personally, I think she hates everything I stand for and loves everything I hate.

"As for the threat, I don't know when or how they'll do it, but I'd appreciate it if they'd at least let me go home to be with my wife this Sunday. I can't explain it, but I feel like the Lord's gonna act real soon on our prayers."

Josh wanted so badly to tell him what he was so sure he knew about Sunday, that if his vision came true, Hampton would probably be safe in Dallas and whatever was left of the country after the meteor shower or comet or whatever it was, they'd need a leader like him. The two men parted company with a handshake and prayer. It occurred to Josh as he watched his motorcade drive away that this was how he'd said goodbye to Dave just three days ago.

****

Thursday morning, Massey called in. He was still sick. Dinkins told Josh to go back home, however, saying he was too valuable to risk losing him to another stroke. Joy was at work, so he could've taken a nap or just sat on the back porch. It was hard to rest though.

Time was running out for America, and here he was playing couch potato. He tried channel surfing for one of his old hunting/fishing shows but such entertainment reminded Americans of the 2nd Amendment rights they no longer had, so most of those shows had faded from the airways two years ago.

The news wasn't much better, biased as always. Some cardinal or bishop or something big with the Catholic Church in San Francisco was talking to reporters about his take on the worldwide revival.

He continued to quote the Vatican position that the *"spiritual awakening"* was a good thing but expressed his concerns that Baptists and fundamentalists around the country were taking advantage of the millions of people seeking spiritual truth by playing to their fears about a coming judgment.

He cited examples in the earthquake ravaged area of San Francisco where *"sincere Catholic Christians"* who *"just happened to be gay"* had visited some *"intolerant churches,"* only to be told they needed to repent and ask God to forgive them for their *"unnatural sex sins"* then ask Jesus to be their *"personal"* savior. Josh wondered how those churches *just happened* to know they *just happened to be gay*. He changed the channel.

A high ranking executive with the Disney Company was found dead in his home near Orlando this morning. Another big wig, this one with Time Warner, was found dead in his car outside his home in a New York suburb. Though these mysterious deaths seemed to be unrelated, Josh's suspicions went into high gear with reports that news network executives with ABC, NBC, CBS, CNN and FOX had also died this morning, no apparent cause of death.

There were similar cases of financial executives found dead in their offices in Charlotte, New York,

Boston, London, Hong Kong and Tokyo and university executives in L.A., New Orleans, Montreal and Milan. By day's end, the death count would show 1,000 of the world's behind-the-scene movers and shakers in entertainment, finance, news media and academia had been targeted by someone for early retirement.

"Coincidence," Josh said sarcastically to the news anchor reviewing the day's reports on the deaths of the world's most important, *unelected* leaders.

Josh turned off the TV and decided to fix a sandwich. There wasn't any luncheon meat, so he decided to check the freezer where he found a pound of Stephens BBQ. Joy had bought it the last time they went there together, probably three months ago.

He could hear her fussing at him already as he placed the container of BBQ under the facet and ran hot water over it until he could get the entire pound of the best of the best BBQ in the world to plop into a serving bowl, which he promptly set in the microwave.

As the BBQ heated up, he grabbed three hamburger buns and a large bag of potato chips. *So what, if it was bad for his blood pressure!* In some ways, he felt like a condemned man; his last meals should be things he enjoyed.

As he was eating his third BBQ sandwich, Josh turned on Joy's radio above the kitchen sink then returned to his couch. Christian radio stations like CBN had pretty much been forced off all FM channels, and those few that survived on AM stations were allowed very little transmission power by the FCC. The sound quality was like something Josh remembered from his boyhood. Lots of static.

"Two FBI agents died in a fiery crash about an hour ago, 15 miles north of Doone, N.C.," the noon hour news began. Josh nearly choked on his last bite. He could only guess who these two agents were and failed to hear the rest of the news as he grabbed the phone.

****

Friday morning's news began with more unexplained deaths of the rich and powerful. Academia giants in Greensboro, South Bend, Berlin and Rome were among the first to be identified. Newspaper, magazine and publishing big shots were also targeted. Even though the list included key players in their own industry, by mid-afternoon a death count of 1,000 more of the world's most powerful was reported like the score of a lop-sided ball game.

News reporters showed more sympathy in hearing about the deaths of a few snail darters than their own top executives. But then, reporters were outer party members and these unfortunates were inner party members, Josh mused.   Initial autopsy results from yesterday's mysterious deaths showed hundreds of cases of some kind of neurotoxin poisoning. Scores of others appeared to have had their necks broken. Hearing this, Josh immediately suspected Jake.

Nah. Even Jake couldn't work that fast. Too many people spread all over the world – *but* foot soldiers trained by Jake could do it. Now he understood what Jake meant when he mentioned the *Invisible Army* starting to march!

It gave Josh something to think about as he filled in for Massey who hadn't even bothered to call in today. No answer at his home phone. Not even an answering machine. Josh figured his wife must have finally taken him to a doctor. He'd try to get up with him this evening.

Messner and Murphy's crash wasn't an accident. Witnesses claimed seeing a construction truck forcing their vehicle into the overpass wall at the intersection of I-95 and I-40. The crash destroyed their small sedan and killed them instantly but barely left a mark on the overpass wall.

But whoever was behind their killing simply traded two FBI agents for over a dozen more. The Bureau didn't take the murder of their agents lightly and had allowed a news leak to express its concern that Homeland Security might be over-stepping its authority and might even be behind the death of its agents and two local law enforcement officers in Benton County, N.C.

Though most of the American press refused to air the leak, foreign newswires picked it up and ran with it. A power struggle among America's top law enforcement agencies was big news, particularly in Europe where the EU was asserting itself more and more while the U.S. declined as an economic and military power.

Still, much of the news media were relieved to have something else to talk about than the revival, which actually seemed to be subsiding now. The crowds that gathered outside churches around the world were starting to grow smaller.

This was welcomed news to mainline protestant denominations and the Catholic Church. Baptist, fundamentalist and most evangelical churches, however, continued to seek the lost and invite them off the street to pray with them and explain the gospel of Jesus Christ.

Missionaries from these churches in distant, third world nations continued to preach the gospel without faltering. But Muslim or Catholic governments in South American, African and Indonesian countries now felt free to crack down on their missionary work. Hundreds were arrested and thrown in prison for "proselytizing" while thousands more were beaten and told to return to their own countries.

Late Friday afternoon, the news media finally got the news story they had been waiting for all year. Chuck Hampton's plane had crashed just minutes after taking off from Tallahassee. The ultra-conservative presidential candidate now with a *70* percent rating in the polls was no longer a threat to the liberal establishment.

Josh felt a wave of nausea come over him. *All the man wanted to do was make it back home so he could be with his wife on Sunday!* Now the magnanimous liberal press was tripping all over itself to praise him, the man they first tried to ignore then tried to paint as an ignorant, intolerant outsider.

Cell phone pictures of the plane as it crashed were already spreading around the internet, though the national press tried to deny their authenticity. The plane was clearly on fire long before it hit the ground in a wooded area near Lake Seminole.

Eyewitnesses of the crash were blogging that the plane's right wing appeared to be on fire moments before an air explosion rocked the neighborhoods close to the crash site. The plane's wreckage was strewn through the woods for half a mile.

Some of these eyewitnesses spoke directly to Hampton's running mate, Big Joe Watson. He was emailed photos of the crash by area residents, which disputed the account of the crash promoted by the FAA, which claimed the aircraft had hit a flock of crows or some other large birds, similar to what brought down U.S. Airways Flight 1549 in January 2009.

"Unless they're gonna claim they hit a flock of *phoenix*, birds don't cause planes to catch on fire in mid-air," Watson told BBC reporters, the only media willing to speak with him. "This crash is a *double* tragedy. We need to pray for Chuck's wife and family, and we need to pray for this *dying* nation – *'cause this crash was no accident.* This crash was *government-sponsored murder!*"

This first publicized statement by the American Party vice-presidential candidate got an immediate reaction from the White House, Homeland Security and even the national media, who immediately descended upon his home in southern Oklahoma. When the FBI's Director suggested publically that Watson's statement might have some merit to it, another media frenzy then descended on Washington.

The president called the FBI Director's remarks "*unfortunate*" and "*irresponsible*" then hinted he might consider replacing him, as this was not the first time he had allowed "*misinformation*" to go public without "*presidential approval.*"

Later that evening media sharks shoved a mic in Watson's face, leading him with the statement that if he believed some government agency was behind Hampton's plane crash, what was his recommendation to the American people?

"*Every American needs to arm him or herself to the teeth,*" he responded like an angry citizen, more so than a politician. "I realize ammunition is difficult to find these days, thanks to this administration and this Congress' attempt to disarm you, but you need to have a basic load of ammo for every gun in your household – that's about 180 rounds per gun. Obviously, *the federal government has declared war against the American people, so the American people had better be willing and able to defend themselves!*"

Hampton had said if they didn't like him, they'd hate Watson. Josh understood why now. Not only were the media pundits having a field day with his statements, several democratic Congressmen were calling for his arrest for making subversive statements, claiming he had called for the overthrow of the government. The U.S. Attorney General's office suggested his statements might be considered an act of treason.

Their charges were responded to by the FBI Director who pointed out that Watson wasn't calling for the overthrow of anything but that the people should be *willing* and *able* to defend themselves since it appeared the government had declared war against them. His statements prompted a public response by the president that the FBI Director was now out of a job.

American Party members of Congress quickly responded that the president didn't have the authority to fire the FBI Director without Congressional approval, that he didn't simply serve at the whim of the president. Besides, they said the director's assessment of Watson's statements were valid. It was going to be a long night. Josh wondered if the country was going to be able to stay together long enough for God to destroy it.

****

Despite all the political smoke that rose out of Washington the night before, the town was peculiarly empty Saturday morning. Congress had cancelled its sessions for today and Monday and left town in a flash. The president, his family, his cabinet and most of his staff members were gone, as were the members of the Supreme Court and their staffs.

In fact, the leaders of every government in the world had literally gotten out of Dodge and were nowhere to be found. The Vatican too was emptied of all but a few staff members. Remarkably, the world ran itself just fine without the tens of thousands of demagogues that usually ruled over it.

In a rare change of behavior on their part, the liberal media was skeptical of the overnight evacuations and for once sought answers, using the wire services, internet and old fashioned journalism to get to the bottom of the story. Since many of the PC police had gone into hiding with government officials, a few reporters thought it was safe to openly question the character of world leaders that secured their personal safety in the face of some unknown calamity.

By mid-morning, a semi-official statement was issued by the Speaker of the House, who along with the president, nearly all democratic representatives and senators and a few republicans with key members of their families had moved to underground shelters in the mountains of Virginia, West Virginia and Pennsylvania because of a *"remote threat"* that some sort of *"astrological shower"* might be eminent.

The speaker personally doubted this risk and was certain of the safety of all Americans but said that it was right that America's leadership be protected, *"just in case"* the worst *did* happen. This official press release failed to mention that all American Party and most

Republican Party representatives and senators had gone home to their perspective states to face whatever fate awaited their constituents. A news reporter at a New York television station who criticized the government statement found himself out of a job before the end of the broadcast. Apparently, there were still enough PC police to keep the bulk of the media in line.

****

While the world prepared for eminent disaster, on a park bench at UNC's Chapel Hill campus, an indigent-looking man sat high on the back of a bench with his feet in the seat. He was reading a small Bible tract that had been given to him 30 years ago.

"How to be Saved," the man read the cover of the tract aloud. Its faded print and frayed edges made it appear like it might fall apart in his hands as he turned the pages. It was nonetheless well-preserved, having been kept in three layers of sealable plastic sandwich bags, along with a picture of his wife and son and his newest fake driver's license.

Jake didn't look the same. His long black hair was cropped short and back to its natural gray. His Elvis sideburns and Fu Manchu mustache were gone, and in their place a seven-day, gray stubble. He wore dirty running shoes without socks, faded jeans with holes in both knees and a pale blue, Carolina sweatshirt with the sleeves cut out at the shoulder.

His tattoos were gone too. Large bleached blotches hinted where they had once been, though partially concealed by his farmer's tan. He looked the part of a street person, except that he wore a shiny gold class ring on his right hand, a ring that when its fake ruby stone was twisted revealed a tiny needle under it.

"*Romans road*," he mumbled as he re-read the passages from the Book of Romans for the thousandth time. "You're right, Josh. This is probably all I need to do to be saved. I still don't *think* I wanna be saved though. At least I *know* I don't deserve to be. So what do I do, Josh? *What do I do?*"

If Joshua Athol only knew how much he enjoyed debating with him 30 years ago, the man's head would be too big to wear an old Army steel pot without the liner. He'd lost every debate with Josh, even this last one. He'd since studied up on every person and every organization Josh had suggested he *Google*, and he had come to realize he was probably not doing the work of an independent group of vigilantes.

In addition to an internet search, Jake had read or re-read five books in the last six days. First, he re-read Robert Welch's *The Blue Book*, which he'd kept long after leaving the John Birch Society. They were useful in spreading a lot of good information about what's been going on in this country over the last 100 year, but JBS folks weren't willing to take action against those causing all the problems. That's was why Jake joined the Klan. He wanted to do something, *even if it was wrong*.

He also re-read an old book by Alexis DeTocqueville called *Democracy in America,* particularly Chapter XVI's prophetic warning that the majority might one day *overrule the rule of law*. Jake read a new book called *Controlling the* [Ignorant] *Masses* after seeing a copy of it in Josh's pickup last Saturday. Not bad though a little too long. It was just the sort of book America's functionally illiterate society needed to read but wouldn't because proles generally don't read, and if they do, they don't understand what they've read.

Another new book he read, he found online. It was David A. Rivera's *Final Warning: A History of the New World Order*. This book was the conspiracy theorist's golden book. It had it all. Jake wasn't sure how much of it he believed, but he believed enough to understand that everything he thought he knew about world history was terribly flawed if not outright wrong.

Then last night, Jake re-read Orwell's *1984* for the fourteenth time. The one thing that bothered him each time he read it was what really motivated The Party. Orwell claimed that The Party wasn't interested in power or money or even privilege of a special class. The Party was only interested in *perpetuating* itself.

"*Jones, Aaronson and Rutherford*," Jake mumbled, tugging on his right ear lobe, which was red and swollen. Two college students walking by turned to look at him, as though recognizing the names he mentioned.

He was repeating the names of three of the founding members of The Party, three men who, for whatever reason, lost their usefulness or became a threat to The Party and needed to be "*cured*" of their thoughtcrimes.

Though they had been responsible for putting The Party in power, each man was tortured in the Ministry of Love until he had no self-will or private thought left in him and spent his days drinking bad gin, waiting for a bullet to the back of his head.

"***That's it!***" Jake nearly shouted. A young woman walking near him hurried to get beyond him, just in case he might speak to her. "This is a *purging*. We're not taking out the bad guys, just those who've lost their usefulness."

The 99 *soldiers* he'd trained were not part of any great army at all. His and nine other *units* were now spread all over the world, each man with seven targets he would take out over a seven-day period.

They were notified and probably tracked via a microchip implanted in their right ear lobe. When it was activated, the chip became hot and vibrated and would remain a steady reminder until all their targets were down.

Though he wasn't privy to all 7,000 targets, he had noticed they were primarily Jewish and Catholic, which he'd thought reflected the Klan's bigotry. Looking closer though, he could see where the majority of the news media and entertainment targets were Jews, and most of the financial and academic targets were Catholics though some of them were Jewish too and vice versa. Someone was consolidating his power by eliminating the competition, a ploy perfected by Joseph Stalin, the original *Big Brother*.

There seemed to be a method to this madness, but he couldn't put his finger on it. One thing he was sure, after he and the 999 other Klan soldiers took down their seventh target, he was sure arrangements were already made to eliminate them.

That was why Homeland Security's henchmen were claiming the Klan was behind Dave and Koz' murder and now the murder of two FBI agents and a presidential candidate! It would justify their police action later when they purged the world of those men they'd used to purge their own devilish ranks.

Jake's blood began to boil. He'd killed 14 men and four women for the Army during 22 years service with Special Forces, not counting those he killed in actual combat. In the last four years, he'd killed half that many men and one woman for the Klan. And why? Because that was what he was trained to do, no questions asked.

But now he was asking. *Why?* Why should he continue to help some unelected elitists or some Stalin *wanna-be* take over the world? But it wasn't that he suddenly felt a burden of guilt for those he'd killed.

Yesterday in Charlotte, he'd broken the neck of a big shot financier who worked indirectly with the Vatican and led a secret Congressional coalition of UN-backed financiers that called for the internment of all Baptists, fundamentalists and evangelicals. Jake never liked bullies, and one of the reasons he'd resented organized religion was because the Catholic Church and its offspring protestant churches tried to control what people believed. *Why not let the people read the Bible and decide for themselves what to believe?*

Two days ago he bumped into a Turner Broadcasting executive in an Atlanta parking lot. The tiny needle in his ring was long enough and sturdy enough to penetrate the man's dress suit, shirt and skin. Ten minutes later, the man suffered what appeared to be a massive stroke. He was a Jew. Jake was a Jew. He thought about it a moment.

He'd only met the Grand Wizard one time and realized even back then he wasn't the one really in charge of the Klan. There were concerns about his parentage, but no one came right out and said they knew his mother was a Jew. At the time, Jake surmised they probably decided that because she was an Eastern European Jew, that he was only Jewish by his parentage, and that his family's supposed *proselyte* Jewish heritage probably had no blood relationship to the Old Testament Jews.

But Jewish blood did run through Jake's veins. His grandmother had told him her great-great grandparents had fled Palestine in the late 18th century to escape the oppression of the Ottoman Turks. They settled in what is now Hungary and quickly adapted their Hebrew to Yiddish but kept the customs of Orthodox Jews.

The fact that he'd killed a fellow Jew didn't bother Jake. His conscience was pretty much seared, but something was stirring in him. His targets were all men and women no one had elected, and yet they were a major influence in the lives of billions. Jake had no sympathy for them, but whoever had ordered their deaths was far worse.

He sighed and looked at his Bible tract again as a mockingbird began singing to him from a nearby magnolia tree. In the corner of his eye, Jake then noticed his target approaching. He had to decide what to do as the bearded old man limped by him, his dress coat folded under one arm, a brief case in his other hand.

"Professor," Jake called to the man as he left his perch on the bench. "Professor Rothschild. Sir, I believe you dropped this."

The old man stopped hesitantly. He didn't think he'd dropped anything but wondered why this street person knew him by name. He turned around slowly and saw the grungy-looking man approach him, his hand extended toward him with what looked like a small brochure or something.

"I didn't drop that," he said bluntly. "How did you know my name?"

"I know you didn't drop it, Professor Rothschild," Jake grinned as he handed the old man his Bible tract, ignoring his question. "But I wanted you to have it. Read it carefully and one day it may save your soul. *It's already saved your life.*"

Jake left the old man standing there holding the tract, which he looked at then thought about what Jake had said. When he looked up again, Jake was gone already. He looked back at the tract, trembling as he realized he'd just seen the face of Death.

Rothschild suspected the recent purging might get to him, especially after a call this morning told him to wait until this afternoon to leave town for the mountain getaway. Here was proof of it in his hand. The more he thought about it, the more difficult it was to breathe. His chest felt heavy, like someone was sitting on it. He was having a heart attack.

Even though Jake had retired from killing, his final target died anyway. An hour later, a McDonald's employee was about to clean the men's restroom when he found blood smeared on the sink and what appeared to be a tiny microchip stuck to the soap scum buildup next to the facet. His supervisor called the police.

****

That evening at supper, Josh tried to enjoy the company of his children but couldn't. They thought his melancholy behavior was due to the loss of his two best friends and having just had a stroke. He let them think what they wanted and only half participated in discussions. Not even Joy's homemade fried chicken, mashed potatoes with gravy and macaroni and cheese were able to lift his spirits. Neither did her special banana pudding sweeten his disposition.

Earlier in the afternoon, McNeilly came by with a bundle of firearms, all belonging to Josh. He returned Josh's Model 700 and his .327 magnum with the bullets in separate plastic bags. He also returned his .45-70 with the unused rounds in a separate bag. He said the Johnson County sheriff's office had brought the buffalo rifle and bullets by late Friday afternoon, saying Josh might need them, giving the current *political* climate.

Josh promptly re-loaded all his guns and stashed them where they would be handy, but he didn't run out to buy a full basic load. He had a couple boxes of shells; didn't need any more than that. A few well placed shots were better than a barrage of bullets, which only suppressed the enemy's fire. A dead enemy doesn't shoot back. Exactly *who* was the enemy though?

After supper, Josh, Nathan, Phillip and Joel sat down to watch the news. Sheila and Will waddled over to Josh's recliner, extending their fat little arms for Papa to hold them. Josh swallowed hard and tried not to let anyone see his heart breaking as he hugged his grandbabies.

World government leaders, including the Vatican, had set up communications through their underground sanctuaries. They fed the rest of the world their encouraging words about the pending crisis, which they were still certain would pass safely, reminding everyone the earth was two-thirds water, that the odds were that these chunks of an approaching asteroid would probably all land in the oceans.

"Yeah, and what about the tidal waves that would cause?" Nathan asked the news reporter, who seemed to be a bit distracted herself. Josh felt sorry for her, and he felt guilty for the knowledge he was compelled to withhold from his own family.

The Vatican issued a statement about the apparent end to what it now called a *"week-long uprising"* started and fueled by Baptists and fundamentalists. Though it denounced the *"cruel crack downs"* taking place in Moslem countries, it said world governments were obligated to ensure radical religious sects would never again be allowed to cause *"a world-wide panic."*

The president issued a similar statement, promising to deal with those who *"preach intolerance and generate fear among the masses."* In reaction to his comments, Phillip and Joel suggested the family pray, so the wives were called into the living room to join the men and children in prayer. His eyes filled with tears, Josh wholeheartedly supported the call for prayer.

****

Sunday morning, Big Joe Watson and his wife went to church as they always did, only this Sunday they were accompanied not only by Secret Service agents but also FBI agents, Oklahoma State Troopers and Oklahoma National Guardsmen. The governors of 27 states had signed a petition and emailed it to the president in his *underground Whitehouse*: If anything – *anything at all –* happened to the American Party's *new* presidential candidate, *Watson*, they would ask their state legislatures to vote on a *"Proclamation of Secession."*

A major problem for the president was that several of these governors were democrats. The news media called it a *"threat from the president's political enemies."* The press failed to mention the governors of Vermont and

New Hampshire, though not signing the petition, had also expressed public support for these rebel states, saying that if it came to secession, they would not support federal military action against these states and would consider dedicating their own Guard units to defend these states right to secede.

By 10 a.m., the parking lot at Northside Baptist Church was overflowing onto the vacant lots beside and behind the church. Though some of the additional cars were from new members who'd joined during the week-long revival, most were members of Back Swamp Baptist. Today was their joint services Sunday with a special guest speaker who was teaching during the Sunday school hour and preaching during the morning service.

"*Shalom*," Rabbi Luke Nydel said after being introduced by Pastor Holmes. A few people responded, causing him to grin. "Let me try that again. *How y'all doing?*"

Most of the nearly 300-person congregation laughed then responded, "*Shalom!*"

"That's better," Nydel said. "But I really shouldn't let you think 'shalom' means 'how y'all doing.' It's really a Hebrew word that sort of translates to mean 'peace' or 'peace to you.' So, let's try that one more time. *Shalom.*"

"***Shalom!***" came the immediate response.

Nydel spent the first part of the Sunday school hour discussing Hebrew words found in both the Old and New Testaments that really don't have a direct English translation, like "*selah*," which essential means "*stop and listen.*"

He then began the focus of his morning message – Jewish holy days and how they relate to New Testament prophesy. Just before breaking for the morning service, he introduced the Jewish autumn festival called the Festival of Trumpets or *Yom Teruah*, which he said would begin being observed in the nation of Israel at sundown today, which was less than an hour from now. He asked everyone to read 1 Thessalonians 4:13-18 during the break then closed the Sunday school lesson in prayer.

Joy, Rachel, Abigail, Jenny and Kathy, and several other women excused themselves to the ladies room. Nathan, Phillip and Joel joined several other men for coffee, but Josh stayed at his pew and opened his Bible to 1 Thessalonians 4. These were the same verses Hampton mentioned just a few days ago, the same verses he discussed with Koz a few weeks ago. He re-read these verses then Chapter 5, stopping at verse 9.

"For God hath not appointed us to wrath," he read half the verse then stopped. "Oh, *Lord. Please have mercy on us this day."*

As he prayed, several men started scurrying for the doorway to the sanctuary, causing Josh to leave his Bible in his pew. He and John soon joined Lopez and Bear at the front door with a dozen other men. Some uninvited guests had arrived, and they'd brought with them two busses. It was Hershberger and Dodds with lots of black-uniformed friends.

"Gentlemen, I think we need to come back inside and have a seat," Pastor Holmes said, his voice filled with fatherly concern. "Let's get our families together, please."

It took 10-15 minutes, but everyone eventually returned to their pews with children in their arms. As he waited at his pew with Joy and his children and grandchildren, Josh's cell phone began to vibrate. The voice on the other end was familiar but a bit weak, like a whisper. He was told that Homeland Security was there to enforce the president's new initiative to deal with all those who *preach intolerance.*

The caller warned the men in the church not to resist in the least way, that they had been authorized to use *extreme* force to make their arrests and take them to the containment camp at Fort Bragg where several other local congregations would be taken this morning.

The caller hung up. Josh patted Joy on the thigh then moved purposely to the front of the church and whispered what he'd just been told to Pastor Holmes who then whispered the information to Dr. Stearns then to his assistant pastor and school principal, Tom Withers. Withers then walked over to Rabbi Nydel and informed him of what was happening. Nydel, the son of a Holocaust survivor looked especially pale on hearing the news, but he recovered quickly and smiled.

"Maybe this time, the Messiah will come for us before they take us," he said.

The operation wasn't going so smoothly outside.

"*Dodds*, is this church really this big?!" Hershberger asked, pacing back and forth, trying to get his boss on the phone. No one was there to answer in Washington. "What's Peyton doing on the phone? Tell him to get on over here. I want him inside watching these people until we all go in."

"They're apparently having some sort of combined service here, sir," Dodds answered his first question, ignoring the second. Peyton was always on the phone to his wife or somebody. "We just got a call from our people at Back Swamp Baptist. There's nobody there this morning, so I'd bet my soul they're here. Anyway, I told them to get everybody over here. We're gonna need more busses anyway."

"Good," Hershberger said, still pacing. "That'll work. I can't understand why I can't get him on the phone. Let me call the New York office."

Inside the church, the congregations of the two churches were seated and for the most part, calm and quiet. Josh took Joy by the hand and smiled. He looked down the pew and saw his children holding hands with their spouses, babies in their arms. John and Kathy were holding hands and babies as well.

Stearns told everyone what was happening outside and asked that everyone give their full cooperation so no one got hurt.

"We're in the Lords hands," Holmes reminded his people. "They can do nothing except what the Lord allows, *and if it's his will that all of us be imprisoned for his name's sake then blessed be the name of the Lord.* Until they come for us though, I'd like everyone to please pray with me at your seat. Just kneel at your seat or bow your head and pray with all your heart and soul. *We need a miracle.*"

It was difficult for Josh and some others to get down on their knees. Most just leaned over and prayed with earnest sincerity. It was an humbling scene for anyone to witness, especially Peyton, who stood in the sanctuary doorway. He closed his tear-filled eyes and prayed with them, *for* them.

The earth itself responded to their prayers. It seemed like little more than thunder that caused the building to shake, making the walls tremble just slightly and the lights flicker. But it was the bellowing sound of something like a distant trumpet that defined that brief, split-second moment. Then it was gone, and with it nearly everyone in the church sanctuary.

A few teenagers stood and looked around for their parents and friends then raced for the altar where they clung, crying to the Lord. One old man and a woman near the back stood and looked at each other then at the clothes, shoes and personal items lying in the pews and on the floors. Pocket change, wedding bands and engagement rings were still rolling down the aisles. Eye glasses, dentures, hearing aids and pace makers lay atop the piles of clothing and shoes or on the floor beside them.

The old man and woman sat back down and held their saddened faces in their hands. For months, they'd taken turns attending Northside, Back Swamp and a few other Baptist and fundamentalist churches in the area. It was their job to report the intolerance being preached here, and that they did.

They'd sat among these harmless people and listened to Bible-based sermons and pretended to pray with them, but now the church was no more than an empty building. It was suddenly a cold place, empty not just of people. A comforting spirit was gone with them.

*"**What happened?!**"* Hershberger demanded to no one in particular as he, Dodds and more than a dozen SWAT-clad agents rushed inside. "Where did they all go? Who's at the back door? I want to know how 300 people got out of this building. Where's Peyton?"

He didn't realize it at the time, but he was standing next to a Peyton's clothes – shoes with socks still inside them, slacks with belt still buckled, suit jacket over his shirt with necktie still tied at the buttoned collar. His badge was clipped to his dress jacket.

Dodd bent down and plucked a Blackberry from its plastic, clip-on case and checked the last call made. Not recognizing the number, he pressed the SEND button. Seconds later, a vibrating sound could be heard coming from one of the pews to his left front.

He found a cell phone vibrating in its leather case, attached to the leather belt of a man's dress trousers, resting in the seat of the pew. As with Peyton's clothes, the pants and belt were buckled, zipper zipped. Clipped onto the belt next to the phone was a badge. This was Josh Athol's phone.

"Peyton was one of them," Dodds mumbled what he'd suspected for months. "He was on the phone warning these people we were coming."

As he turned to go, he noticed three shiny, silver pins on the floor next to Josh's suede leather shoes, which were stuffed with nylon socks as they would be were his feet still in them.

Dodds pick up one of the silver pins, the one that used to hold Josh's hip together. He'd studied Athol's file and knew all about his service-connected injuries and just about everything else worth knowing about the man – *except where he was right now.*

"I just don't understand how they all got out of here, and who did they think would be fooled by these '*Left Behind*' movie props," he said out loud, dropping the pin to the floor.

"They ain't *props*," the old man spoke up from the opposite side of the building. "I saw 'em *disappear* while they were praying. They're gone, really *gone.*"

"Yeah, *right*," Dodds mumbled, refusing to believe his eyes. "They're here somewhere."

The three teens still crying by the altar were left to themselves, but for the next half hour, agents went room to room, pistols drawn and M-4's at the ready, like they were clearing a building of hostile forces. Every classroom, every closet was vacant. They then checked the area outside the church building, looking for any hint where all these people had gone. The old man was right. They were gone, just *gone*.

Hershberger could only think about how he was going to explain letting 300 Bible thumpers escape. He hurried back outside and tried phoning the New York office again. No answer. He called Chicago and got nothing then tried Atlanta where he was put on hold. Dodds walked around the outside of the building, checking to see if there was any way possible for that many people to slip out some other exit. Even if there was, the very old and very young couldn't just disappear across that field over there that quickly.

As Hershberger finally got someone on the phone, sirens began going off in all directions, some as distant as Fort Bragg, most from nearby fire departments. The loud wailing only added to Hershberger's frustrations.

"I've gotta problem here," he told the agent in Atlanta. "A bunch of people have up and disappeared on me while we had their church surrounded. Do you have a number for anybody that's still in Washington I can talk to?"

"*Washington?!*" The agent repeated, "Man, don't you know anything? *There is no Washington anymore. It was hit by.....*"

Hershberger's Blackberry went dead. He checked his battery to see if he had any bars left. It was dead, and it had a full charge this morning. He was about to ask

Dodds to give him his blackberry when he saw the huge ball of fire moving across the sky from east to west. It was too large for a plane. It disappeared over the horizon, north and west of them. He frowned and shook his head, puzzled. Again, he started to call to Dodds about his phone when he and all those standing around him saw a brilliant flash of light.

"Oh my...." Dodds mumble, finally realizing the salt that preserved America was no longer there to protect them.

The light brought with it a wave of heat. It was so intense, they couldn't see it anymore. Tears filled their eyes to the point they were blinded. When Hershberger put his hands up to shield his eyes, he realized he had no eyes at all. They had melted. Only then did he also realize his hair and clothes were ablaze. He opened his mouth to scream in terror, but the heat had swallowed up all the oxygen, sending the scorching hot air down his throat.

The pain was excruciating, but it was only for a moment. By the time he and his band of culture warriors realized they were about to face the Christ they'd persecuted, they and everything around them disintegrated into millions of pieces, which quickly burned up in the flame that swept over them.

Everything within 70 miles in any direction of what had been Raleigh, N.C. was nothing but black smut. When the world's leaders emerged from their caves later that afternoon, they found things very different. When Jake ventured from his mountain cabin near Taylorsville, he could feel the change in the air long before he could see or smell it. Josh Athol was right all along. Now Jake understood he had seven years of *trouble* to look forward to.

The ash cloud that covered most of North America was spreading around the globe, leaving the world beneath it in a state of darkness, like wintertime above the Arctic Circle. The world in fact was about to have an early winter. Many of the same false prophets who'd preached about Global Warming would soon be singing the blues about the New Ice Age.

Tens of millions in America were dead; tens of millions of others were missing. But those that were missing were not confined to the former U.S. Hundreds of millions were missing in Europe, Asia, Africa, South America, Australia and New Zealand. Thousands of prison cells in Muslim countries no longer contained any prisoners, and the homes of tens of thousands of radical Christians being watched by their governments were found to be vacant.

Not to worry though – contingency plans had been in place for 20 centuries, just in case those crazy Baptists-types were correct. Sunday evening, the Vatican sent emissaries to London and all the major protestant denomination headquarters. Their story had to be the same, especially since Baptists were not the only ones missing.

Millions of Catholics, Anglicans, Presbyterians, Lutherans and Methodists were conspicuously missing. On the other hand, hundreds of thousands of name-only Baptists had been left behind with the other religious heathens who called themselves Christians but never knew Christ. Now it was important that churches of all denominations be united as one, or they'd lose all their followers.

The former leaders of what had already become the Divided States of America had half as many people to rule over when they finally slithered from under the rocks they'd been hiding. But at least they wouldn't be bothered with those intolerant Bible thumpers or Constitution-quoting, right-winged radicals.

For the most part, the last Americans left with the Bible thumpers. The country – *what was left of it* – was entirely in the hands of the proles.

www.ingramcontent.com/pod-product-compliance
Lightning Source LLC
Chambersburg PA
CBHW070440120726
47910CB00003B/862